THE CALLISTA

THE RETROFIT

B. WILLIAMS
J. J. WHITE

Copyright © 2024 by B. Williams and J.J. White

All rights reserved.

No part of this publication may be reproduced, distributed, or transmitted in any form or by any means, including photocopying, recording, or other electronic or mechanical methods, without the prior written permission of the publisher, except as permitted by U.S. copyright law. For permission requests, contact mossandwolf@gmail.com.

The story, all names, characters, and incidents portrayed in this production are fictitious. No identification with actual persons (living or deceased), places, buildings, and products is intended or should be inferred.

Book Cover by Michelle Hermes Art

Typography by GRBookCovers

ebook ISBN 979-8-9907660-0-6

Paperback ISBN 979-8-9907660-1-3

Hardback ISBN 979-8-9907660-2-0

1st edition 2024

The Callistar

The Retrofit: The Callistar 1.0
Thin Ice: The Callistar 1.5 (Coming Soon)

contents

Dedication	VII
Prologue	VIII
Chapter One	1
Chapter Two	15
Chapter Three	25
Chapter Four	41
Chapter Five	52
Chapter Six	61
Chapter Seven	71
Chapter Eight	88
Chapter Nine	103
Chapter Ten	115
Chapter Eleven	130
Chapter Twelve	136
Chapter Thirteen	154
Chapter Fourteen	162
Chapter Fifteen	178
Chapter Sixteen	195

Chapter Seventeen	210
Chapter Eighteen	220
Chapter Nineteen	236
Chapter Twenty	257
Chapter Twenty-One	269
Chapter Twenty-Two	287
Crew Files	306

Stars above know we don't change easily,
but our heart is so easily swayed
before the mind is even touched.

This is for those who fall first
and ask questions later.

Prologue

RUMORS ARE A CURRENCY all their own in the depths of space. Deceit and ingenuity play their part in establishing the baseline for all that occurs; but rumors help guide all that along. Space was too large to just take a stab in the dark without coordinates. You needed guidance- a way to find your way. Navigation pings only got you so far when the expanse before you was much larger than anything you'd ever faced before. So rumors, the information trade, they helped fill those gaps.

Until things went downhill and it stranded you among the stars. Every spacefarer knew sending an S.O.S. was a dangerous business. You never knew who'd pick up the distress call. The woman in the shuttle's pilot chair prearranged her rendezvous point to make sure this didn't happen.

They're nearly here, Captain.

Kira tilted her head as the implant passed along the AI's message. The innocuous speaker rested right behind her ear. A lima bean-shaped insert pushed under the skin, the procedure done minimally with a small dermal incision that healed over so no scar rested above it. The only sign of its presence the bump under the skin. A thin wire ran off towards the inner ear canal making it so all communication was heard only by the person meant to receive it. Any communication back had to be said aloud. But since she was by herself, there was no concern of anyone overhearing it.

"Thank you, Watson."

Her voice was so different from Watson's, smooth and easy to the ear. The voice that shot back to her was harsher, the tone almost banal other than a slight accent that matched her own. Normally AI's had specifically clear voices, accents were hard to detect without it being forced through the programming.

Should I bring us about to the other side of the moon, Captain?

"No, I can handle that, Watson. Thank you."

Leaning over the console, the glass reflected her back as clearly as any mirror. Dark hair almost black, purple in the right light, which the fluorescent sheen hinted at. Long fingers trailed along the console, the flat surface reacting to the heat of her touch. Flicking a reading upward of their current positioning, it expanded across the wide front view screen.

Numbers scrawled in a pale neon blue against the inky black sky behind it, every line perfectly straight. It reflected in her eyes, covering liquid amber with an unnatural light. The same light that made dusky skin off-colored.

A rapid proximity beeping came off the scanner. "Watson?"

It's not the Callistar.

"Check its signature."

Captain, it's Praetorian.

Her mouth formed the beginning of a curse that did not drop from her full lips, the cupid's bow of the top forming a slight dent as she bit her lower one. Watson automatically shifted her initial readout to the other side, allowing her to see the projection of the radar.

Cruiser class, non-military, possibly a privateer.

"You couldn't have mentioned that sooner?"

The statement sounded unconcerned, even if her heart hammered, every beat sending it banging against her ribs so hard she could feel her pulses extending into her wrists.

Do you want an apology, Captain?

She snorted as she realigned their trajectory. The shuttle moved into the moon's gravity. With any luck, they'd be a bleep on their own monitor, so quick they didn't bother looking into it further. A sharp veering of the other ship told her one thing- they'd seen her and they didn't fancy an interaction either.

It appears they're moving away.

"More power to them," sarcasm mixed with relief painted her tones.

The console pinged for a message relay, causing her to purse her lips before Watson came across the com line.

You were right, Captain. We're going to be recalled back for repairs.

"It feels like there's more to it than that," she sighed, leaning back in her seat piloting around to the light side of the Callian moon. "I suppose we'll find out soon enough."

I'm sure we will.

Chapter One

KIRA

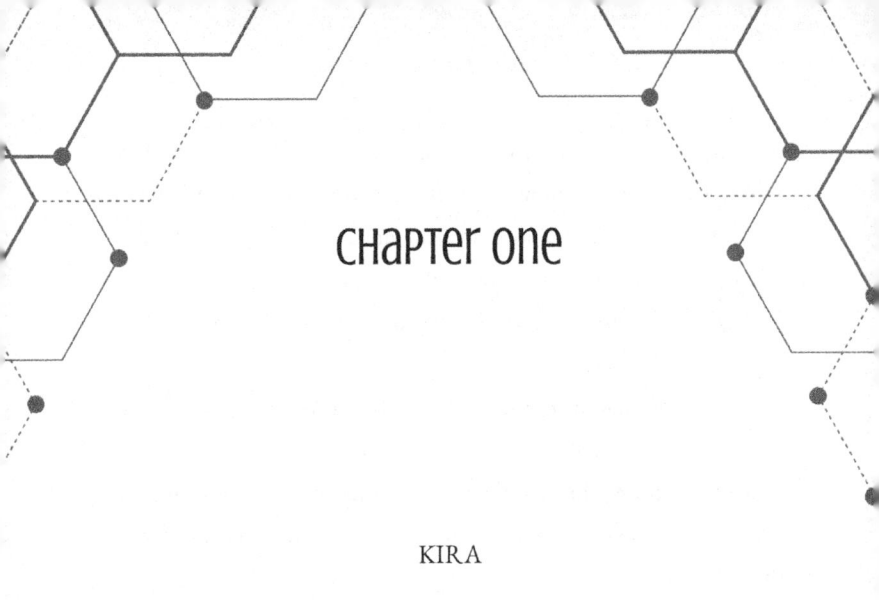

Watson sounded off in her inner ear, **Your heart rate is up.**

Kira waved her hand dismissively, but realized he couldn't see the gesture. She was in the cargo bay by herself. Max, their Vicar, pestered Morgan, their resident pilot, with questions, while she paced.

"I'm concerned about the changes."

Alec may keep it together, but progress was never made through steady work. Updates are required if we're going into deep space.

Kira clenched her teeth together. Her ship, the Callistar, was a freighter, one of the largest classes of ships in the galaxy. After being decommissioned, they retrofitted the entirety, transforming it from a warship to one for mining and cargo transportation. They left it in orbit, choosing a smaller vessel, the Valstar, Morgan's pet project, to make their way down to the Meeting Place.

Unsurprisingly, Max had also chosen to go along with the pilot and captain. He'd been quick to volunteer his services. Kira had snorted at him, like she did Watson from time to time. His original goal had been to gain entry into the Meeting Place, and here the Vicar was. He'd spoken extensively about his motivations behind that goal with Kira.

And no one else questioned the Captain. They came from all walks of life, and if she said the Vicar was clear, then he was clear.

A voice came over the intercom, "Fixing to land, captain."

"I'll be right there."

Passing through the magnetic doors, they made a shppppp sound as they pulled aside. She settled into her seat.

Morgan, their pilot and fellow Praetorian, turned about in his, joking to her, "Doubt you would have even noticed we'd landed back there."

Kira fastened her seatbelt.

"I trust you," she told Morgan with a wry smile. "It's the others I don't."

Sir is requesting our ETA.

"Pass it along then, Watson. There's no reason to keep him waiting longer than necessary," Kira replied smoothly.

Morgan landed without guidance from the system as per his usual coming down with the slightest oomph on the landing pads. The vessel incessantly beeped at him while he flicked off the active warning against it. Kira knew he preferred landing manually in order to practice what he would otherwise miss in the long run. Outside, even the loading dock personnel commented on how smoothly he'd done it, the crew hearing it in the background of Morgan's transmission to confirm engine shut off.

Kira didn't care how he managed it, only that he had. Max came hot on her heels as she unclipped, walking back into the cargo bay before the shuttle's 'parking brake' could be applied.

"I've not forgotten," she told Max with the slightest smile behind it at his eagerness. "I told him I would be bringing a friend."

The Vicar smiled openly, pulling down the edge of his tunic, a muted gray shift somehow managing to ride up, despite its stiffness. Bearing a high collar, the tightly fitted material, and broad shoulders beneath gave him a commanding look as he trailed after her in shining, simple, black knee-high boots. If it weren't enough that he dressed like a member of the clergy, his closely cropped hair and beard, both white, and his stern, disapproving look, were a bright red neon sign that said it for him.

Kira dressed much less conspicuously as the area they were in was one where fashion had taken its leave or arrived. Really depended on who you talked to. The upper district resembled a hodgepodge of the naturally rich, those who were wealthy because they'd risen through ranks, and traders who'd made good early on. Therefore, it had those who dressed like old money, those that dressed like new, and some who simply wore what suited them best.

Surrounded by muted suits, bright contraptions of netting in pinks and turquoise, high collars, low collars, sleeves three times too large with fitted waists on the bodice, it was an eccentric variety of alien fashion and concepts. Kira could have sworn one person they passed wore scales individually sewn to one another.

Kira blended into the crowd with black leggings, knee high reflective black boots, and an orange jacket that fit tight against her forearms. It remained loose around her breasts before the elastic waist helped it slim to her waist. Tucking her long hair into a reggae style cap, it fell at the nape of her neck, keeping small tendrils from escaping. Next to Max, they made an odd pair, her bright, him subdued, but they walked together all the same, matching pace.

"That is a-?" Max asked with gray eyes flashing.

Kira interrupted him, "A Mosin, yes."

"I thought they were-"

"Uncommon, unfriendly, barely capable of being in society, all of the above?"

She grinned in his direction as they gave the creature with eyes like pitch and a hairless head a good bit of distance. Kira kept her eyes down, putting herself between it and Max, guiding him by his shoulder with a light bump of her own.

They turned onto a short catwalk, crossing over a section open to the universe below the invisible barrier. There was no comfort when the expanse of space rested below like a blanket, welcoming but entirely cold. The transition from the stockyard to downtown went from wide open landing spaces to cramped quarters and shops, giving the impression of stacked housing circa early twenty-first century China.

Turning down the main walkway, it transformed into an industrial area. What looked to be a line of bars with bright advertisements surrounded them the closer they came. Some were holographic in nature, popping up out of nowhere and being waved aside absentmindedly. Others were neon signs blinking spasmodically, the oldest were physical ones attached to the shops or pasted on the inside of the glass like force field.

Max glanced at one, the neon reflecting off his peppered hair but not his muted suit, and asked, "This is supposed to be inconspicuous?"

Kira laughed at his words and touched his shoulder lightly. "Business is never conducted in the same place with Toke. It's wherever he feels like that day."

At least his schedule was unpredictable enough that it was difficult to hunt him down, unless one went through the Keepers. Basically, the scheduling secretaries for Rumor, who coordinated rendezvous and transports. You had to know someone who belonged to even find them.

A turnstile door awaited them under a pink glowing sign. The text was alien, but the other signs made it clear it belonged to the same class as the rest of the line up, something that did not truly waver from an Earthen experience even in space. The floors were a tacky olive green color, sticky from spilled drinks, and the walls weren't much better. This was a place for live music, the atmosphere of smoke and intrigue more gritty than interesting.

They entered, and Kira barely had to raise her hand before a Talcien, a humanoid form with lizard-like features, hissed out, "You're late."

He came through shadows next to the door, as if coiled, ready to strike. Talciens were similar in nature to a cobra, with the large arching hoods on either side of their face and a pointed mouth, slits for nostrils on top. His mixture of black and silver scales intermingling gave him a severe look complimented by obsidian eyes. Crossed arms revealed three fingers on each hand, a thumb like appendage and two longer ones, lacking scales and silver with completely smooth skin.

Kira glanced over with an amused grin. "I never truly gave him a time Bi'ast."

The suited man managed a smile, which looked more threatening than pleased, long fangs settling back over the bottom part of his jaw. "It isss good to sssee you."

"And you."

"Follow me," Bi'ast turned, taking one step back before shifting his feet. He kept Kira next to him in the motion while side-eyeing the Vicar. He did not question his presence, but lowered his voice hissing out to Kira, "Toke hasss company asss well. It isss-" His s's elongated slightly like a lisp that no one pointed out since in front of that lisp rested poisonous appendages.

The man paused, looking back, but no one could overhear in the environment, but he did not wish his opinion known openly was what the pause told Kira, "It isss not polite, but he sssaysss it isss necessary."

Kira lifted her chin at the alien creature, as he beat her height by well over a foot. His scales gleamed even in the low light, the reflection a sign of good health. "Necessary for what?"

Bi'ast slipped his forked tongue out and up and down over the front of his mouth, as if tasting the air. Kira read the action. He was uncomfortable. It was a nervous gesture, and she'd comfort him if only for a second, "Nevermind old friend, I'll see soon enough."

They passed several unmarked doors, then turned a corner. Two men stood beside another unlabeled door, leaning towards one another, as if having a discussion, but neither spoke. One knocked with force enough to send the rapping through the thick metal which sprang open without delay.

Toke is in a hurry, Kira thought. She gestured to Max as she asked Bi'ast, "Will you entertain my friend until this is finished?"

Neither were in a position to refuse. Kira ranked higher than Bi'ast, and Max needed her to vouch for his honesty. To be impolite now risked her not giving him the introduction he sorely wished for.

That was until a voice came from inside the room. A low smooth baritone met them with exasperation. "You may bring him Kira, I am aware of his presence."

Kira shrugged. Bi'ast stayed outside.

The 'office' for the club wasn't redecorated for the meeting, the only sign of Toke's presence came from the rather large blue-prints of the Callistar. Hanging in the air and holographically lit from below, the emitter laid flat across the desk while the ship hovered an inch above it. The rest of the room was the sort of thing one expected from a manager's private office, seats that resembled leather for easy cleaning, a pole in one corner, cushions in an alcove for comfort, and a secondary bar that a few of the black suited cronies remained by, another Talcien in the mix.

What did interest Kira was the company that Toke chose to keep outside of his personal guard.

Before the desk sat two chairs, one empty, which Kira quickly conceded to Max. For once, he did not argue. A man with shockingly white hair filled the other. Judging by the pale skin, rounded ears, and general lack of correct posture, she guessed he was human, mid-twenties, if she'd learned from the others she'd seen. His face had hard angular features, and his expression, a scowl that looked baked on permanently. A quick glance at his legs, *tall*, she thought to herself, but the leather jacket he wore was too baggy to reveal much more.

"Thank you for coming Kira," Toke spoke directly to her, drawing her attention away from the other man. She returned her gaze to the stern leader who'd requested their presence.

"Of course, Sir," Kira wasn't quite monotone, but her voice remained steady.

Toke was essentially the head keeper of all rumors. He garnered respect. She perched behind Max, her hands on the edge of the upholstery. With him seated, she would address Toke once again. "It is good to see you, and to see that the Callistar will be brought into this century."

A fire flashed in her eyes at the upgrades. Deep space was dangerous and their exploration of it in search of Listium, a rare metal, might run them into raiders or new species.

The politeness came to an immediate halt as the white-haired stranger spoke in a broken Irish accent, "I beg yer fekkin pardon?"

The white-haired man sat up, his eyes glaring first at Kira, then at Max. "Who the absolute fek, brings a fekking priest ta meet a bloody criminal overlord?"

Max reacted first, just the slightest upturn of the corner of his lips. Kira hardly found it amusing. She itched to backhand the man with no qualms about doing so in front of almost anyone other than Toke. Who took the situation in hand rather quickly, preventing her from doing as she pleased.

"Kira, that is Quinn. Just Quinn. I will get to him shortly." Toke turned his gaze onto Quinn. Barely concealed anger hidden underneath the surface of his severe features. "Quinn, did I not tell you to keep your comments to yourself unless you are asked to speak?"

Quinn's response was childish. He rolled his eyes dramatically before returning to staring at the ceiling. His behavior eerily similar to a teenager's, despite his apparent age.

"My apologies for him. He thinks he is smarter than everyone in the room. And as much as it pains me to say it, as near as I can tell, he is right. It makes humility and respect hard for him. I could give you an extensive list of what I speculate his issues to be, but I am sure you can guess. What do you want to know first?"

Kira bit back the obvious question of why Quinn's insolence was tolerated, and instead said, "I've seen the schematics. Alec let me peruse the copy that you sent to him. I assume this is to be the head of the project?"

Max shifted in his seat, glancing over to Quinn. Kira saw it happen almost instantaneously and fought the desire to groan. Max was curious, and his curiosity was bad news for the insolent man sitting next to him.

"Smart girl, someone raised you right." Toke grinned at her, clearly pleased that she showed she'd paid attention to his memo, just as he'd taught her once to read between the lines she had to read the actual lines first. "So, I'll tell you why he is the head of the project and see if you can connect the dots."

He gestured at the schematics. The screen changed to a company logo. Paradigm Enterprises, Kira recognized the name. They were one of the "big three" tech companies in the entire galaxy. Earth-based, they manufactured ship parts of every kind from civilian to military use. It was the best of the best.

"The replacement parts that are going aboard the Callistar will be of Paradigm Manufacture. Not just that, but it's going to be from their Q series."

Kira kept up on major ship changes. She knew the Q series was a part of the newest line from Paradigm. It was their cutting edge equipment. The Q series went on Capitol Class Dreadnaughts. The Earth's Dreadnaught Gemini was newly equipped with a Q series experimental plasma rail. A weapon, according to reports she wasn't supposed to see, that fired tungsten steel rods from a rail gun with near-light-speed acceleration suspended in a field of plasma. They were called Dreadnaught killers as they shredded through the thickest shields and hulls like a hot knife through butter.

"So Kira, based on what I've told you so far, care to make any guesses?"

"I am assuming that Quinn here-" the lack of last name made her use his first, but she knowingly left out a proper title. "Is behind the Q in Paradigm Enterprises, though how you managed to pull him away from Paradigm would be a guess, and I don't like drawing at straws."

Max showed surprise at her statement, but only to Kira. She caught his curious look earlier and knew quelling it would be impossible now. His hands, which had been on the armrests, moved to his knees, rubbing the edge of them in a telltale sign.

"Clever, clever girl," Toke said with an absent shake of his head. "Yes, Quinn here is the brain behind pretty much every breakthrough in ship design over the last decade. And he is going to do a complete overhaul of the Callistar. By the time he's finished, she will be the most advanced deep space exploration vehicle in the galaxy. So, my dear Kira, that's the good news, and you were smart enough not to guess the bad."

Reaching up, Toke rubbed his eyes. "I didn't get him away. Quinn here contacted me himself. Paradigm held him as a virtual prisoner inside of their headquarters on Earth. They couldn't risk the company's most valuable asset by having him going around living his life. He wanted out and for payment he has agreed to retrofit two ships."

Toke gave a brief pause as he let that detail sink in. Kira deduced she was getting one, and he surely had gotten the other. If the man only wanted to escape, why he'd agree to two ships was beyond her. Each retrofit surely took months of labor. She needn't wait long for an answer as he continued. "On the condition that one of those ships be used to take him into deep space. To an uninhabited, uncharted planet of his choosing where you will leave him. Then you are going to wipe your ship's A.I. and nav charts of the location and do a memory modification of your knowledge of the location."

There it was, Kira thought. Toke got a new ship, and now she had to uphold his end of the bargain. In exchange, she also got a new ship. It was the best kind of deal for him. Oh sure, he likely had to orchestrate an escape, but even that Toke wouldn't have done directly. He got to benefit without getting his own hands dirty. But what he suggested, what he wanted, messing with the mind was always dangerous no matter what assurances they made otherwise.

"True shore leave then, and longer than I thought," she said, her gaze falling to Quinn, then back to Toke. "We'll have time to make proper preparations. The supply list is already prepared. I've forwarded it, but some things have yet to arrive."

Quinn kept his eyes on the ceiling. Max side-eyed Quinn, looking back to Toke as if this phenomenon was vastly amusing instead of worrisome. This explained exactly how he'd ended up on the Callistar to start. No one simply hopped on the ship willingly or remained on it purposefully after all.

Toke chose not to meet either of their looks, dismissing the blueprints, causing the hologram to dissipate. The program shut down. "There is one last, tiny catch in all of this. You can't kill him."

That earned a sharp breath that was perhaps a laugh, or it wasn't. Something in-between due to the seriousness of such a thing that he said on the matter. The memory wipe was the first insult, now he simply added another, "You expect me to-"

Toke did, and even with her interruption, he proceeded to do the same back to her, finishing his train of thought, "Or turn him into Paradigm, under any circumstances. I would not feel right without telling you to do this without clarifying those circumstances. Quinn has placed some serious personal boundaries into his technology in my ship and is soon to be in yours. Any attempt to hack it results in an immediate lockout of every system and for the ship's reactor to go into overload. He is the only one who can disable the program and he will only give you the codes to do so once you are in orbit. He has a neural link with both ships. He can remotely trigger that override at any time for any reason with a thought."

Kira knew, then, he did. Toke expected her to hold her tongue, and she wasn't the type to do so for very long. Disrespect didn't last long on her ship. Not necessarily short-tempered, but there was a spark that tended to light itself into a flame when it came to the management of 'her crew.' Not a boss, but a leadership role in her opinion. Getting dirty was what she lived for, and she was always with the rest of them in the muck and the mud as quick as possible to prove this.

But Quinn, so far, didn't sound like a team player. Non-team players were shot out the airlock, as were smart mouthed passengers.

Max, who had been watching and waiting, reached a hand back up to the one over his right shoulder, the one that tightened without knowing it. He patted it lightly as a show of support for the young woman. He still kept his silence.

Kira would not change her mind from a simple touch. "You place too much trust in me with this." Kira drew her hand out of Max's to the back of the chair so that he did not feel the wrath that displayed in the further whitening of her knuckles. "I think it is best that my posting be temporarily filled by another."

"Your ship doesn't run without you and you know it," Toke said

Toke was well aware the crew she'd put together would not listen to anyone else. He could get another captain, sure, but they wouldn't be loyal to the new captain. Which was a big problem for a long-term trip into deep space. The crew had to be loyal, especially when their cargo was as volatile as Quinn.

"Look, as I understand it, it's a Quantum computer core. So, he can detonate my ship from anywhere in the galaxy. Which means that I need this done properly. Therefore, you are doing it Kira," Toke said. He brooked no arguments in tone or expression, but he took a breath as he looked to Quinn for aid. "Please say something to placate her on this."

The man finally looked up and snorted. "Aye, ye want me ta dig ya out of this hole?"

Quinn cracked his neck and turned his attention to Kira. "While I appreciate Toke telling ya ta mind yer P's and Q's-" a pertinent level of sarcasm in his voice made it very clear he did not. "And I appreciate that ye would apparently rather give up yer ship than be forced ta be polite ta someone." Surprisingly, this lacked the same sarcasm. It almost sounded like grudging approval, if anything. "I'm not going ta blow myself up just because you call me a fekking nitwit. I might do it iffin ya decide ta try slapping me around more than I think I deserve. And if ya kill me, my neural net is set up to detonate all of my locked tech. But other than that, I don't give a shite what ya do or say as long as you get me away from people. You are all fekking terrible, and I am sick of dealing with the lot of ya."

Something in his explanation that told her he wasn't talking about anyone in that room specifically. He referred to other people in general, as in, every other sapient being in the galaxy.

Watson sounded in her ear. **Your heart rate's up again.**

Max chimed in, giving his two cents. "Captain, if I may. I believe I would also like to stay on board."

Kira looked down to the holy man. He would not be asking to stay on board if he did not have a reason behind it, which was beyond her own reasoning at the moment. Then, it dawned on her recalling how he looked at Quinn. Something else caught his eye.

Letting out a deep sigh, she said, "If you have some sense of self-preservation, at the very least, then perhaps this will be a suitable arrangement."

"I should fekkin hope sa. Yer getting basically a trillion dollars worth of experimental ship parts to act as a glorified taxi. Seems ta me yer getting a pretty fekkin cherry deal, even if ya have to put up with my surly ass." Quinn snorted before he let his head roll back to rest against the chair as he returned to staring at the ceiling. With the matter at hand settled, he seemed to have decided his input was no longer required.

So, maybe he really is as smart as Toke says.

Toke let out a slow breath this time through his mouth, his patience wearing thin. "Thank you Quinn. Now, is there anything else we need to cover?"

"I would seek a private meeting with you," Kira addressed Toke directly. "Since we will be here for some time, there is nothing so pressing with you it cannot wait for another time."

There existed a slight strain at the edge of Toke's features. His expression turned to a thin line of obvious displeasure. After a moment of taking another calming breath, he said to her in very clear, clipped, and precise tones, "You can have your meeting after you take your ship to the shipyard. It's in orbit around Eikos."

"At your leave then," Kira said, bringing her hand up to her shoulder over the symbol of Rumor imprinted there. A mark she'd never be rid of, no matter how hard she tried. It wasn't visible, but Toke knew exactly where she'd chosen to have it imprinted, and therefore could recognize the gesture as one of fealty.

Max remained seated. Kira gave a soft nudge, her way of silently saying they were to leave, and he was coming with.

There was one other matter that needed sorting. Kira cleared her throat before looking at Quinn. "Are you using us as a ferry, or do you have your own transportation?"

"I've got my own transport," Quinn responded without actually lowering his head to look towards the captain.

"Excellent. Glad we got that all figured out. Now get to work." Toke waved his hand at all of them, indicating they should take their leave.

Chapter Two

KIRA

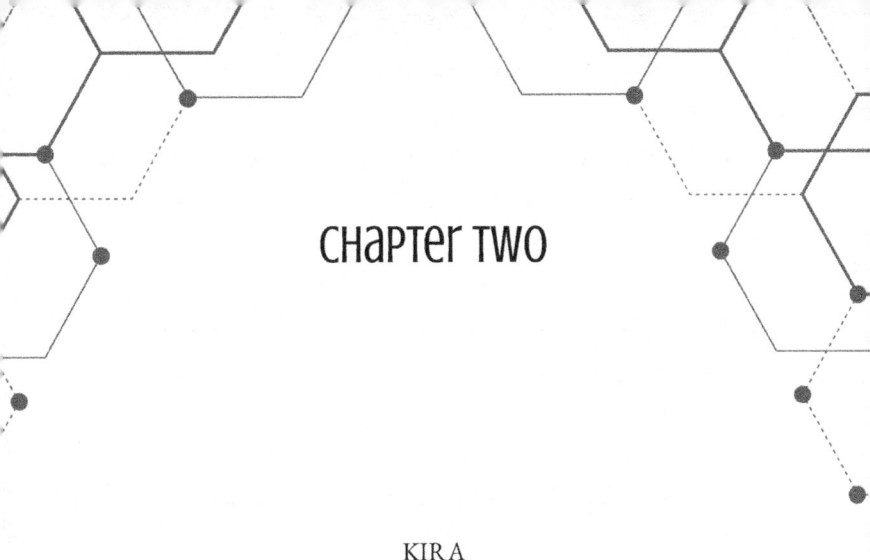

"That was certainly interesting." Max put his hands in his pockets, sneaking a peek over to Kira as they walked back down the hall.

"It is... unexpected," Kira grimaced with her reply, showing far more to Max than most anyone else. He was a trusted confidant, but this wasn't the place to discuss such matters, something she passed along with a look.

"Shall we return to Morgan?"

"You should. I have something that I need to take care of."

"Ah, I am-"

"I will walk with you to the transport," Kira smiled at Max. Despite his earlier forwardness, the man did not want to be left alone at the Meeting Place. She couldn't blame him.

The floating station had become a collage of all that happened within the universe, steel mixed with glass and technology along with Praetorians, Verdissians, Humans, some Talcien's and a mix of other sentient creatures that chose to skirt the rules of society. It was where Rumor ran out of, and it was where rumors simply existed. It wasn't a place for someone to roam if they did not have allegiances to one of the major syndicates. Which meant Max should not be walking out along the falsely lit streets on his own.

Bi'ast waited for them at the bottom of the stairs, his long split tongue flicked out, retreating just as quickly, "Ssso now you sssee?"

"I do, Bi'ast." Kira covered her emotions outwardly with a placid mask of indifference when possible, but Talcien's, Talcien's could practically taste your emotions by the release of pheromones. Making it nearly impossible to lie about being stressed. Still it was worth a shot, "It'll be fine."

Narrowly slit pupils became thin lines, an almost imperceptible snout shake following it, "You ssshould join me for a drink. I will find you sssomething real."

"We're short on time, perhaps next time we visit." Intercepting and refusing before Max could open his own trap, Kira guided the man with a swift hip bump, pushing him towards the door, "Bye Bi'ast."

Bi'ast performed a fealty gesture, his three fingers wrapping up his upper arm on his left.

"Another discussion for later, I assume?" Max said outside.

"You're a quick learner." Kira beamed at him and escorted him back to the Valstar.

Dropping their resident holy man off with Morgan, who seemed delighted to see they'd be off earlier than promised, until he discovered they weren't leaving, and was then put off. Kira slapped him on the shoulder and laughed before departing, once again heading down to the inner market.

I do not approve of this, Captain.

"Since when have you approved of anything that I do?"

You should have brought Max or Morgan. It is not safe here.

"It is safe enough. No one would dare touch me."

You think that your status protects you, but it makes you more likely to be kidnapped and ransomed back. Just because Sir has taken you in as his progeny does not give you protection, just the opposite, in fact.

"If you had a hole to shut, I would tell you to do so, Watson."

Watson kept the line quiet instead.

The main marketplace was reminiscent of a street market from Earth. Vendors who did not have physical shops rested under broad pieces of brightly colored cloth with floating storage trays. They rolled the cover back over when the day's business concluded. Those with physical shops used screens, force fields of a sort, turned transparent for the day so one could see what goods were for sale.

The translator installed in her implant worked overtime, bringing every language into the common tongue. She programmed it that way instead of on her native Praetorian. Advice from Toke, once upon a time, that had rather been like an order. She was not to represent Praetoria to the outside world, even if her appearance hardly fooled anyone.

Weaving in and out of the stalls, she had a specific destination in mind. Slipping into a side alley, a chill went up her spine. She ducked behind an old solid sign for a pharmacy, hung only for looks, and waited. Peering out behind it once she caught the reason, Bi'ast trailed behind her.

Kira leaned back crossing her arms, Watson spoke in her ear. **I would say something about warning you or about Toke being concerned or-**

"Watson," her seething effectively hushed him.

Once she was clear of Bi'ast's range, the sensation that rolled through disappeared. Skirting to the left instead of the right where he'd gone, she made a quick deal for a black overshirt, swapping it out directly for her coat in front of the woman selling it. Leaving the orange monstrosity, as Watson had called it once, she went the opposite direction, traversing the narrow side areas to avoid being monitored.

Adraxsions never set off her sixth sense. Praetorians were born more attuned to their instincts, a byproduct of old wars and enemies. But, Adraxsions, they were an enigma because of their ability to almost magically appear. It caught her off guard when the store owner did it. That and the drawling, deep voice unnerved her. But the mystery of the species scratched a part of her brain that sorely wished to uncover it.

"That is an excellent choice." The pale man reached over her shoulder. His impossibly long fingers wrapping around the neck of the bottle, tilting it up towards the light. "An earth vintage," he informed her. "Quite strong and aged."

Kira froze. She was of middling height, between five and six feet. He reached almost seven. He did not exude a scent that she could pick up. His hand drew back, and the air felt undisturbed. Had the edge of his sleeve not brushed her shoulder, she might have believed him a ghost. His coloring was light enough, and dressed in a suit of muted gray, cut to fit him perfectly. If it weren't for his eyes and hair, both dark as raven wings, it would have been believable. But his features were humanoid, lidded eyes like a human, formed lips, straight teeth. It was those eyes that differentiated them, no discernable pupil, just black in a circle.

"Then I'll take it."

"Excellent."

Trailing after him to the counter, she set it on the edge. "Do you have anything put back for me?"

The Adraxsion laid a package wrapped in a silken blue fabric, tucked and tied with a singular ribbon in the same color on the counter.

Kira felt a lingering excitement at the sight of it. Months had passed since they'd come anywhere close to the Meeting Place. The temptation to open it then and there was almost overwhelming until he spoke. "Shall I forward this to Sir's tab?"

"Ah, no, this is personal."

Flipping her wrist over the scanner, she performed a mental calculation of her credits even as her implant advised her of the purchase.

"Thank you. I appreciate your time."

"It is nothing for one of my favorite customers." His fingers came together, the tips pressed loosely against one another. Again too long, too thin, but the right number of joints in each one.

Kira wished her ability to sense more was the reason behind the chill she felt. She deposited both the bottle and the wrapped package into her messenger bag and departed only to run into- "Bi'ast!"

"Kira." the Talcien cocked his head in a bird-like gesture. "You are outsssside the parametersss ssset."

Should I-

Kira tapped the piece behind her ear to shut out the A.I. temporarily. "It seems I am. Would you be so kind as to escort me back?"

Bi'ast hissed with his tongue flicking forward. "Follow me."

The sensation of something watching had not quite faded. So many eyes in one place had that effect. Kira noticed Bi'ast tensing. Every muscle tightening making him appear rigid as he leaned forward. Then backwards towards her, so far, it was clearly not intentional. His feet pointed out, making him top heavy, as like a chess piece being pushed for checkmate, he fell onto her.

Kira didn't have time to react. One minute he was speaking, and the next she knew a stunner, which froze him in place, had him keeling back. Whoever shot the blaster wasn't out to kill, which was a minor relief from the current predicament. Who hit him was less obvious, and there was no time to focus. His dead weight pinned her. His head hit her over her heart, knocking her to the ground. Sharp pain shot through her spine sending a tingling sensation down through her toes.

The rough landing earned an expletive. She thrashed, maneuvering her feet to gain traction as she fought to get out from underneath Bi'ast.

"It ssseemsss we caught more than we intended."

Kira stopped her escape attempt to take stock of the situation. Three more Talcien's strolled up before Bi'ast, and her prone body beneath him. They were darker creatures than him. Their black scales were mixed with copper, but the same lisping speech would have given them away in a dark room. The one in front held a sleek blaster the size of a sawed off shotgun. The metal gleaming from the neon light of a nearby shop.

"What do you want with me?" Kira felt for her own blaster, her right hand shifting near her hip. She'd clipped the slimmer, more feminine version into her back waistband the instant she'd known they were coming down.

"You?" They walked in a triangular formation with one leading. He was the one that spoke, slit eyes blinking as the secondary eyelid slid across. "We have no quarrel with you. We want what we are owed."

"From Bi'ast?" Kira moved her hand in infinitesimal movements to avoid attention. *Keep talking.*

I will alert Sir.

"No," she whispered.

Luckily, Talcien's had very little in the way of hearing.

"Yessss." The leader tilted his head. "You ssseem familiar little one..."

"Oh yeah? I mean, I work in the market sometimes, so maybe you've seen me here."

Help is on the way.

"I thinksss thisss isss not it."

"Well, I think-" Kira did not wait to finish her sentence. With a slight heave, she got her hand free and reached for her own blaster. She didn't hesitate, firing directly at the leader, hitting him square in the chest with maximum voltage. She'd stalled long enough to turn up the firepower. It wouldn't kill him by any means, but it would stun him for a good hour. The blaster beeped in her hand, indicating the next charge was ready, but she didn't need it.

The other two collapsed to the ground almost simultaneously. Both had been reaching for their own weapons strapped on their hips, but their hands never made it. The Adraxsion shopkeeper stood behind the pair.

"Great timing," Kira said with a grin.

"I cannot afford to lose one of my best customers," he spoke in his long, drawling voice. He sidestepped the pair, walking up beside the leader. "I daresay you should make yourself scarce."

Bi'ast laid half on her legs, still frozen. He could hear but not move. She scuttled out from beneath him. "Hey Bi'ast, looks like I wasn't the one that needed saving. Now, I'd love to keep this between us. How about it?"

Bi'ast blinked.

"I'll take that as a yes. I'll be out of your hair. Watson's already got help on the way. Toodles."

You should wait, Captain.

"For what, a spanking?" Kira tapped Bi'ast on the side of his face, giving him that same mischievous grin, grabbing the thin canvas bag with her items, then pacing down and out of the alley. She walked with some haste towards the shuttle bay.

To give a full report. Sir will not like you simply leaving.

"That Sir does not like a lot of things. It doesn't change the outcome, Watson."

The approval codes will be locked out until this is settled.

"Not if I get there before he knows to do it."

Clearing the bustling part of the market, she moved from a swift walk to a run, hitting the shuttle bay at full speed.

"In a hurry there, Captain?" A ground crew worker shouted as she ran past.

There was no answer as she rushed inside the Valstar. The little transport ship's cargo hold was long enough for four seats along each wall in the cargo area, and four forward facing ones in the main cabin.

She hardly broke a sweat as she hit the back ramp. Max already stood there, his arms crossed. "Are we running from something in particular?"

"Parental disappointment," Kira said.

She hit the button to close the back hatch before heading directly into the small cabin.

Max pursued. "Kira, what have you done now?"

"I actually didn't do anything. It was Bi'ast's fault."

Max frowned. His evident disapproval formed like a rain cloud over his head that was about to turn into a full on thunderstorm.

Morgan, who'd just turned as she entered, caught part of the conversation. "I take it we're leaving?"

"Speedily, please." Kira let out a half laugh. An ache in her side throbbed from where her blaster dug in when Bi'ast fell on her. Reminding her of their reason to hurry.

THE EIKOS

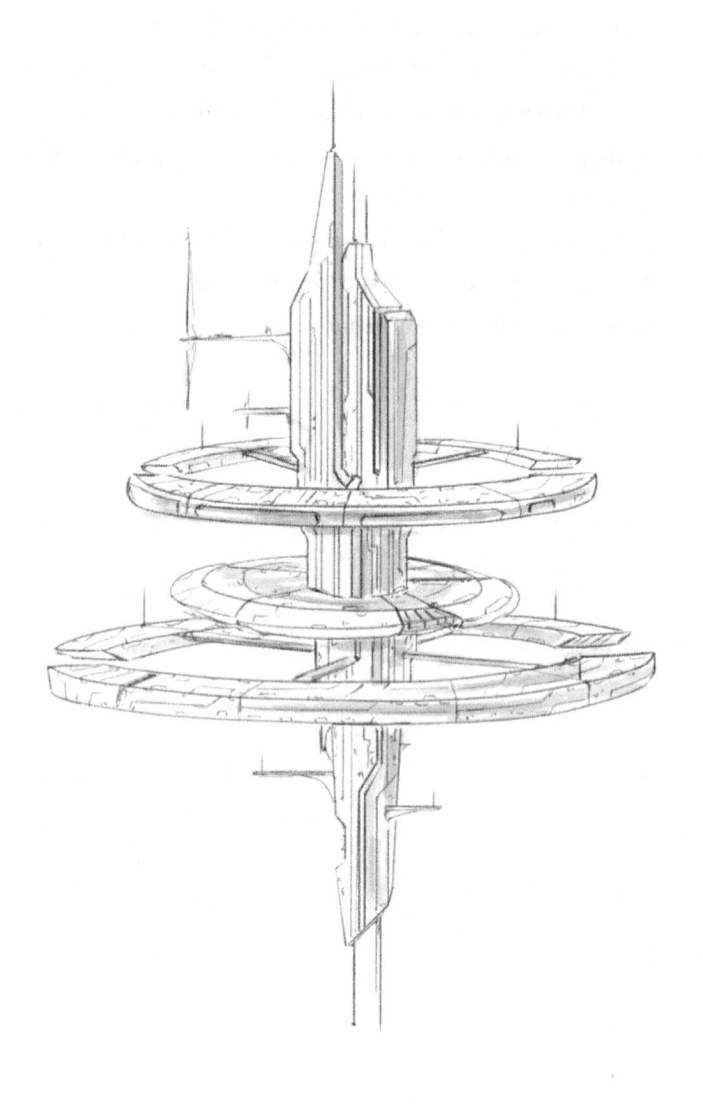

Chapter Three

KIRA

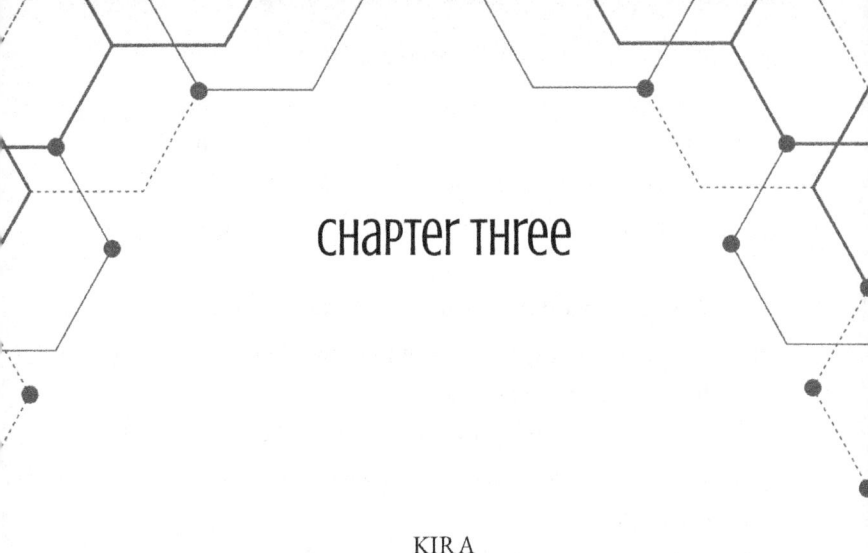

Circling the Eikos Station, the ship docked in the outer ring. The Callistar was once a Verdissian warship. It carried rail weapons and shielding, which was sometimes shaky from that time. It'd been converted for transporting supplies, typically of the illegal nature, considering who they reported to. Their current reason for deep space exploration was to mine Listium, a precious resource. It was rarely found in the known quadrants due to over mining. The retrofit of the ship was scheduled in advance; the addition of Quinn was, while inconvenient in Kira's eyes, not a change to their initial mission or purpose. They docked, and most of the crew went their separate ways. Kira pushed through the paperwork that listed them officially as off duty, doing so through their contacts within the Verdissian government, since their licensing existed in their systems.

The day after, Kira lounged in her room when Watson alerted her through the primary communication system, which he utilized when they were on the ship.

Captain, we have a security breach. They've accessed one of the data ports and I am being shut out of all sys-

Watson's voice faded to static. An unfamiliar voice sounded over the comm. This one far more robotic.

"Intergalactic planetary, planetary, intergalactic, intergalactic planetary...."

It became apparent that the initial interruption was some kind of song as a human voice joined in. The music blared over every speaker inside the Callistar, including crew quarters.

Watson switched to the personal system after he was forcefully removed out of the main soundboard. His next line rattled directly through her skull.

Captain, I do believe our guest has arrived.

"I do believe you're right," she murmured, slipping deeper into the armchair in her private quarters. She'd been nursing a bit of dark liquid in a decanter, and while she was not absolutely plastered, she wasn't quite in a state to be running about the ship either.

Sliding down a bit more, her feet dangled her toes reaching the floor as she put a hand to her forehead. "Just get the blasted music off."

Watson grumbled over the line, which translated to forced static, like a tv with rabbit ears being adjusted. He attempted to short circuit the music and not fry the whole system, or at least to get it shut off in the crew quarters, updating Kira as he worked at the task.

It cut out a moment later, and Kira lifted her glass in a silent salute the A.I. couldn't see.

QUINN

The ship automatically allowed Quinn's shuttle to dock. As the doors opened, a host of drones came rushing out. Each unique in function and design.

Small flat ones scuttled across the floor like spiders, miniature arms attached to a flat body that turned sideways to get in small spaces. Hovering ones with multiple attachments, which included pincer like limbs for grabbing equipment split apart from him going left and right. Larger ones to carry heavy equipment came out last. Approximately a three by four foot empty flat surface in the center with short sides to prevent any items from slipping off. All were in shades of varying gray and black, with blue lighting to signify their current status.

One whizzed by Quinn, flashes of white strands flitting into his field of view before settling down back over his crown as if constantly pushed out of his vision.

The Irishman lit up a smoke as he read through the diagnostic readout being fed by the drone he'd sent ahead. The text pulsing across reflected in his eyes, moving at a speed humans weren't supposed to read, much less comprehend. Especially when it was all the barely comprehensible language of ship programming.

"Jay-sus, this thing has seen better days," Quinn muttered under his breath, clicking his tongue as he headed to the engine room first.

Quinn took it all in and found it to be almost exactly as he expected. A simple industrial design, he was near the top of the ship so the corridor had a lopsided hexagon shape; the walls sloping outward until about knee height, where they sloped back inward. At that point a solid beam of white lighting ran across. The lighting was clear enough, but it seemed like the only section that someone had cleaned meticulously was the clear covers over them. There were scuffs on the lower sections and wear and tear on the top. They may have once been a bright steel, but the remnants were dull.

His drones scanned the ship as he walked, various alerts piled up. Everything indicated clear and loving maintenance, but age, wear, and tear were causing structural problems for many of the plates. Underneath, the mega-structure was in good shape. It had suffered no major damage that he could see, so that would be salvageable.

Arriving in the engine room, he knew he had his work cut out for him. The outdated reactor was nowhere near good enough for the overhaul. An automatic alert indicated the ship's A.I. was trying to regain access to the ship's communication systems. He'd dispatched one drone to plug into the computer core, which allowed him to control and shut out all other programs.

Still, it was slightly annoying. He'd have to do something about that at some point. A blip on Quinn's screen alerted him to Watson's change in tactic as the A.I. tried to access only a non-essential system. A quick scan on life support explained why.

"Whatever."

He gave a mental command, and the A.I. gained access to the intercom system in a limited overwrite capacity. Anywhere Quinn went, the music followed, blaring at the level he preferred, but Watson could shut it off to the rest of the ship.

The life support system showed three souls aboard.

The one he was concerned about was in engineering. An older man wielded a stun gun in the process of giving every speaker a short blast. It sent back feedback and flipped the array to that specific speaker. They'd have to be manually switched back on, as the system was not advanced enough to function without toggle switches.

The man's back was to Quinn, but as he turned to get the last speaker, attempting to quell the noise, Quinn got a good look at him.

Wild eyes framed with broad, thick brows furrowed in anger. A slight quiver went through a full mustache that traveled into his beard. He had silver hair, hands that no amount of washing could clean, and his personnel file had stated a tendency towards anger. The years of anger showed in the lines of his face, which made it apparent just what he thought of the music. "What sort of blasted noise are ya trying to blow me ears out with?!"

That file also filled in other relevant information, Alec O'Malley, Chief Engineer, human. Not that it mattered to him.

"It's fekking classical music yer desecrating with that bloody stun gun of yours." Quinn shot off as a drone split off from the following set to repair the breaker. "And why the fek are you on this ship? I don't need idiots running around my workyard, making a bloody nuisance of themselves."

"Because it's my bloody ship!" The mustache bristled, and the man's cheeks went a ruddy shade of red that flared to his ears.

He fired at another speaker. The man had the sort of aim that any security team would admire.

With the noise cut off, his mustache stopped its quivering as Alec said, "And your 'workyard'," He made finger quotes, "Is my engine room. You're here to make your adjustments, but I've got upkeep, too."

"There is probably a way I could say this without offending you," Quinn said, his own expression impassive. "But I don't fekkin care to. Fer the next three months, this ship is my bloody workyard. And whatever ya do on this ship is going ta cause more harm than good because, frankly, ye aren't smart enough ta handle any of this equipment. I've seen the outdated equipment yer trained ta work on, and I don't have time ta give ye a fucking lesson right now."

The speakers turned back on, flooding the engine room with music. Quinn raised his voice to compensate, "Now, unless ya accidentally want to set off a cascade that will result in this ship and your boss's boss's ship ta go up in a fusion explosion with enough yield to level everything within a hundred kilometers why don't ya go take some fekking shore leave and let me work?"

One drone flitted around Quinn. Equipped with a large electromagnet, it ripped the gun from the Alec's grasp. Behind him, the reactor core popped out.

A massive circular ring had been visible before the removal with a viewing port, but the entirety being yanked from place gave one perspective of the size. Powered by an antimatter reactor it flooded the ship with raw power, this one ventured on sixty years old, the technology outdated even by regular standards. The side maintenance accesses were open, the wiring severed cleanly at the hub, so as it passed by Alec he could see every hatch open and only remnants of the original hook ups.

Removed through a new hole formed straight through the hull of the ship and out into open space, a shining force-field let the metal head out while keeping the air in.

The engineer twisted to observe the deconstruction. The furiousness of his expression and his anger were so well displayed to someone who understood expression. But there was tension in the way he stood, something Quinn didn't recognize.

"Oh ai," Alec said, looking back to Quinn. "You think yer clever don't ya son. Well, I'll be damned if imma listen to such a farce while you do yer so called work."

Quinn rolled his eyes. This job was already giving him a migraine. He rubbed at his temples in irritation. A drone swung around in front of Alec and a holographic display popped up, showing a spaceship part. Using it to prove the updates were well out of the range of his comprehension, the hologram winked out of existence a second later.

"Instead of fekking around in my workyard making a nuisance of yerself and setting me back the time it takes for me to repair whatever thing you break in a petty act of revenge. Why don't ya find yerself a nice beach off this fekking ship and try to learn how to repair it after I am gone? 'Cause yes, I do think I am fekking clever, pops."

"Never much liked beaches," the engineer said. "Nor do I take leave if the Capin' ain't leaving either."

The pulling of spit sounded. Alec drew a bottle from the pocket he had his left hand in. What came from his mouth was dark, but the metal cup hardly showed it other than a fleck that he wiped from his beard with the back of his hand.

"Oh fer feks sake!" Quinn swore in irritation. His neural net tapped into the intercom system and he found the room he wanted with just a quick scan on life support.

"What the fek are ye still doing on the ship?" Quinn's voice crackled over the speakers in Kira's room. Interrupting the previous silence Watson gained. "Rhetorical, don't care. Your annoying ass of a mechanic won't fek off if ye won't so fek off."

Quinn couldn't see Kira, but she was still halfway down in the chair. Her glass dangling from her fingertips, which hung off the armrest. Hearing him come over the intercom, Kira let out a heavy sigh and rose, setting her cup down on the table.

"So polite Mr. Quinn." Her words were intelligible, but the pitch was high enough that it was clear she was smiling at the way he told her to leave. "For your information, Mr. O'Malley is working on some interior structural issues that should not interfere with your own work."

"I really, really cannot wait ta be away from all ya gormless fekking idiots."

Killing the call, he removed Watson's access to the ship's non-essential systems, putting his music back on full blast. He'd tried his version of being nice, letting them control the volume where they were so they didn't have to deal with it. But if they couldn't even get out of his way, he was done being considerate towards them. He was going to act like they weren't there.

Quinn locked every access door to the ship's systems, having his drones put signs everywhere that read clearly: "Authorized Personnel Only." He gave them full access to the living area and similar cabins within the ship but anything technical was off limits.

A group of drones floated around Alec, monitoring the mechanic to ensure he didn't get in anywhere he wasn't supposed to be while forcibly making him walk by prodding his back.

With that all done, he went back to work. No threats, no nothing.

Alec spit in his cup and replaced the cap, screwing it on before sliding it back into his pocket. His head tilted for a moment, a clear sign he was getting a communique Quinn couldn't hear, not that he was paying attention to him. He grumbled as he walked off, smacking at a drone, "Watson, get that blasted music off."

Alec grumbled further at whatever reply he received, pulling a thing of wax out of his toolbox. The item rolled behind him, levitating as he moved. Slipping it into his ears, he left Quinn, who'd shifted his attention back to his work.

KIRA

Kira knew she was going to have to listen or destroy her own speakers based on the report of the situation. Watson had the personal interface to relay anything pertinent, but she didn't mind the music. It might have been loud and intrusive, but it drowned out her other thoughts as she took another sip before the glass clinked down again on the metal tray that was next to her.

Deciding to make her way down after a few more slow swallows, the pounding in her head from the music overrode her usual sensibilities when there wasn't alcohol involved.

Watson was her conscience, **Captain, I would advise against this.**

"Yeah yeah."

Captain, his voice repeated. Instead of keeping the general tone of indifference most A.I.'s carried, he sounded irritated. **You promised to keep things civil.**

"I'm going to be civil," Kira said as she worked her way down through the ladders that were a part of the manual override system. There were still ways to move about without having to actually go through any of the doors with security systems. It was difficult, and one needed to have insider knowledge of the ship that was almost impossible to memorize.

It took her until the Beatles came over the speakers to pop down from the ceiling. An irksome grinding noise echoing as the hatch gave way a fine layer of rust sprinkling like pixie dust downward. Yanking the ladder, it fought against being extended. Every inch was an effort. Deciding on using her body weight instead of fighting, she hung onto the rungs, then hopped on the bottom one. It gave her a whole three feet in a room with twelve-foot ceilings. Monkey barring the last handle she landed on her feet, heavily, swaying into a standing position.

The engine room no longer looked like her engine room. A massive amount of drones circled in a symphony of timed reactions. Panels were laid flat on the ground after being removed from the walls. Stripped wires in assorted shapes and sizes littered sections along the side walls, a larger drone grasping them and throwing them onto a transport.

Grudgingly admitting it was impressive beyond that she noticed the amount of changes he enacted in but a few hours. The room was the same shape, but literally, everything inside had been gutted. While they were in Eikos station, the ship was being powered by the external feed that made sure the life support, gravity, and other systems all stayed online while the reactor was being worked on. *He isn't just updating the reactor. It looks like he's going to do a complete overhaul of the ship*; she thought.

Toke was correct. Quinn was the sort of genius that Paradigm would have exploited without looking back. She remembered how they operated, as she'd done some work with Paradigm once upon a time in order to relocate some supplies.

Or at least she'd called it relocating. They may have called it something else.

Cheeks flushed from the exertion of the journey down through the manifold pipes and something else, she started forward, each step carefully placed. Had she been a little less under the influence, she might have avoided some of the grease that rubbed off on her clothes, and the line on her cheek, but she'd not been paying much attention and she didn't wash her own laundry. Taking a few settling breaths, she gingerly stepped around one of the smaller drones working on a piece of the wall next to where she'd landed, taking off at an uneasy walk, one hand on the wall to find the culprit of her current mood.

Locating him, she watched Quinn absently pop a gum bubble as he ripped out the transformer array that currently powered the ship's non-essential systems. The new one he'd fabricated was a quarter of the size. Slapping it in, and bolting it, he cracked his back, stretching before he started stripping and connecting wires. His gruff voice parroted the song. He didn't sound very good, but at least he was on key.

"Quinn?"

She caught the exhale through his nose. His eyes closed before he looked down at her. They were electric blue, illuminated by an unnatural light that came from behind the iris. Like electricity powered his very sight. It struck her as funny to wonder if in complete darkness he could be used as a flashlight.

It reminded her of Toke's warnings to treat him kindly. While he may not be capable of blowing up her ship, yet, he could certainly blow up Toke's at the moment. With that in mind she backed down from responding with equal zeal to the 'what' he sent her way and kept herself from cackling.

Hands on her hips, her position denoted power, but being looked down upon did not aid her in making herself appear more than she was.

"Look, O'Malley can be stiff about what's been his home for some time, but he needs to make some structural repairs while we're in dry dock. I've asked him to stay out of your way as best as possible and work in different locations, but he cannot do that if he's locked out of every area."

It was as close to a please as he was going to get. Her tone had been cordial, overly polite maybe. The slight making her a little more pleasant than she might have been before.

"I, strictly speaking, don't have an issue with that. However-" He gritted his teeth as each word left his mouth like he tore them out. "He would waste his time. Ta accommodate yer new engines, I am going to have to repair and reinforce any structural weaknesses myself. So anything he does, I will likely wind up having to redo, anyway."

"Well, at least turn off the music then, so I can think long enough to figure out how to explain this to him." She rubbed at her pounding temples.

Watson came over in her ear. **Mr. O'Malley is pacing in the mess hall.**

Gritting her teeth, mimicking Quinn, she was going to grind them into nubs by the time this was all over. Kira could already feel it happening. She shook her head minutely at Watson, both at him simultaneously warning her and giving her Alec's location. Quinn barely did anything to the man, and he was already under his skin.

"Ya know, when I got on the ship and learned people were still around, I gave yer fekking A.I. the ability to control the volume, hoping it would lead to me not having any conversation about it." Reaching up, he rubbed at the bridge of his nose. "If I let your A.I. control the music in the crew living quarters, will you and yer mechanic stay in them? All I fekking want is to be left alone. I don't even think I am being unreasonable here."

Her mouth pressed together in a thin line, and the little sway she made on her feet either denoted she was about to vomit or she'd been dizzy for a second. She'd not reached for anything to stabilize herself, knowing the nauseating feeling came from hearing him talk like he'd been the most polite creature on the Eikos at the moment.

Swallowing the bile in her mouth, she gave him a fake salute. She knew if she opened her mouth, something rude would come out. Something vulgar.

With that, she turned about face muttering out loud. "Watson, get me a blasted transport to Maudlin."

Yes, Captain.

Backtracking to the ladder, her mind wasn't clear. The cloudiness made her believe her best bet was to head back the way she came. Which meant a jump to catch the ladder and a pull up to get her the rest of the way up to it. A good few feet of leaping, and she grasped it, but when her left hand tried to grasp the next rung, it all went to hell.

The fall back was comically done. Her hands flailed due to slowed reflexes, and a word slipped out in Praetorian akin to a four letter word on Earth that would cause mothers to cover the ears of their children.

Laying flat on the ground, staring up at the hole of the chute, her mind wasn't full of regret, or thoughts about her past transgressions. It was mainly full of the idea that her bottom was going to be bruised and her ankle throbbed. If she looked down, that would mean facing the fact that it felt like it faced the wrong angle.

Therefore, staring at the ceiling seemed like the right move.

Watson, being blocked from the area still, only heard her outburst, but he did not know the result of it. Her heart rate spiked but was already stabilizing. **Captain?**

"Watson," she replied. Warmth flowed through her leg, and pain, but she ignored the latter.

Quinn appeared over her after a short tick. Kira, later, when her mind could string together a coherent thought, considered that his drones probably caught the whole thing on camera.

His unpolished Irish accent did her no favors as he said, "Ya broke yer fekking ankle."

"Is that what I did?" She asked feigning shock.

He started muttering so low she couldn't hear him. It didn't surprise her, but she'd yet to look down. It would be difficult in the current position she laid in, and she really had no desire to do so.

"Aye, ye broke yer ankle. I am reading up on how ta fix it now."

Quinn scratched his chin and shrugged. One of the large cargo lifting robots came over, lowering and sliding lift bars beneath her which emulated a bridal style carry. Surprisingly gentle, the ride did not jar her as she came off the ground. Quinn led her out of the reactor room, towards the med bay, pulling out his communicator as he absently blew and popped a bubble.

"Did ya think I wouldn't let ya leave by the door?" Another bubble popped.

"You know, it was questionable." Leaning back, long tresses swayed beneath her, a breeze simulated by movement. Her vision flipped upside down, so she giggled. Honestly, to her, the situation wasn't funny. It was clearly just the end of a long few weeks that she'd not taken the time to sort properly.

"I feel like explaining that my goal is ta be left alone. Therefore, I would not, in fact, have stopped you from leaving in the most expedient way possible just to piss ya off."

"It's not what you say, it's how you say it, Quinn." Inhibitions were down still, clearly. "But if you want to be a lonely little man, that's your business."

Letting him read for a moment since he didn't decide to immediately have an issue with her correcting him about pissing her off, she didn't know how to control herself like this and she'd add, "Good taste in music, though."

Shifting in the drone's arms to bring her head upright, Kira decided she needed to look at the leg. That was clearly a mistake because she'd not been fully feeling it before but once she glanced down at the appendage, and the angle it protruded at, she let out a groan of irritation at her own self and the true throbbing set in.

"I do want ta be a fekking lonely little man," Quinn muttered after her groan, evidently deciding that the drunk Kira was worth a little triad. "Because when you are around enough people, they keep ya in a gilded cage. They take what you build and claim it's their own. You give them the key to galactic peace, and they turn it into a bomb to nuke a fekking planet."

Despite the obvious grief and anger in his voice, he wasn't yelling. His tone had fallen flat, nearly emotionless, but the anger was there just under the surface. "So yeah, maybe I am not polite and cordial and all the other fekking shite ya might want from others, but frankly, I don't care. I'm done with all of you and you can all fekking burn a million fekking light years away from me. . . and music is about the only use I've found fer people."

Food for thought, Kira mused. Enough to chew on at least until they entered the medical ward. She let out a slight hiss as the drone literally dumped her without the politeness or cordiality that Quinn had spoken upon. Before anymore choice words slipped out, Quinn got to work. She knew it was unlikely the man had ever done anything like this before, but his hands were quick, confident, and professional. He scanned the cabinets visually, found what he was looking for, to temporarily numb the limb, broke it free of the package and jammed it into her leg. The pain vanished rapidly under the anesthetic.

Evolving from injections that required needles now they worked through air pressure, uncomfortable but not painful. Kira couldn't watch, so she took the opportunity to wave off the medical drone after it activated and floated over. It was an assistant only and required direction directly from a physician registered to the ship itself.

Quinn grabbed the medical scanner and moved it over, making minute gentle adjustments to her ankle until it faced the correct way before engaging the 3D printer. Medical technology had come a significant way, but Praetorians required a cast with advancements. Their bones were thicker than humans, built of something akin to calcium, but with a density unmatched by their counterparts. She'd be in a splint for a few days while it reconnected.

For her part, she allowed him to work without speaking. It seemed kinder than interfering, but something in her wouldn't allow what he'd said to just be dropped. Watson remained quiet, but listening. *He is always listening*; she thought.

When he finished she said, "Quinn?"

If he looked at her or not, she wasn't certain. She tested the muscles in her calf flexing.

She swung her leg over the side. "Thank you." For that statement, she'd look up at him. Arguing semantics at the moment didn't help either of them. So, she let it go. Rather magnanimous of her in a current state, but she was slightly more sober than she'd been when she'd came down the ladder.

The man didn't turn, but he stopped in the doorway. He grumbled out, "Yer welcome."

Chapter Four

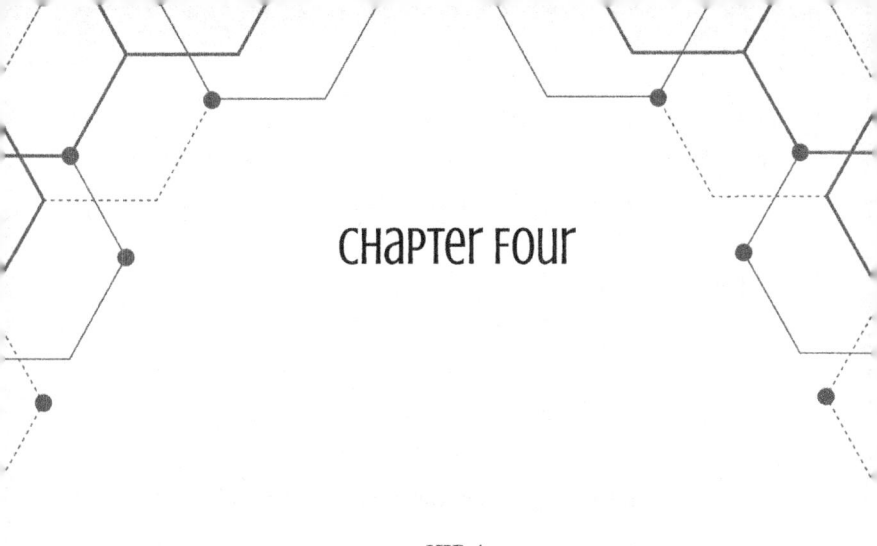

KIRA

C**APTAIN?**

Flopping back onto the cold metal surface of the exam table, Kira felt this was the last thing she needed. Covering her face with her forearms, she let out an aggravated, "Yes?"

I -

A normal A.I. didn't stutter, or stop. Their minds worked too quickly because of their programming. They were numbers that computed and spat back a response based on what was expected of them and what they had learned.

"I don't need a lesson right now, Watson. I've learned it already."

I'm not sure you ever really learn a lesson.

Kira snorted. "I'm not sure you ever do either."

I learn much faster this way.

"You do." Kira pushed back up into a sitting position. Searching the room visually, she found what she looked for: a transport table. It levitated and held up to seven hundred and fifty pounds of weight. The table worked by either lightly touching it on a handle that slid out the bottom, by using a remote to move it, or setting it to follow said remote. Shuffling on one foot across the room and awkwardly hopping over the short side rail, she picked up the datapad that controlled the inputs.

That's a clever idea.

Kira snorted. "I have those from time to time."

The transport table was about two feet wide by four feet long with a two inch raised edge, and appeared to be made of stainless steel. A rounded handlebar on one side could be adjusted for the handler's height. Beneath it rested a small slot where the datapad went for controlling it and for keeping track of the supplies on it. When Kira sat, the tablet updated automatically to reveal a Praetorian lifeform sitting on the table.

Zooming out into the hallway, it had a total grand speed of up to five miles an hour, which sufficed to move her into the wide halls.

"Watson, connect me to Alec, please."

Yes, Captain.

A second later, the man came over the line. "Aye, Captain?"

"Meet me down in the mess hall, please?"

"Aye, Captain."

The mess hall was once the size of a full football field. It'd been quartered and butchered for other uses as space became a commodity to be used for storage rather than entertainment. Leaving the dining space a fraction of the old space. Two long sleek tables with bench seats in the same finish occupied the area left.

The kitchen, just off the dining area, had avoided being gutted. Originally meant to feed an attending crew of over one hundred, a pass through section, reminiscent of a cafeteria, remained on one side for trays to be slid back and forth across. The inside resembled a reminder of humanity's contribution to cooking. There were still large ovens, along with dehydrators, old-fashioned bin sinks, large working countertops, and cold storage. There was not much to be improved upon when it came to preparing food in any society.

Alec worked in the kitchen upon her arrival, arguing with the oven. "Infernal thing! Work dag nab it."

Kira laughed while pushing the forward button moving into the kitchen but hopping off after getting close to the counters, hobbling forward around the center island to steady herself. She laid both hands flat on the cool surface. "I daresay, if it had feelings, you would have bruised them by now."

"Oh aye, just as my own have been." He continued to poke his finger against the buttons to set it properly. "A child kicks me out of my engine room."

The word room became elongated with his accent. The more flustered he became, the more he relied on it. Kira stifled her laughter so as not to offend him further. "Toke wants the upgrades done quickly, and it makes sense that we will only be in his way. From what I understand, the superstructure will need quite a bit of stabilization to withstand the new engines."

"Toke can-" Alec paused, a sharp breath exhaled from his mouth. Condensation grew on the oven as it finally beeped and showed the right temperature. "Toke can do what he wants, lass."

"He does pay for this whole-" she did a vague hand wave upward at the ship. "Operation."

Alec shifted his weight back and forth, finally turning to look at her. His cheeks were ruddy, but his eyes remained bright as always. "What have you gone and done now, lass?"

"Fell out of one of the old shafts. Well, fell trying to grab the ladder that retracted but." She shrugged.

Alec sighed heavily. "You need to be more careful, Captain."

"A few days in a cast never hurt anyone."

"Oh aye, a few days in a cast actually resting to recover never hurt anyone, but yer not gonna do that are ya?"

"I might."

Kira slipped around him to pluck a strawberry out of a bowl he'd set aside for part of their dessert. Alec smacked her hand. She shrieked a sharp 'ow' and he let out a peal of laughter at her shock.

"You're not funny." Rubbing her hand, she side eyed him, but didn't attempt it again.

"And you're not thieving before supper is done."

"Spoilsport," Kira grumbled.

Alec pointed a spoon at her as if it were a sword. "Child."

"Old man."

Alec plucked a strawberry out of the bowl and tossed it in his mouth. Kira gasped dramatically before a fake sword fight ensued with long, metal serving spoons. They fought to keep each other from the bowl.

It ended with a fake death on Kira's part, her pretending to be mortally wounded. "Grant, a dying woman, one last wish?"

Alec eyed her suspiciously. "Aye."

"I just want," dramatically clinging to the cabinet, she clutched her shirt wrinkling the fabric, "One... last... strawberry."

Alec guffawed before they both dissolved into fits of laughter, and he granted her request.

Kira and Alec crossed over to the Eikos station. A large bridge connected the station to the Callistar, remaining in place to allow supplies to be shuttled back and forth. The bridge provided a regulated and pressurized atmosphere for the safety of all passing through.

Alec and Kira met at the gate in the morning. Alec's old leather bag hung loosely over his left shoulder, the thick strap digging down. He would take the shuttle Kira ordered to Maudlin. Kira waited impatiently, tapping her good foot. She'd skipped the transport table and had gone for a stiff boot instead. If their chief medical officer, Bre, had been aboard, she would have torn her a new one about keeping off her leg. However, she had matters to attend to.

Kira started on the first. "This is the tablet with the new specs on it. You'll have everything you need to look over the new systems before you return. I've sent everyone else's homework on an encrypted line."

"Oh aye, shore leave isn't really shore leave without an assignment, is it?"

Kira smiled. "It's not."

Alec tucked it into this bag, swinging it back into place. "Are you walking with me, Captain?"

"To the shuttle. Then I have a meeting with Commander West."

Alec smacked the button on the lift a little too hard as she said the name. Both were silent on the matter as they waited for his floor. He hit the next door with the same pent up anger, and it swished open to the Eikos' outer ring.

The Eikos served as a shipyard repair station. Staring inwardly there was a tube-like center, then a large lower ring and a smaller upper ring. The lower ring was where the larger galaxy class and mining ships docked. The inner part of the large ring was for smaller ships, cruisers and the like. They could fit in the space before one reached the towering center. The center being the primary hub of activity. The upper ring was where shuttles and transports docked, dropping off supplies. Everything had to be cleared through customs in the center before being transferred to the lower ring for customizations and repairs.

The pair made their way across one of the permanent passages on the outer ring to the main column. Passing security, they scanned access badges coded for their ranks before they could grab a tube heading for the upper ring.

"You're sure you'll be alright by yerself, Captain?" Alec was keeping the shuttle from leaving by lingering, rechecking his belongings as if he had forgotten to pack something.

"Right as rain Alec, don't worry." Kira waited until he stood up all the way. She leaned in and embraced him.

He returned it after a second, wrapping one arm stiffly around her back.

"Take care of yourself, old man."

Alec didn't return the jest, but squeezed her a little tighter before making his way onto the shuttle, still patting his pockets restlessly.

Commander West liked to keep people waiting. It was a power move, schedule a meeting, then make sure that you were 'busy' when they arrived. The tactic was as old as time and Kira expected it, not that she'd stand for it, but she certainly knew it was likely.

She'd passed through the Eikos station, taking a few shortcuts over to the tube that hit the officers' quarters and offices. The principal thoroughfare on the station had been about what it was on the Meeting Place. A collection of strange faces and races all obtaining last minute supplies, hashing out deals for repairs or upgrades, or visiting one of the many on board spots for entertainment and drinking. A one stop shop for some and reputable enough they had upscale clients as security kept the station clean and the janitorial staff kept it well cared for.

Kira popped down a side hallway that ran the outside ring to avoid some of the open areas. They'd boarded here before and she'd be recognized, and she wasn't in the mood to be trifled with, nor did she want to be late. The Eikos was familiar enough to her that she could skirt around the crowds.

Hitting security again as she came to the commanding decks, she flashed her pass, explained she was there for a meeting, and was given directions, unnecessarily. Rolling her eyes after she passed the scanner, she hit the alert button for West's office.

"May I help you?" A decidedly feminine voice came over the line.

He's gotten a new secretary, Kira thought, "Captain Starling here to see Commander West."

A beep sounded and the familiar swishing of a door showed she was free to enter. Crossing into the room, she left a metal platform for something much more plush, actual carpet. The Eikos itself was what one expected of space, modernity in smooth lines and harsh metal mixed with a few sparse touches of luxury, but the Commander... well he liked to have a mixture of what the 1960s might have looked like if they'd been in space. Oval-shaped desks, odd egg chairs, and the plush bright ugly orange carpet.

Kira hated the sinking feeling of softness under her heels, but she moved forward, giving the secretary a passing glance walking straight to the next door.

"Captain Starling, I'm afraid he's not ready yet," the woman rose to stop her from entering.

The door auto-locked so Kira pivoted towards the woman, getting a good look at her. She was West's type, blonde, curvy, and possibly dim-witted. They'd find out in a moment. She adopted a bright smile, stalking over like how a predator stalks their prey.

The blonde woman sat back down, satisfied, not knowing what she'd gotten herself into. Kira planted her hands on the smooth white table, the shellacked surface threatening to make them slide across.

"Let me guess, the Commander is entertaining another guest?" Kira leaned over her hands, every word bringing her just a little closer to the woman.

Blondie swallowed at the proximity. Her robin egg blue eyes were wide as saucers, "He's, uh…" She licked her lips, "He'll be done momentarily."

"Mmm," Kira was inches away now, her own amber gaze trapping the woman in place, "I'm sure he will be. The problem is that I don't intend on waiting."

"I'm afraid-"

"That I insisted," Kira spoke over the woman, "Hit the button. Please."

"There's no need to assault my staff, Captain," the Commander spoke from behind Kira. She recognized his voice immediately. It wasn't one she'd soon forget because while he acted like he was a Talcien's relative in his actions, that snake charmer oil salesman's voice just sealed the deal.

Kira shot upright, turning about. "Commander! Lovely to see you again."

Centered in the opening between the two offices, she noted his hair had been slicked back, possibly with the oil she joked about him selling privately. Chopped at the nape of his neck, it all landed perfectly there from where he'd combed it that direction. His uniform fit tightly, the black polyester mix straining across a muscled chest, and his broad shoulders, but his nose had taken one too many hits and was a little crooked. Ones he'd probably deserved if anyone asked her.

"As it is always lovely to see you Captain, now if you're done disturbing Miss. Donahue, you can follow me."

"I'm done," Kira winked at Blondie before following the commander into his office, which was even more repulsively decorated because there were bright neon orange accents on top of shag.

"Would you like something to drink, Captain?"

"No, thank you."

"You can take a seat if you'd like." West poured himself something out of a decanter. Fake booze, she guessed. It lacked the smell of ethanol but provided the same kick if one allowed it.

Kira eyed the furniture hesitantly. Anything covered in fur was questionable, so she'd politely refuse, "I'm good standing, thank you."

West took his time, adding in one ice cube after another, each clinking against one another.

Captain, how long should I give you?

Watson sounded off in her ear. His reminder he was present with her as he always was. When she crossed the threshold from her personal quarters, Watson automatically rerouted to the implant with standard permission protocols in place.

Kira tilted her head, her eyes flicking to West, "Five," she muttered low enough he would not hear her.

Might I remind you we will be here for some time, it would be best to keep your temper under control.

Kira snorted.

West added in his last ice cube, "Everything alright over there Captain?"

"Peachy." Assuming a relaxed stance she said, "I'm only here to make sure all of our paperwork is in line? Since we were allowed to dock I assume we crossed all our t's and dotted our i's?"

"Not here for a friendly chat?" West raised his glass to his lips. There was something extremely wormlike about them, Kira decided, as he took a drink.

"Usually summons like this are about protocol."

"Ah," West fiddled with his cup, sending his ice spinning around in it, "Miss. Donahue personally processed your paperwork. Everything was in line. I simply wanted to check in with you... Kira, I was informed you were supposed to be staying on board the Eikos."

That earned him a sharp look, both for the use of her name and for the fact he wanted to check in, "Commander West, I do not believe it is any of your business whether or not I remain aboard the Callistar."

"You know I do not mean it like that," he sighed and set his drink down, "There is always a place for you here on the Eikos. You'd be safer here-"

"Safer how?"

"Well, for one you wouldn't be on a ship with a stranger without proper security, and two-"

"Watson is there," Kira interrupted him, not allowing him to give a second reason.

West frowned, his chin dropping a little, "And two, it's not healthy to be alone like that. Besides, you don't think Watson can't be worked around? Toke didn't spill all the beans, but he gave me enough to know that the retrofitter of your ship can work around an AI."

"Well, one," Kira raised a finger and her eyebrows, her tone sarcastic, "I'm a grown woman who can look after herself, and two," a second finger shot up, "I don't like the accusations you're making about my new crew member."

Kira knew Quinn was not quite a crew member, but for the sake of arguing with West it wasn't worth the semantics. Shifting her weight to her good leg, her ankle ached inside the boot. She'd covered it with loose pants, but a good look down would give it away.

Which was exactly what West did when she'd moved. "Kira is that a medical brace?"

"It's the new style these days," she shot back venomously. The anger there made it clear. It was best that he dropped it.

The room speaker beeped before Watson came over the line, "Commander West, sorry to interrupt, Captain Kira, you have an urgent message from Sir."

Kira breathed in a slow breath. He was early, but she thanked the stars he was. "Thank you, Watson. Forward it to my communicator."

West stepped towards her almost physically, barring the exit, but she was quicker.

"Thank you Commander, I'm glad everything is in order. I really must be going."

"Kira-"

"Bye Commander."

His door wouldn't auto lock from the inside, so she was out of it and past a very confused Miss Donahue in a matter of moments.

Taking a few deep gulps of air in the corridor like she'd just left a stuffy room, which she had, she'd grin like a Cheshire cat. "Good timing, Watson."

Someone had to save you from yourself.

"You're a good man," she'd chuckle under her breath, starting a very painful walk back to the Callistar.

Chapter Five

KIRA

Hitting up the med-bay first, Kira was immensely grateful that Bree, their ships doctor, was an organized little critter. She also liked labels. "Bless her," she said as she opened the medicine cabinet.

Most of the prefabricated meds that were prepared as time savers, analgesics and nausea medications. Both fixed two of their main problems: people getting hurt, and newcomers not used to space travel chucking their cookies.

Grabbing a labeled vial, she popped a pill in her mouth, swallowing it without a chaser. Praetorians lacked a gag reflex because of their primary diets, once upon a time, requiring some rather unsavory things. Their anatomy differed from humans regarding their trachea and esophagus being completely separate, so they couldn't suffocate from choking unless someone jammed it down their nose.

Easing back onto the counter, she grabbed the unobstructive scooter Watson had insisted she bring back with her to the Callistar.

I told you. You should have grabbed those last night.

"Just because you kept me from making a fool of myself earlier doesn't mean you get to chastise me now, too."

Where would I be without my 'I told you so?' His voice was generally bland, but he could push emotion into it and he was clearly amused. It was like how one knew someone was smiling on the phone.

"Still-" Kira stopped herself before she could finish the sentence. Telling Watson that he'd still be in the system was an absolutely no go situation. He couldn't help it.

Still here, I know, I'm still grateful to be anywhere.

"I couldn't just let you go." Kira looked up at the ceiling, blinking away emotion.

You'll never have to.

"Heh." Kira pushed off. The pill already kicked in, and her stomach growled. "I think I'll take our guest some lunch."

The Eikos can send over a tray, as was arranged. He went back to being emotionless.

"Yes, but where's the hospitality in that?" Kira chuckled, wheeling her way out to the kitchen.

All the doors she'd tried allowed her access, even where Quinn worked, despite the fun little signs she passed everywhere, so it wasn't necessary to take the access panels. Rolling through and munching on an apple, she carried a brown paper sack in the hand holding onto the handlebar of the scooter. Watson still did not have access to a lot of systems on board, but after checking where the speakers were active, he'd been able to pinpoint Quinn's location, nestled in the reactor.

The entire area was an organized chaos. Drones flew back and forth, causing her to stop and go as if in traffic. The rewiring in process impressively done, the array torn back to reveal the innards. Kira looked on in curiosity at each part as she passed by it before becoming more focused on hearing some sort of techno music.

Following her ears, she came to one of the floor panels that he'd tossed aside to reveal an engine shaft. She got down on one knee to knock on the side before backing up a little. She waited on either a sign he heard her or a sign he hadn't. Considering the volume of the music, she prepared to knock again when she saw movement.

Quinn popped up like a prairie dog. His white hair slicked back with grease. Unlike West, it didn't look purposeful, just as if he'd been putting his hands there absentmindedly trying to get the locks out of his face while he worked. His glance seemed accusatory. Not that she blamed him after their last interaction.

Kira waved the doggie bag with a grin.

Quinn grunted before stepping back down the ladder, disappearing.

Kira shrugged and left it on the side of the panel, figuring he'd be back when he was ready for it. Or he wouldn't, and one of his drones would dispose of it. She'd done her fair share.

Rolling away like a nineties kid on the scooter, she'd be popping wheelies if she could.

"Well, that could have gone better," she said aloud.

The man wants to be left alone.

"Oh pish posh." She wheeled around a corner, leaning into it as she sped away. "He's gotta eat, and it's just as easy to make a little extra."

It's just as easy to leave him alone.

Kira didn't reply to that one.

It developed into a pattern. She'd drop off lunch. He'd grunt or barely acknowledge her, but later she received a message through the com system to the tune of 'Thank you, it was good.' Considering his original attitude, she found that downright polite.

The third day, he was stuck inside the reactor core. Quinn couldn't get out without a struggle, and she left laughing when she heard him grumbling, "It's a bloody frictionless environment, no good gosh darn reason they couldn't have made this space a little bit fekking bigger except ta save money on materials."

There was far more colorful language from what she could hear up top before she rolled away. Just like the day before, there was a message from Quinn thanking her for the meal.

A full week passed, and there were no changes. Minor exchanges here and there, but nothing major. She dropped off a cupcake on the sixth day, which was a Saturday. Out of the cast, and no longer reliant on the scooter, she was in a good mood.

Setting down the wrapped plate, she put the cupcake on the side of a table that had once been where Alec used to set things when he worked. It would keep it well enough until he was ready.

"I'm doing waffles in the morning," she said to him, knowing he couldn't care less. "It's Sunday. With strawberries," she added, since that was her favorite.

Quinn paused in his work at the addition. For once not in the reactor, but in the hall, so she didn't have to wait for him to appear. Their exchanges had been bare bones, and this was more than she'd said to him in quite some time. She caught a muscle ticking in his jaw.

She wondered what he thought. Would he think it was even an invitation? Clearly, he considered something because it took him a second to conjure up a reply. When he opened his mouth, he only said. "Alright."

The muscle in his jaw relaxed. *Baby steps*, Kira reminded herself.

She knew the problem with olive branches was that they were in short supply, just like the amount of flying birds he gave at any moment. She was shorter than most in that department as well. Betrayal, even the slightest, would get them bumped off her radar. A thing she believed Quinn understood better than most.

Figuring that was the best answer she was going to get, she'd turn to head the other direction leaving him with his lunch, and the cupcake, which looked to be covered in icing in such a way as to distract from the fact it was slightly lopsided. While she had not learned to bake things well, even with a tin, it was as delicious, being made with raw ingredients.

You invited him to breakfast?

Watson came over the line the instant they were out of earshot, so she could reply freely. Quinn may have been keeping him out of most things, but he could hear her side and most of what came through the communicator.

"I did," Kira said lightly, taking the shuttle up.

Do you think he'll actually accept?

"Probably not." Was that disappointment in her voice? Kira had a sort of curiosity that couldn't be denied, or easily subdued. Quinn's previous confession had only strengthened her need to figure out what lay beneath the exterior. Her crew was important to her. It was key to her effective captainship to make connections with each member.

Watson made a sound that resembled a 'hm', as if he considered it as well.

"Watson, you never keep your opinion to yourself for long, so you might as well say it."

We're only transporting him after he finishes this work. Hela can ship his meals to his room, and he'll want nothing to do with anyone else.

Kira quieted after that. The only way to tell if things would change was if he showed up the next morning.

Right as she'd begun cleaning up, the man in question, for the first time, appeared in the kitchen.

He looked like a steamroller had run him over. With bags under his eyes, Quinn grumbled under his breath. The only words Kira caught were, "way too fekking early."

The man yawned as he scratched his cheek and blinked as if he realized he was late. "Buggering fek."

"Good morning to you too, sleeping beauty." Kira stood by the waffle iron which she'd been turning over.

The grunt Quinn offered in return sounded almost like a snorted laugh, or perhaps a disgusted one. He wasn't looking her way, so it was hard to tell. In fact, he sat at the table with his head face down on top of his arms, shielding his face.

Kira laughed brightly and opened the old-fashioned iron by flipping it back over. Pulling the waffle out with tongs, she'd been about to put it on a plate and leave it for him since she figured he was just being unsocial. She'd ate in the kitchen, so she piled up the syrup, strawberry bowl, and the butter between her two hands. Kira also grabbed a glass of milk and somehow delivered it to the table without spilling a drop. She rearranged the table and sat down across from him.

"This is just fekking, sugar." The man sounded a bit shocked by the revelation.

"There's some stuff in the strawberries that's good for you." She told him as she set the syrup next to him. "Try this on it."

She plucked a strawberry out of the bowl. The Callistar boasted a hydroponics bay in which most of their vegetables and fruits came from, perhaps a little rushed by the ability of the fertilizer and current technology, but still fresh. That was where their fruit hailed, the wheat as well, which was Hela's business. Kira stayed out of her way and just used what she needed with approval.

Quinn eyed the bottle and Kira with a frown, but shrugged and did what she suggested. He took a bite, chewed thoroughly, then nodded his head. While he still scowled, it wasn't like he could deny that he enjoyed the meal. It vanished fairly quickly.

Still, he wasn't chatty. When he finished, he cracked his neck, making an audible sound.

"Thanks," he muttered to her as he eyed the dirty plate. Kira caught a flash of blue, and a moment later a drone showed up, clearing it away before she could react.

"You're welcome."

Kira expected very little out of the man. He was clearly a loner. She kept him company while he ate, only picking out the occasional strawberry and enjoying the quiet that built up. It was not as awkward as she might have believed it could have been, but the Vicar had not yet returned to make things interesting with Quinn. She knew Max was going to be shut in a corridor before things were over- by Quinn.

Watson butted in after she finished that train of thought. **There's a message from Toke.**

"Is it urgent?" She had to ask aloud for Watson to hear.

It is not flagged as such.

"Then it can wait." Talking to oneself wasn't seen as a psychiatric disorder with the matter of futuristic technology. One was most likely talking to an A.I. or talking on a cross line in the ship.

Watson made a clicking sound, which made her grimace in return. She hated that sound as it rang loudly, vibrating her ear drums. It was his way of expressing his displeasure.

Quinn didn't seem to register her talking at all. If he did, he didn't seem bothered by it. The drone that cleared his plate came back for the rest of the supplies. Quinn ducked out before she could get another word in edge-wise.

The message from Toke was simple and to the point. A date, time, and location. She had asked for a meeting before the Callistar left Eikos, and he'd given her about a week to cool her heels. Kira mused he probably hoped she'd come to something akin to peace with his orders, to avoid yet another argument.

The Valstar

Chapter Six

KIRA

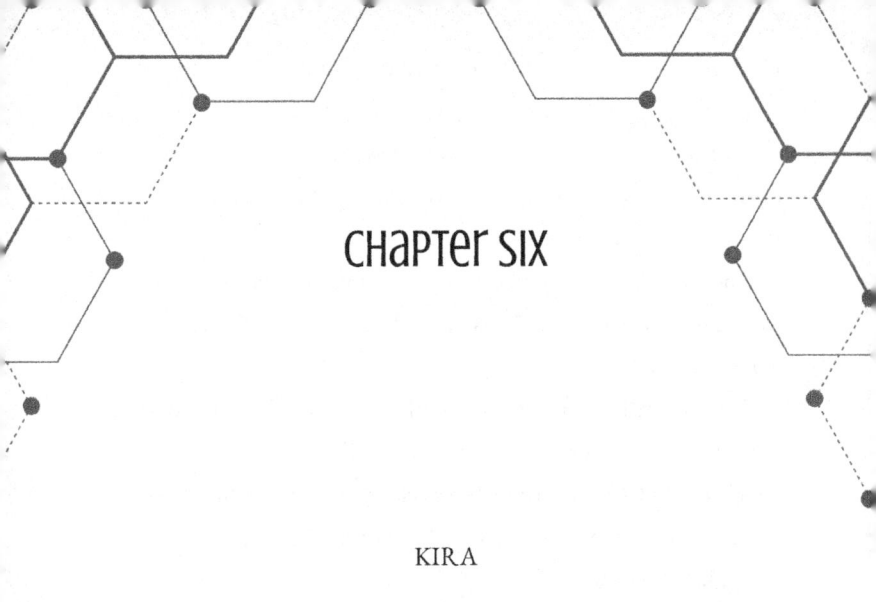

Their normal schedule resumed for the next day. Quinn being left to his own devices. Lunch, or something closer to breakfast, considering his schedule delivered by Kira around his workspace. Tuesday brought a change as she waited patiently for him to appear, all while hearing a distant grumbling.

She stopped one of the hovering drones by touching its side. It looked like another octopus that simply floated with its legs swinging about. It turned, presenting its front face, which was a rather large viewing screen.

"Would you let Quinn know I am here?"

It beeped acknowledging her before swinging around and heading up to where the new reactor core was being installed. Quinn popped out feet first, crawling backwards.

Kira kept quiet until his feet hit the solid platform that he'd raised up for his work. "I will be gone for a week. Would you like me to have someone on the Eikos bring you something for lunch?"

"Why the fe..." The man started. He paused, working his mouth closed with an effort, frowning slightly.

To Kira, he looked like a fish out of water when his mouth was open. The gears weren't quite visibly turning, but it amused her to think he had to process how to reply.

The same awkward gesticulating of opening and closing came before he struggled out with, "Thank ye... fer asking... I will have a drone get my lunch."

She could tell he was trying to be nice, and possibly trying to resist pointing out that he'd been capable of handling his food before her, which would have been rude. It was clearly painful for him to piece together a reply that wasn't telling her to fek off in the strange Irish accent he'd concocted.

"Oh, that was hard for you, wasn't it?" Perhaps teasing him wasn't the right move, but she wasn't drunk this time and she'd seen the frown before he'd haltingly got out his words.

"Oh, fek off, I tried." Quinn flipped her the bird, vanishing back into the reactor core.

Kira covered her mouth to stifle a bit of laughter. The ambient music, which she hardly even noticed anymore, changed drastically. It had been more mellow and now was suddenly harsh and deafening.

I think you made the poor boy angry.

Kira could not reply without yelling, so she'd walk back the way she came until the music didn't threaten to burst her eardrums. "Oh fek off," she told Watson, mimicking Quinn.

The burst of short static that sounded in her mind was almost like a snort coming back across the line.

Are we no longer respecting his privacy?

"I am respecting it to the extent that I expect he respected mine."

Watson repeated the fuzzily gray noise. It hit intensely sharp in such a short burst.

"You know I hate that Watson, if you need to scold me, just do it verbally."

This is more effective.

"If your goal is to get me to shut you off."

...

"That's what I thought."

Offloading onto the Eikos early, Kira took advantage of the main ship's log to do a thorough analysis on Quinn, or rather Paradigm Enterprises. But looking into him proved to be a fruitless endeavor. His name wasn't in any record database. Considering his implants, it wasn't surprising to her. The inside of his skull was completely illegal. That extensive amount of work had been outlawed because of the intense side effects, mainly death.

Putting out a few feelers with her contacts in Rumor had turned out to be equally useless and a waste of a favor. No social media, no official record of him existing, not even a picture of him at a Paradigm facility. The galaxy was a big place, and some people slipped through the cracks, but a guy like Quinn? It seemed impossible that he could be so utterly off the grid.

But the event he'd told her about, she hit the jackpot there. A planet being destroyed didn't go without some news coverage, especially on covert channels. The publicly available information indicated that it was some unforeseen geological occurrence that cracked the planet apart. The military report on it was a much more fascinating document. It was a weapons test. A Paradigm weapons test.

"Quinn couldn't possibly have known what he was working on."

The man couldn't *not* know what he was working on. You've seen the ship upgrades. Hell, you've seen the implants. He probably has a processing system installed inside his brain.

Kira's face scrunched up a little at the mention of his processing system. Watson sounded almost matter of fact, but the use of the word 'hell' told her plenty. He still felt peeved she'd not dropped it.

"I've seen his eyes too."

The words dropped from her mouth with the softest inflection. They sparked with electricity, with light. Beneath that, she wasn't sure what color they really were. All she could see was the ring of unnaturalness when he focused upon her.

That is exactly the reason you should walk away now, Kira. He's dangerous.

"He's lonely."

That's not your problem to solve.

"The Valstar?" Kira rechecked the log. The transport she'd requested had been a general request, or so she'd thought that's what Watson had applied for.

Yes, Captain. When I contacted Sir, he made the arrangements.

"Recalling Morgan is overkill." Rubbing her eyes, she'd been staring at the screen for too long. Blue light was no longer a concern, but too much intense focus still could be harmful to the eyes of non-human races.

Should I ask for another? Watson sounded almost amused.

"I prefer Morgan's flying," she spouted off, kicking the desk to push her chair, sliding away from the console. On her feet in a sharp turn, the door opened as she approached.

I am simply glad I do not have to feel it.

Kira laughed. "Just because you know the math of what he does now doesn't mean you would have before."

Some stunts he's pulled have been outright impossible. There is no reason he should have survived them.

"Yet he does." A matter of pride for the Captain as most everything was. "Morgan is a boon to this ship. Well overqualified. We are lucky to have him."

You are lucky to be alive. The scorn he managed to get through his processor was impressive.

Kira laughed again. "There is truth in that statement, but it's not about Morgan's flying."

Arriving at the main shuttle bay for the Eikos, Kira initially expected to hop on a regular transport to Maudlin, not to be catered to by Toke to the point he used her actual pilot. When she'd checked the transport list looking for her arrangements, she'd discovered the switch. It wasn't an unpleasant surprise, but still a surprise all the same.

The shuttle bay encompassed a large section of the outer ring, with a landing platform inside one could board smaller shuttles, usually for less than twenty passengers, that passed through the barrier to land. It spanned across a wide open area with an almost translucent field that kept the environment, and gravity settings, alive within the bay. The faint purple tint made one aware of its presence. Passing by several smaller eight passenger vessels, Kira came upon the Valstar.

The familiar paint scheme of navy blue and yellow stood in stark contrast to the usual gun metal gray of every other ship. Morgan stood at the back, the ramp let down before him. Shoulder leaning into the side of the vessel, he had an ease about his stance. Morgan was the only other Praetorian serving on board the Callistar. Like Kira, his skin had copper in its tone. His physique resembled someone who just got off work on a shift at Abercrombie later, but he possessed quicker reflexes than a human. When he pushed off the side to greet her, it was unnaturally fast.

"Captain!" His grin widened, resembling the Cheshire Cat as he stalked forward, a model on a catwalk, arms outstretched as he embraced Kira, lifting her up in a bear hug. "Long time no see!"

"It should have been longer." Kira could not resist smiling back, giving him a once over to make sure he looked alright. "I'm sorry you were recalled."

"Nah, don't be sorry." Morgan made a tsking sound, turning back on his heel, motioning for her to follow him.

Kira avoided looking down. Morgan wore his flight suit, and for a semi-fitted onesie, it did wonders to highlight his assets and if he caught her eyes anywhere near his ass, she'd be hearing about it for weeks.

Morgan smacked a side console on their way in and the ramp lifted, making her half-jog the last few steps down at an angle. Landing firmly on her feet, she followed him through to the small bridge. The Valstar was a wonder of technology. Twin side engines, transport and cargo space, small crew quarters, only two, but efficiently sized above the cargo space in the small common area, and the bridge which housed four stations. Two were directly in front of the large windows, the other two were behind them flanking the side walls for monitoring, but the chairs and a smaller extension area could also be turned forward on a pivot. Kira strapped into the front station on the left in front, as the right was the main pilot chair.

"How's the upgrades coming?" Morgan flipped switches, preparing for takeoff. Both knew they should clear the Eikos with minimal fuss due to the ranking of his vessel.

"More like a retrofit than an upgrade," Kira said with a sigh. "The entire ship is being torn apart. Quinn is making sure everything is up to his standard. I doubt there will be anything original left, other than the meal trays."

Morgan laughed good-naturedly as the ship lifted, turning about to clear the interior docking bay heading for open space. "Can't beat the original design on those."

"It's a classic," she agreed half-heartedly, still managing a smile for him.

They lapsed into silence for a short while. Morgan didn't need to fill the space which left her with her thoughts, and Watson buzzing around somewhere. He remained on the Callistar, splitting his consciousness in order to accompany her. It was the practice for away missions as well. He would re-upload anything he gained on the mission on their return. Not that this was a mission, it was simply meeting Toke and making the introduction for Max. Something she could quite do without having him in her ear.

Meeting up with Max for pick up went smoothly enough. His pleasure at seeing Morgan was purely genuine, as was it at seeing her. Then the meeting with Toke went semi pleasantly. She did their introductions properly this time and left them to it. Toke clearly wished to discuss Quinn. He pushed on the subject before she'd dismissed herself, but she refused to elaborate other than he'd been diligent.

QUINN

Quinn, back on the Callistar, met the expectation of the word she'd used to describe him. He gave no words of luck or goodbye when she'd departed. But he'd kept tabs on her movements on the station, and noted the ship. Tracking its progress, he had slipped a small tracking beacon and drone in Kira's luggage. It concealed itself well in the suitcase. While not hyper focused upon the results of its feedback, certain words were flagged for review. His name, the Callistar, Paradigm, anything that was concerning enough to review in case there was a lapse in the security of his position.

A conversation between Kira and Toke that had been flagged, was one he heard even if he could not see it…

"And Quinn? How is his work coming along?" Toke sounded curious, or so the filter that he put the conversation through told him.

"Good," Kira replied. The word came too quickly. "He's practically making an entirely new ship."

"That's what he did to mine as well."

Kira was silent for a full ten seconds.

Toke spoke again. "Have you had any contact with him?"

"I leave him to his own devices. You said it was best not to interfere," she lied openly, but while he knew it was a lie, the system pinged nothing awkward about the words. She sounded bored, according to the analysis.

"That's… good."

"Mhm," Kira hummed back. "Well, if there's nothing else, I'll be on my way."

"Kira?"

"Yes?"

"Be careful," fatherly, compassionate, loving. The system told him that about those two words. How he packed it in there in such a short two-word sentence was something Quinn couldn't explain. It didn't matter. She'd not said anything concerning.

Still, the man sulked, though he'd never admit it. Kira had really pissed him off since he'd been making a concentrated effort to not be rude to her. Then she'd gone and been rude to him and he did not know why she would do that.

Teasing was not a concept that he was familiar with. He didn't know that she was just trying to be funny. The man was about as socially maladjusted as they came. Just shy of a feral child raised with no human contact for their entire life.

They took great care to curate and filter everything he could access in his youth, so as not to harm his development as a child. So he didn't even have many common movies and books to base things on. The reason his taste in music was so ancient was because he'd found out that the content filter didn't sort classical music by sub-genre.

In terms of gaining Quinn's trust, her decision to be rude to him and laugh about it appeared a total betrayal.

One he was unlikely to forget.

He closed his eyes, resting his head against the cool metal of the reactor. The music had returned to its normal volume a long time ago. With his eyes closed and the music playing loud, he could almost drown out his own thoughts. Kira was only part of his focus. The memories of what he'd learned and what he'd seen haunted him. He'd given Paradigm the key to galactic peace. They'd used it to destroy a planet.

The image played over and over in his head. Not only had they blown it up, but they'd also sent down drones to record the footage.

He'd gotten to watch as tens of millions of innocent people were consumed in an energy burst. They didn't even have time to scream, as their bodies were reduced to nothing more than cosmic dust.

It wanted to play over and over in his mind. But if he kept busy and kept the music loud, then he could keep it at bay. Pushing away from the metal, he let out a long, low, exhale of breath, shaking a bit as he shrugged off the memory. Then he got back to work.

Chapter Seven

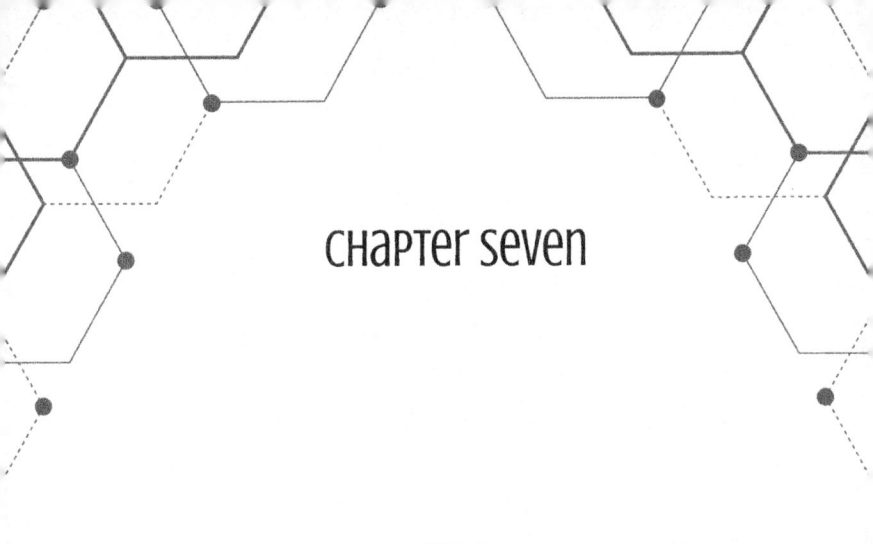

KIRA

KIRA LAID AWAKE AT night while off the Callistar. She knew it would solve nothing, but her mind raced constantly. Watson attempted to distract her by laying out some of their plans. They were going into deep space, but they would travel through some of the known quadrants before making their leave into the unknown, the uncharted. Morgan should have been involved in the conversation, but the AI seemed to know what her mind lingered on, as if he could read it himself. Morgan left after dropping off her and Max on Maudlin, back to his shore leave. She caught a regular shuttle back to the Eikos with a trader.

A full week passed before she finally returned to the Eikos, mainly to confirm that the supplies she had ordered were being rerouted properly. The Eikos would store some items that required cold storage. A precaution, just in case Quinn turned off power to that part of the ship. Her arrival at the station, and her checks, went without incident. She even chatted with the crew before taking the passage corridor to the Callistar, happy to return home.

Reaching the access door to the Callistar, she found it locked. Not unusual, but when she punched in her entry code, the system denied it.

Then, her override code was denied.

Standing there, hands on her hips, her expression, which had been so pleased at being home, contorted into something between anger and rage. Which for her were completely different emotions.

"Watson?"

I cannot access the ship's systems.

There was only one person who could be responsible.

"He's locked me out of my own damn ship." Her hand came down hard on the freshly fitted metal paneling. Newly reinforced; before it might have buckled, leaving an imprint. The harsher contact prompted a program, a hologram projecting out of the pin pad with various diagrams.

It appeared Quinn had compiled the likely reasons and questions that she might have when she returned to the ship. A shipping manifest of what she'd ordered on there, as well as where each item was currently being stored. A percentage bar for each major system on the ship, showing the current progress. The Reactor at 100%; the engines were at 52%; the rest were all sitting under 20%. Then a timer showing the estimated project completion time, which updated every few seconds.

He'd even built in a query function, so if she had questions not already covered in the report, she could ask them. The only thing she couldn't do, her furious typing of commands on the screen trying to subvert it, was communicate with the inside of the ship.

Her fingernails bit into the edges of her palms, leaving small crescent moon indents white from the pressure. "I'm going to strangle him."

That goes against Sir's orders.

The lack of reply on Kira's part should have been the first part of a warning to Watson. What was to come... Well, it would not be pretty.

For all that she knew, Quinn may have been angry. He may have misunderstood her, but she also knew he did not understand that there was no fury like a woman scorned. Being denied entry onto her own ship was the last straw, and it threatened to break her own barely established truce. Leaving her stranded on the Eikos' desert, as there was nothing there for her, was unacceptable. Crawling back to Commander West for quarters was inconceivable. She'd sooner walk on hot coals than that shag carpet again.

Turning on her heel, every footstep became punctuated with the weight of her fury. The Eikos had suites available to be checked out on demand, available for outer repairs on the ring. A sharp right and she entered the small mechanics room nearest to their docking site. One of the staff, a smarmy man, gave her an immediate smile as he rose out of his seat to offer his help.

Put straight back into his seat, Kira exerted a quick pressure on his shoulder and a sharp, "I can help myself," as she yanked down a bio suit.

The side airlock had two sections, one for dressing and preparing, then an outer for decompression and exit into space. Settling in the first chamber with the neoprene like suit, she drew it up over her waist before she'd begin securing the buckles along the thighs. Thick, heavy loops rested on her hips. Meant for tool storage or supplies to be rigged in, she left them empty.

Drawing the zipper up to her throat, the black fabric fit like a second skin. Reaching onto the wall for the respirator, she attached the inconspicuous black metal triangle to the center of her chest. It created a film with a translucent appearance, not unlike a bubble.

The triangle sat there with a sharp point down and the other two pointing at the shoulders. It wrapped the breathing space over the shoulders to encompass the head. Lightweight and invisible to the eye of the one wearing it. If the suit was a second skin, this was the original, so close and moving as she moved. After testing a few breaths to reassure herself of its working order, she felt satisfied enough to enter the decompression chamber.

The outer door reflected her appearance as she stood waiting to leave. It showed her the level of irate calm that possessed her. Her dark hair plastered against her neck, the suit fitted in all areas revealing her shapely figure, but her eyes, the deep pools of amber surrounded by thick lashes, flashed impossibly with fire, glinting. No internal processor needed.

Kira, do you really think you should do this?

"Watson?"

Yes?

"Get out of my head."

The suit ended in heavy boots containing magnets to attach to an outer hull. Boosters on either side provided propulsion and stabilization. The guidance worked by a built-in controller resting on the forearm, a quick pad system that used single finger movements to direct the amount of force exerted on the bottom of the boot while one moved their feet to direct themself.

Air flooded out. Space flooded in, and she kicked off the edge, heading around to the side of the Callistar, looking for one of the maintenance hatches that were accessible, hoping he'd not thought to change the codes on every entry point. At least if his logs were anything to go by, he had not gotten to fixing them yet.

Clasping the side's riveting and the handles a quick scan and the door popped open. The smaller compartments had a miniature version of the two-room system but made for only a few souls.

Grumbling as her feet landed, she tugged the door tight behind her, beginning the sealing process. Utilizing the manual system of turning bars, unlike most current ships, what she'd failed to realize was that it had already been upgraded. The hinges automatically retracted, sealing for ease of use, which happened as she leveraged the door back.

Thinking she was in the clear to hit the lock for the hall, she started for the interior door, only to be sucked back out into space. The cold violent wrapping of nothingness pulling her out by the sudden negative pressure flooding inward.

Flying outward, kicking out her feet and hitting the jets, she pushed back towards the side of the ship. A swarm of drones came out of nowhere, surrounding her next to the lock where she landed. A quick glance backwards and...

"I'll teach you to cut holes in my ship!" She screeched the words while waving a fist at the drones. Knowing how unlikely it was he'd get the message from only that, she included a rather coarse gesture. She hoped they were recording this, capturing her intended vulgarity.

A team of drones with laser cutters huddled outside the newly done hole where she'd been ejected. Two shield emitter drones on either side corrected the atmosphere while four cutters had been used to make the hole; basically a perfect trap. Which meant it was a good thing she'd not yet taken off her environmental suit.

"Child," she added to her tirade. Maybe Quinn had been playing fair before because he hadn't actually been angry with her. Maybe this time she had hurt him, and he lashed out like the child she labeled him as, inarguably overreacting in the extreme. It showed why Toke had given up on trying to get to know Quinn in any capacity. He may have been a pacifist, but he was a pacifist with an army of drones.

She returned to the Eikos mechanic station. The same grimy worker attempted to rise out of his seat. He got the same treatment he had the first time. Ripped two stun guns off of the wall, inserting one into the side loops, she hit up the security panel next. Counting on the fact that his drones weren't specifically shielded against an EMP, she hoped it would put them out of service until he could replace the internal chargers. But betting on his ability to quickly adapt, she'd bring true projectiles. Kira hit a switch on the one still out and ejected a magazine out the bottom. Previously empty, she took dummy projectiles loading them in one by one, each a heavy rubber-like ball. A quick adjustment to the setting and the rifling in the barrel clicked into place.

Her aim would have to be very exact to not cause the sort of damage one wished to avoid in space. Toke made sure she'd not been brought up to be anything but excellent at meeting expectations in all fields. Firing a phaser took very little skill, firing ammunition with accuracy took true sighting.

He'd caught her off guard once, she wouldn't let him do it again. Piloting towards one of the farthest entrances, betting he'd assume she'd go for the next one on the line, she mentally continued her tirade. Activating the mag boots on the outside, she flung open the hatch, deactivated the boots, and went through like a submarine sailor tossing herself feet first until she plopped on the ground in the artificial gravity.

Her left side held the modified bullets, her right hand scooped the handle of the regular phaser, setting the stun into place and taking a defensive posture, she proceeded. She did not dare to deactivate her suit. Not trusting Quinn, pacifist or not, enough to think he'd care if she could breathe or not. This time, she made it out of the decompression room.

The same setup as before approached her. Laser cutters and shield emitters, both the octopus-like drones that floated with the specific attachments on their long appendages. A ball joint inside each one allowed them to move almost organically, except for the fact they could twist any section in a 360 degree movement.

Ducking behind a ballast, it was no contest as she let loose a few shots. Each drone deactivated. The satisfying thunk of metal on metal as they collapsed made her smile. She stepped proudly over them until shell-shocked into silence the shield emitters suddenly had her by her arms, putting her in a crucifixion-like position, locking them out thrusting her bodily out of the ship again.

You should return to the Eikos.

"Like hell I will."

Kira, be reasonable, what are you even going to do if you can get to him?

"I don't know yet, but I'll figure it out."

Blowing a puff of air to push away a stray piece of hair, it remained locked in place, unshifting because of the sleek design of the emitter she wore. A few more quick blows followed out of irritation. Retreating to the Eikos for a second to rethink her plan, Watson remained blissfully quiet while she did so.

She considered destroying his drones. The action felt appropriate. The complete calm that settled over her as she enacted a new plan was... well, a bad sign. Grabbing tools from a welding crew- they'd almost refused to lend them to her, but the look she gave them of pure determination inspired second thoughts. It instilled a terror by design almost like she'd touched them physically.

Shoving back into space, she grumbled, and Watson chose only to give a warning about the equipment she utilized.

She didn't even make it to the ship.

The drones flocked out the moment she came close enough for a life sign to be detected drifting toward the Callistar that couldn't be on the Eikos. They zipped out in a swarm. She fired off a few shots but, especially in space where she wasn't particularly maneuverable, she wasn't able to stop them before eight got into formation and created a shield cube. Quinn literally put her in a box.

Then, her communicator toggled on like Watson meant to talk to her, but it was Quinn's voice. The man sounded as angry as she felt.

"What, the buggering fek, is wrong with you? I try to be nice and you throw it in my face and laugh at me. Now, you are distracting me from my work, so you can what? Prove to me you can get aboard the ship? Let me guess, because it's your ship? Well, I don't give a shite. Just leave me the fek alone. Let me finish my work, and I'll just stay in my fekking room until you find my planet and it will all be over. You never have to see me again. So please just leave me the hell alone."

Towards the end of his impassioned speech, she could hear the anger fading to hurt as he lost his accent too.. He just sounded tired, depressed, and done with everything.

"I made one joke at your expense and you've decided to absolutely lock me out?" Talking back she wasn't even sure he was still on the line. "Are you so absolutely unable to understand even the smallest nuances of conversation with others that you couldn't tell it was friendly banter?"

She managed to be civil enough to not raise her voice the octave it wanted to go to. But it felt like admonishing a toddler that taking someone else's things was wrong. If he understood others well enough, he would have heard the tension in her voice, the tightness, the heavy breath that came as she kept control of herself. Banging her fist against one of his drones, she turned off the communicator for just a moment to continue her barrage of words that he definitely would not understand.

Watson still had access- she didn't keep him out- and he came across with a soft **Kira you should just let this one be.**

"Shove it Watson." Lashing out at him, even if it wasn't his fault, was unfair. She had no control of the knee jerk reaction. She'd feel bad for it later.

Quinn clicked back on in a voice unknown to her, the inflections were gone, the emotions were gone. It sounded like she was talking to an A.I. that lacked a personality module. The only reason she knew it was Quinn was the smoothness of his voice. Even the best A.I. had some processing in their voice without a module. "I was raised in a *lab*. Anyone that was too friendly with me was fired. Paradigm was worried interpersonal connections would inhibit my growth as an asset. I was not a person. I was an experiment.

"So no, I don't understand the *subtle nuance,* as you call it. Such things were considered unnecessary to my directives. However, people have proven to be a constant disappointment to me, so I do not feel particularly bothered by this. I made a sincere effort, and you mocked me for it. I would like to be left alone, Captain Starling. Please respect my decision. As previously stated, once the ship is complete, you can have full access back. I will remain in my room until you find me a suitable planet and our business will be completed permanently. I do not think asking you to find other lodgings while I work is an unreasonable request. If you continue to persist, I will break my deal with Toke and find someone more willing to be reasonable."

"Stars Quinn." Relaxing her hand against the drone she just touched, Kira spread her fingers wide arching the tops of each one back until the tips drew down. Softly, she said, "Just don't do anything to Watson's systems. Please."

She begged. It wasn't a request. It was a very odd, strangled, ask that he would not mess with him. If he did, he would learn his true origin. If he made even the smallest change, he could destroy him. Quinn was updating all systems, but Watson was the one that needed to stay exactly the same.

Watson could hear them both, but he did not comment upon it.

"The Digitized Praetorian Consciousness you've designated Watson will not be harmed. The last step in the retrofit will be reconnecting him to the ship's new systems. He may be pleased to learn that this will include the new drone bay for emergency external repairs, reactor maintenance, and general maintenance, as this will give him some physical agency once again. By personal choice, I have decided to do no further harm, as I have seen the purpose many of my inventions have been turned to. I consider digitized consciousnesses to be a valid form of life just as any other."

That voice of his remained placid, but there'd been a break in it. She heard that small fracture when he mentioned his inventions. She knew Paradigm was responsible, but he felt guilt. The mental abuse weighed heavily upon him, that much was clear. Neglect could be as harmful to a person's psyche as anything else. Combine that neglect with knowing you had played a role in countless deaths? It was little wonder he wasn't good with people.

She realized the depth to which she had wounded the man on the other end of the communicator. It had been a joke to her. For him it had been yet another time an attempt to connect with a person had ended with pain.

"I'll take your silence as confirmation that you find this agreement equitable. Thank you for your cooperation."

The shields clicked off, and the drones retreated, Kira floated alone, drifting in the void of space.

Are you alright?

"I feel like you should be asking him that."

I'm not worried about him.

Adjusted the aim on the control pad, the thrusters kicked to life. She had supplies that needed to be returned to the Eikos. She let out a shudder at the idea of having to arrange quarters under West and instead sought the station's quartermaster. Arrangements were made with a little bribing to keep the room under a different name.

QUINN

Quinn found, on the third day after she'd taken up residence on the Eikos, that his drone came back with a little paper sack instead of the usual food tray. With the bag under the thin wrapping rested a box of chocolate-covered almonds with sea salt wrapped and tied in a neat bow.

He met it with a frown. He eyed the treat for a moment, then opted to open the paper sack. Par for the course, there was a sandwich. No note or anything. Just a plain thing that had some sort of mixture in it. The sandwich smelled vaguely fishy, but not in a bad way. The chemical analysis showed eggs, mayonnaise, and pickles.

He chose not to respond, giving no message of thanks this time. The bag and box were returned to her room neatly folded. Not quite forgiveness but he did, in his own way, say that he understood that it was meant to be an olive branch.

The next day was the same: the generic meal the Eikos provided, then a bag lunch from Kira, and a snack of some sort. The Eikos crew only sent what was of nutritional value with nothing special. Kira usually did earth inspired food, but occasionally she would give him something alien yet certainly edible.

On the third day after she started the deliveries, Quinn pinged her communicator with a single verbal message: "Thank you, your food tastes better than what Eikos provides."

The following day, his lunch included a handwritten note on the sack itself. "Any preferences?"

His response came at an odd hour. They usually did. He didn't treat his body well, often ignoring its physical demands far longer than he should. "No."

After several minutes passed, another response came. "Not being difficult, I haven't tried many things."

Trying to peaceably make amends in some regards, even if it was beyond him why he was doing so, he kept busy to ignore analyzing it.

The next night, with his supper, sat an insulated silver cup with a mixture of sugar, water, cream, and crushed vanilla beans, a straw beside it and another note. "Had to sneak this one out."

Quinn returned the silver cup to her in the evening via drone. It had been cleaned so thoroughly, she could see her reflection. A note left in the cup.

'Thanks.'

Later, when he retired for the day he decided to ask reopening a line of communication audibly, "Is there anything you would like to know about the status of the ship?"

"No," she said softly in return.

He didn't disconnect right away.

"I trust your work," she continued.

"Okay, thank you." He'd paused before saying it, then the communicator went silent. He manually flipped it off.

Sometimes he'd get something special with lunch, sometimes with dinner. In one package, she threw together some snickerdoodle cookies. His readout said she'd substituted cinnamon, but found a suitable replacement.

Quinn felt mildly confused about Kira. The woman had hurt him deeply. He respected her obvious pride, and once they'd reached an easy truce, he started feeling a bit more at ease. He felt terrified of letting people in. People either left him, by choice or force, or betrayed him. Underneath the layers of rough Irish accent and sarcasm was just a lonely kid who'd been hurt so often he hid himself underneath a layer of surly anger just to keep people away.

He wouldn't admit it, but he wanted a friend. So when Kira had laughed at his attempt at being polite, it had felt like a betrayal. His natural response was to curl in on himself, covering himself in spikes, to keep everyone at bay. Yet here remained that woman, against all odds, getting through his spikes and, well... he wasn't actually sure if she felt sorry for what she did. Nor could he even guess what she was trying to do now. So the next note she got from him was simple and to the point. One word, with punctuation, "Why?"

He did not get one back at lunch, but when dinner came around, he found a sheet of paper tucked up under a bar of chocolate. "The Vicar taught me that there is always more than meets the eye to everyone. I think there's more to you, too."

He didn't reply, besides his normal thank you, for several long days. He could think on several things at once, but he pushed off his thoughts about her choosing to keep her intentions unknown. Then, one evening, her communicator clicked on, and Watson and Kira both found themselves on the line.

"I'm sending a few sets of rough schematics for a drone body. This one will have a quantum computer core capable of housing Watson's entire consciousness if required, but it can also be piloted as a primary body. Let me know which one you would like, and what features you want me to include.

The line clicked dead and both of them received an alert that of a rather large data package being transferred. Quinn included a variety of options. Simply put it was essentially a build your own body kit. He included options for polymer skin with haptic feedback. This gave Watson the option of having a full human android shell. It wasn't, strictly speaking, getting his body back, but it would mean he could feel and act like a man again.

He found a full cake with his dinner which Kira had attempted to ice with the words 'thank you'. Kira's attempt to present a clear message shown in the smudges of icing smeared across the top. Quinn could guess just how many times she had erased the words and began again.

It won her quite a few points. Mostly because one of his few fond memories was a lab assistant sneaking a slice in on his "birthday." The nice young woman had been a lab assistant, and she'd been celebrating her own. Quinn had asked about the colorful birthday hat she'd been wearing and she'd explained birthdays to him. When he'd informed her he did not have one, she left, got him a piece of cake, and told him he could share hers.

The cake had tasted good, but the display of humanity had kept the memory.

She'd been terminated once they analyzed his stool and found abnormal sugar levels.

People with more power than the singular kind soul took what humanity was freely given away.

When he uncovered a note inviting him to an actual meal, he simply didn't respond. Two days later, Kira's communicator dinged again. This time there were no words, just an alphanumeric string which he knew she could deduce was the new access code for the door of the Callistar. Going into the station would be too much for him, but he was willing to let her come back into the ship.

KIRA

This is an entire build.

Watson turned off his emoting. His voice lacked the normal inflection he usually attempted to relay- that all A.I.'s relayed in order to make their voice more personable. Kira knew he did so when he didn't want to display how he felt.

The schematics were splashed across the display. The program presented the framework for building an entire android form, as if one were selecting character features from an old human style video game. It made it incredibly simple for Kira, but it was not her decision what he looked like.

"But not flesh and blood."

It's close. Better even, less destructible, more capable.

The emotionless nature in the way he said that made her shiver. Had he really been a part of the system that long? He didn't have eyes in her quarters, so he couldn't see her shake. He constantly tracked her vitals. As he did, everyone on the crew could see some synaptic feedback to reconfirm their status. But other than knowing their general location because of his tracking, he could not see her shrug, or nod, or several other more finite movements.

Shifting uncomfortably in her seat, she flipped through some options, waving her hand at some configurations for the computer to stow them for consideration. Mainly standard looks that were put together by the algorithm. She paused on one that looked akin to Morgan. Was that on purpose? The two hadn't met each other, but he'd probably had access to his file. Her file as well, no matter how much it lacked.

"These look so real."

This isn't new technology, just expensive. I saw them on Praetoria. No one could tell a difference unless they ripped off an arm.

"I thought most of the higher class preferred clones?"

Some prefer these. They keep the consciousness in a small disk that they insert into the spine. It is heavily protected, and almost impossible to destroy. Therefore, it is safer and has less risk of mental degradation.

A tightness blossomed. Life was meant to be lived and felt. A program simulating life made her nervous. Pinpointing the exact reason was impossible. Beneath all those gears and mechanizations was a consciousness, but how much existed from the original?

It will be like flesh and blood still and operate the same.

Watson took advantage of the silence. Kira looked up at the ceiling, tossing a small ball into the void, allowing it to rise and fall. The sound of the ball smacking her hand carrying.

Kira...?

"Hmm?"

Say something. Please.

Kira nearly popped off with a sarcastic retort, but stopped herself, frowning. "You still deserve a physical body."

And how am I supposed to get one?

"I've been putting back almost all of my wages."

The ball smacked back into her hand before she tossed it upward again.

That's what you've been saving for?

Smack.

"Mhm."

Smack.

Kira?

Smack.

"Mhm?"

Smack.

Nevermind.

Kira caught the ball, holding it firm in hand. With a quick decision, she threw her feet down and gathered what little belongings she'd taken off the ship when she'd left to meet with Toke. It took all of five minutes before she was ready to return. She had no intention of being off the Callistar long, so her luggage had been the bare minimum.

Chapter Eight

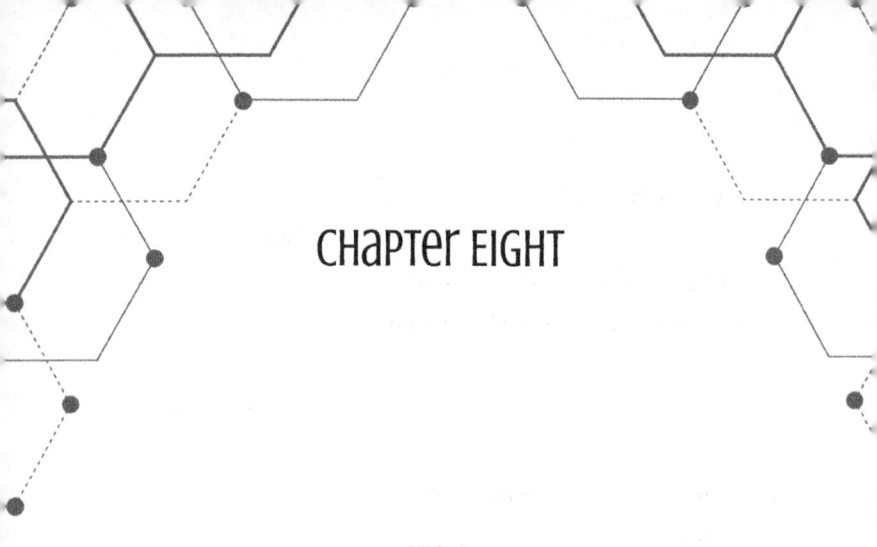

KIRA

Whatever time period he'd extended, she was within it when she crossed the bridge to the Callistar.

She entered her own ship, only to find it almost entirely alien to her. Not that the floor-plan had changed, or that anything obvious added to the distant halls. It was just clean in a way it hadn't been since it had been manufactured. The stains were gone from the walls, some she'd not even realized were that. Her reflection peered back at her through the metallic panels that she passed.

It was eerie to be in such a sterile environment. But, no sign of Quinn.

Only her, standing there, really tempted to touch the clean walls, the intrusive thought similar to mussing a new desk or a clean mirror. Resisting the urge, she made her way to her quarters, which were the same. Then she followed the halls to the kitchens. Late afternoon had fallen, and it was nearly time to start dinner preparations.

Quinn being human, she opted for a fully human meal, steak, and potatoes. Hela, their cook, had left her some frozen pies. Kira chose an apple pie and shoved it in the oven. While she could bake, her lopsided cakes said it was best left to the professionals on that front.

Setting out the steaks, she'd seasoned them on the Eikos, letting them marinate. Heading to the back cabinets, she withdrew a cast-iron skillet. A family heirloom for Hela's. She'd been the one to show her how to use, clean, and re-season it with express instructions that if it was messed up in any way when she returned it, her bottom would be so raw she wouldn't sit for a week.

Putting their plates on the long table felt unnecessary, so Kira decided they would eat at the pass through counter. There were a couple of bar stools nestled beneath it. Putting him on the far side where the overhang came out, she moved one inside the kitchen, facing the inside cabinets. She could sit close enough it wasn't a bother.

"This seems... fancy."

Kira had heard him come in, but she'd been bent over, pulling the pie out of the oven. His voice back to the gruff fake Irish accent. Why exactly he talked like that was still a mystery since she'd heard his real voice- computerized speech- from a living mouth. While the Irish accent wasn't the most pleasant, it was less unnerving than that had been.

The man looked a mess. Bags under his eyes, and he could probably use a shower. There was an air of tension about him, like a piece of chewing gum being stretched almost to the breaking point.

"Smells good," he said, taking his seat.

"Thank you." Setting his plate down in front of him, everything still steaming. A knife and fork followed. "What do you want to drink?"

"Uh, water?"

She poured herself something dark red and had the slight aroma of alcohol from even a distance. The genuine kind was hard to find and something she might have gotten from Toke's stores. Whether stolen or asked for, it wasn't a light thing to share, but she'd happily share it with Quinn after having seen the ship. Pouring a second glass anyways, she set it beside his ice water.

Settling on that topic she chose it as she didn't think commenting on his appearance was likely to make him want to stay for dinner. As she set a glass of water before him, she said, "I've never seen the Callistar this clean, thank you."

"Yer welcome." he shrugged his shoulders. "I had to sterilize some places and figured I'd do the rest."

Reaching up to her ear, she put a finger behind it, touching her communicator. Tapping it once put all non-emergent communication off for an hour. It also kept Watson out of her brain for the same amount of time. Not that he could not listen through the main communication array, but she wanted to focus on Quinn.

"Are you getting enough sleep?" Eyeing him, she pushed his silverware over on an old-fashioned cloth napkin.

Quinn picked up the wine and sniffed it before frowning. He took a small sip, his lips curling around the curved goblet, his frown remaining. "It's a bit…" He trailed off, choosing to answer her question instead. "Naw, probably not. Not much I can do about tha' though."

The tinkling of silverware on their plates followed his ambiguous statement. He chewed with his mouth closed; she noticed. "Do you just not sleep well? There are some aids down in the med bay that can keep dreams out."

Watching for his reactions, she realized her statement sounded concerned, but to him it could come across much differently. He may have believed she worried about him being able to finish his tasks, so before he could reply, she added, "You should take some breaks too, Quinn. Constantly working is not good.

"My brain has a quantum computer core embedded in the soft tissue. Sleeping medication doesn't work on me," Quinn grumbled softly. "Can't take any medicine that messes with my brain chemistry too much."

He worked methodically while eating his food, formulating a science experiment across the fine china. The potato dissected into sections, each one with different toppings as if he were testing the combinations.

She outright starred, not because of the way he ate, but because quantum computers were insanely complex, insanely expensive, and insanely experimental. Even the most diehard cyberware junkies didn't get machinery directly placed into their brain. They had some neural implants that would connect to a person's brain, but only superficially. However, that was a far cry from opening up your skull and sticking a computer inside of it.

"Is there anything that helps?" She could get him something from Eikos or have it brought in.

"Music. It's why I keep it so loud most of the time. Helps drown out other thoughts. People can't multitask, just split focus. I can think about two things, or more, at the same time. Makes it hard not to always be thinking, but if the music is loud enough, then I can focus most of my mind on the songs while I work. Doesn't help as much when I'm trying to sleep."

Quinn answered methodically. Falling back into his mechanical voice. She discovered through further probing that she could inadvertently put him into the headspace he had been when he'd been somewhat incarcerated and his handlers were checking on his "health." Automated responses explaining what details they wanted to know.

"Is there anything else you enjoy?" Keeping the focus across the table didn't feel wise, but her curiosity drove her forward.

"Working? I enjoy making things... or I did." He wore a frown, as if it were permanently implanted as well. "I guess just music otherwise."

"You need a new hobby then," Kira suggested. "What about painting? Or drawing?"

"Hobby?" He looked up at her. The ring of light inside of his eyes seemed to flash brighter for a moment. She'd seen it before, when he worked.

Is he looking for an answer? She thought to herself.

"Yes." Drawing her knife down, it screeched on the plate and she readjusted her angle, catching an annoyed look Quinn cast in her direction.

"Harm," he muttered. "Doing something just because you enjoy it... Maybe you are right, I could try a hobby."

"You'll find most of the crew have them. Max's is getting into others' personal business," she joked lightly, giving him a smile that quickly flatlined. "He means well, of course," she spat out quickly. Her last joke hadn't been taken well, and the rush gave her away. She worried about this one as well.

The quizzical look she received and accompanying silence made her feel guilty. Her face blossomed red across her cheeks. Attempting to move along quickly, she asked, "Is there anything you want to know? About the crew or the ship?

"Know about you or the ship? You mean, besides, what's in Toke's records?" The man confirmed that he had read up on all of them. That he'd sliced into Toke's computer network and took what information he wanted was no surprise. Thus far, as it related to anything scientific, there seemed to be nothing Quinn couldn't do. It was people that were far too much for him to handle. "I... huh... never thought about that. It was discouraged."

"This isn't-" she was about to say Paradigm, but the reminder might have been too much for the man. Choosing her words carefully wasn't a particular skill she was great at. "You are a person, Quinn, not some piece of property. Normal people can have a conversation and ask questions in return."

"I'm a pretty far cry from normal," he said with a snort. Closing his eyes, he let out a long breath. "Where are you from?"

Was that a joke? Maybe there was hope for him yet. She swallowed down the laugh that wanted to come up from deep within her at hearing him say something akin to normal.

"Preatoria I believe." She wasn't completely certain it was the major planet of what made up the Praetorian system, but her heritage was that, as far as she was aware. "But I grew up on Toke's coattails. I never stayed in one place for long." If she asked him in return, it might dredge up memories, so instead she'd ask, "What's your favorite thing you've ever built?"

"Preatoria? A whole 'nother world. I wanted to be from somewhere. One of the nicer researchers was from Ireland. I thought the way he talked sounded interesting. I copied it." Reaching up, he scratched at his chin. "I guess Gary."

He let out a low whistle, and a pocket on the front of his coat wiggled. A gecko popped out, or it had the shape of a gecko, but it appeared to be made of crystal with gigantic eyes the color of jet. The little thing shimmied its way out of his pocket, down his arm, and onto the table to explore.

Kira felt enormously giddy. Creatures in space were rare, leaning across the counter lowering herself a little to look at his creation. Her enthusiasm carried over into her speech. "Gary is adorable! What sort of gecko did you base him off of?"

Quinn blinked slowly at her reaction. Gary seemed thrilled by it skittering up to her, leaping onto Kira's hand and heading up her arm. Its little paws had just the right amount of warmth to almost feel real. If it wasn't for the impossible coloring of it, she might have thought it a living animal.

"Uh, leopard. I took a brain scan of a gecko, tweaked the intelligence enough to understand basic human language, and added in an imprinting subroutine for loyalty. I uploaded that into a neural net that replicates a gecko's body perfectly and grew a polymorphic crystalline gel compound around it to simulate muscles, skin, and bone before covering it in the smart diamond scales."

"Well, he's super sweet." She rubbed his head. Gary stuck out his little tongue to 'taste' her skin, perhaps in order to judge her even if its sensors depended on its similarities to a real one.

Letting him walk over her hands, he climbed up her shoulders. When he hit bare skin around the collarbone of her loose black shirt, she giggled and told Gary, "That tickles, bud."

Raising her hand to get him down, she held the creature gingerly, even though it would be extremely hard to break him. Moving him back down to the table, holding him in both hands, she smiled from ear to ear. Apparently, all it took to break her composure was an animal, and it didn't matter the sort.

When she looked back up, she found Quinn observing all of this with a slightly disbelieving look on his face.

"He looks like he's smiling," she said, running a finger under his chin and lifting it up a little. The sweet little smug thing the sort of critter she used to fall for on alien planets, but would never take. They were wild and meant to be wild.

Kira still smiled like a fool. "This is brilliant, Quinn."

Both knew his talents, and she should have been saying that about the engines or the new manifold, but no, she said it about a gecko made of spare parts.

"Uh, thanks. I just wanted..." Quinn shrugged and looked away, staring down at his dinner before returning to eating his meal without comment. Gary hopped out of her hands and crawled his way back up Quinn's sleeve, vanishing into his jacket.

Finishing up her own meal with gusto, she never turned down food or waited until it got cold. So she dug back in, but she tried to keep the conversation going since he was doing so well. "May I ask how you found Toke to begin with? I would have figured you could have just commandeered a ship on your own-" that made the thought process kick in, "But you need enough supplies to live on. That's a little harder, I see now."

Quinn nodded his head in agreement. "Toke is an expedience. In theory, I could manage to get everything I need with enough time, but not easily. Getting money without making it obvious is hard. Buying large quantities of supplies is hard. Retrofitting a ship is hard. These things would take time to set up. With Paradigm putting all of their resources into locating me, speed is important. Toke already had the resources and network to get what I needed, and barter is the oldest form of trade.

"As for how I found him, I got access to an unsecured terminal with unfettered galactic-net access while at a shipyard. From there, I already had a script prepared to scan for what I needed. Someone with resources, connections, and connections to illicit resources. Toke came up really fast."

"Toke runs the largest illicit business with ties to every major government in the galaxy to do their dirty work. They all know that he does business with everyone else. It's common knowledge and yet the whole thing is called Rumor." She snorted. "It's no surprise you found him first, honestly."

Toke hadn't hidden himself very well, but when you were as powerful as he was, you really didn't have to. He was the pirate king of smuggling. No one dared defy him, and he was so well protected it was almost impossible to kill him. The bar they visited had no actual clientele that day. Kira knew it even if everyone in it had not known that they were all working for the same man. It was a brilliant scheme, if not a dangerously wicked one.

"Yes, it wasn't very hard, seeing as he was already a man with everything. It seemed offering the one thing his wealth could not yet buy him would make him keen to do whatever he could to assist me." Quinn said.

"He's stayed in power so long by knowing a good deal when he sees it." Her tone then wasn't loving towards Toke. She knew who he was, who she was to him, and the debt that she owed. The memory of that fact brought her to down the rest of her 'wine.'

Glancing at the bottle, she knew she did not need another glass. Being a lightweight for real ethanol meant knowing limits. They chemically altered the fake substitute to allow you to be sober in an instant if you wanted to be. This… well, she could hardly account for who she'd be later.

Besides, if the conversation hadn't turned to Toke, she wouldn't be considering it. She wasn't an actual lush.

Quinn finished the last bite of his meal as a drone came in to clean up the mess. "Thanks for the food. It was good."

"Quinn?" Waiting for him to look back, she asked, "May I show you my favorite part of the ship? Before I leave."

He paused, one brow lowered, and the other raised. "Sure?"

The relief she felt showed in a genuine smile as it spread across her face, making her much more likable than the sullen looks he'd gotten thus far.

"Come on," she almost took his hand to pull him along. Her fingers graced the edges of his palm before she realized her mistake. He flinched while she attempted to pass it off as a case of walking too close as she passed him. Awkward, but she tucked her hands into the pockets of her pants, hoping to prevent herself from doing it again.

They went down the hall through the maze that was the Callistar. Heading down a slim working corridor, she explained, "It was closed in because of being nonessential when they did the first renovation. So the only access is through the tubes."

"Hrmm, I think I know which room you're talking about from the diagrams," Quinn said. "I was debating going down there and seeing if I could do anything with it."

Unused space was rare on a spaceship, considering the cost of making one was huge. Kira clearly did not feel bad about it admitting, "To be honest, I blocked it off. Although, I thought I had it removed from the maps as well, that is, unless you cross-referenced and found the space."

"Hrmm? No, I just did a deep spectrum scan of the hull and superstructure. Like I said, this ship is going to be moving faster than what it was graded for. In order to stop the ship from shaking apart, it needed to be graded. If it failed, then it needed to be replaced. A new section that meets stress requirements put in and dry welded together."

"Ah."

The old maintenance tubes, basically large round pipes with ladders, were still there for quick access to interior systems. Opening the latch, she went first, leaving him to close it. Putting her hands on the rung above her, her ankle completely healed she took off, going up it at a moderate pace. Her hair swayed behind her as she climbed, and something else was definitely in his view since she led the way. One quick glance down told her he had no interest in the female form. He kept his eyes firmly on the ladder.

Popping out on a level tunnel, she turned right, hitting a small corridor with a keypad lock. The system remained offline to the main ship, running off its own battery power for the door. Jimmying it open in an emergency would trip an alarm that would alert her immediately. She did not bother hiding the code. She figured he could sort it out if he really wanted.

Punching it into the keypad, the door slid open. Peering inside they were met with complete darkness, other than the illumination that came from behind them. She touched the wall and a ring of light went around the room at the ceiling. It brought into focus a table in the center that had a rounded glass top in the form of a half sphere. A slim counter ran around the circumference in a slick black, cool to the touch. Beneath it, the housing came directly down to the floor from the globe wrapped in black metal.

Kira shut the door behind him.

Figuring if he didn't recognize the item he could look it up she didn't explain. She knew it was an old star projector, one of Astromech's creations from when the company was still booming. Charting in an old-fashioned manner by projecting out systems and planning leaps, it had been critical to that function once upon a time. Then when it served its use, it became a novelty for projecting constellations one could walk through, mainly used to educate children.

Beside it a thick pad with a blanket laid out on the floor, with a few pillows. "Even Watson can't reach me here," she told Quinn. She wanted him to know this was special to her, and special for her to bring him there.

Quinn examined the device in the center of the room before visually scanning the rest of it. She knew he was possibly checking her words. He would find no cameras, no sensors, no connected intercom system. A small communicator rested on the ledge of the star projector, but that was it.

"So, just a little private viewing room?" He sounded distracted, the way he did when she brought lunch and his hands were busy, but he didn't stop at that. "I can see why you'd like having a private place to get away." That sounded more human, more feeling, as if he wanted to clarify that he really got that. "If I had a place like this, I wouldn't tell anyone."

Kira settled down on the thick pad, grabbing the blanket, patting a spot a little way from her. She made sure plenty of room existed between them and she listened to him before leaning back and tapping something on the pedestal bottom next to her. A hatch released sliding backwards allowing it to be programmed from below a simple input system with a visible keyboard and search query function.

"It's a little more than that," she said with a smile. "It used to be one of the astronomy rooms where the crew plotted where they would go next."

The invitation triggered a slight frown from Quinn, but he joined her on the floor. He leaned against a pillow, folding his legs up to his knees and wrapping his arms around them as she turned the device on and the room exploded into brilliant light. At waist level, there were stars. The device displayed beautiful reflections of the constellations and planets, which could be manipulated to almost anywhere in space.

If one were laying down, it felt as if they were looking up to them and stargazing.

"Oh." Quinn murmured softly as he took it all in, silent as his gaze traveled over it all.

Blue flashed in his eyes and he snapped them closed. He placed a hand against his temple, his lips moving, but the sound inaudible. When he dropped his hand, he returned to watching the stars. The electronic blue that his eyes usually had, unless it flashed a brighter shade, was gone. Just normal, pale sea-glass blue took it all in now.

His tells were not so absolute that she found it easy to gain any kind of true understanding of what went on inside his mind, but in that moment she could see just how wrong she'd been about him.

He craved human experiences and kindness, though he'd never say it out loud.

She relaxed and leaned back fully at first, but now she came up slightly onto her elbows. Watching the sky, she whispered, trying not to ruin the moment that had been created between them. "I like to watch recreations of the comets sometimes. The ones that mining processes have destroyed."

"That sounds interesting," Quinn said, keeping the same gentleness as she had when she spoke as he continued to stare up at the starry projection.

Twisting, she'd run through the screen until she found a favorite. It lasted over half an hour, in which the sky became full of projections of falling rock that fell into fire and ketone bursts.

Coming back down, she left a serene silence as she settled into a large pillow that held her up at just an angle to be comfortable. There were a few other blankets around them. The temperature dropped, making it just a little cooler in the room. If she was sharing, she was going to show him what it was like to sit with a blanket and just stargaze.

Then it hit her and she asked, "Do you need music? I can put some on the console."

The sudden question made him blink in surprise. "I was... playing music on my neural net during dinner. I just turned it off... I'm fine." The way he said it made his surprise at this revelation more than apparent. "But, yeah, maybe something in the background."

Flipping through the selections, she settled on classical music, not too far off from what he listened to, but this music only used acoustic instruments as opposed to his electric ones.. "If you need vocals and lyrics, I can switch it again."

He shook his head. The song went from one to another, the second featuring only on a single classical guitar. Halfway through the piece she heard him snoring. Smiling to herself, she listened to both before draping a blanket over Quinn and allowing him to sleep without someone staring, leaving the door open.

Heading back to her own quarters, she wasn't sure about the invitation- if it was okay for her to stay or not, so she collected a few items to head back to the Eikos.

You took him there?

She almost jumped out of her skin at the interruption. She'd cut off communications during dinner and never turned them back on. Watson was patient, but apparently not *that* patient. She let out a snort after her heart calmed a little. "I did."

Why?

She shrugged her shoulders out of habit before remembering he couldn't see it. "I dunno."

Kira wondered if Watson had a lot on his mind, the question faded, because she certainly did.

QUINN

Quinn did not wake for... Eleven hours, thirty-two minutes, and eleven seconds. Give or take about thirty minutes for the time his net had been off before he'd fallen asleep. System alerts piled in as he reconnected. A few projects called for his attention, but most work had continued under an emergency drone controlled A.I. he'd put into place before the neural net had been turned off.

Crawling off of the cushions, he rearranged them to the exact specifications on their arrival. Heading back to work, he sent out a short, "Sorry this took so long. I just woke up. Thanks for last night."

"You're welcome," was the response he received. Warm and lovely in tone, but with some background noise- people laughing. A quick check showed that Kira wasn't on board the ship anymore.

It passed from his mind for a few days before he updated her. "Might take me longer to finish than I thought."

"Take your time, setbacks are normal," was the message he got back and something akin to a care package with his meal. A warm blanket, a collection of music on a data drive, and even some muffins for breakfast.

He, in return, sent her something equally precious as the care she'd put into the package. "I didn't change the door code."

Chapter Nine

KIRA

Kira stared at the message and the little box that had accompanied it. It had been almost a full week since she'd returned to the little apartment-like box on the Eikos. She'd ingratiated herself to some of the crew serving on the station, so she'd not been lonely. Kira wondered if Quinn was and shrugged it off. Aside from the few messages she'd sent, she assumed otherwise.

Are you going to open it or stare at it all day?

"Why, Watson? Are you curious?"

...

It was unassuming- a small metal box with a simple clasp that no wider than her hand or taller. Tempted to allow it to remain a mystery, just to mess with Watson, she popped the edge and leaned it back.

Inside laid a gecko, just like Gary, with skin made of violet so dark it was almost obsidian, but still crystalline, a gleam reflecting off faceted edges. A note rested under it that said: Her name is Gabby, just say it and she will turn on.

"Hi, Gabby," she peered down at the creature, absolutely as fascinated as she had been with Gary.

The enormous eyes opened, and it raised its head, tilting it as if adjusting the way its neck attached and placing it into position. Making a full circle before it spotted Kira, it raised the tip of its chin, the brighter violet eyes blinking once. A flash of light passed through them, which reminded Kira very much of Quinn's net being turned off, before it rose, pulling itself out the side of the box and scampering towards her open hand.

Kira laughed.

Gabby?

"He made me my own little pet, Watson, oh I wish you could see her. She's precious."

Gabby crawled up her arm and under her chin, nuzzling there and crossing over her collarbone and down her other arm, completing a full circuit.

I'm sure she is.

The hour was too late to wander through the Eikos so she chose to stay one more night. Gabby slept curled up on Kira's pillow, nestling into her hair, hiding in the dark locks matching the very color and disappearing into them. Morning light broke the nighttime, a simple subroutine to mimic the passing of time, with lights dimming and rising at set times.

Kira readied herself before leaving to find sustenance. But the gecko had other plans. When the door opened it took off like lightning, leaving the Captain chasing her across the deck.

"Gabby!" Frustrated cries followed the critter. Kira did not realize where they were going until they'd arrived at the corridor that led out to the Callistar.

A return meant exploring the changes Quinn made. Gabby's tiny little pinprick claws scrabbled at the door insistently. Scooping up the tiny traitor, she'd tell her, "I get the point, we'll go in."

The gecko stopped resisting, turning the half smiling face upward as if it were pleased with victory but Kira met it with eye-rolling.

Their entrance became punctuated by them passing several new devices throughout that she'd never seen before, even on Toke's ship. It felt as if she were rediscovering an old friend who had been through a major life change.

There was an entirely new room Quinn had somehow added to the hydroponics bay. Which he'd made large enough to run an industrial multi-tiered hydroponics farm to grow a variety of vegetable matter. All of it could be processed into the raw caloric and nutritional requirements a human body needed, and injected with a flavoring gel to make them taste like whatever you wanted, or used in actual cooking. It was a self-sustaining system as well, with some creative re-working of the ship's sewage system and a composting system. It was what would let the Callistar be out in deep space nigh on indefinitely.

Hela would be extremely pleased at the addition, surely, as the large orange tree was still cooped up over in its corner. Walking down the rows, she knew this was what deep space required, but it was still a wake up call. They were leaving for a good while. Things were changing.

Leaving hydroponics and traversing the halls, she suddenly noticed the silence. Usually, there was the low hum of the reactor that seemed to move through the ship. The sound of pipes in the walls moving liquids, the low whirring of hidden machinery in the walls. Now though? It was almost utterly silent, perhaps a bit of a low hum she could just catch, but other than that... it barely *sounded* like the same ship.

Your heart rate spiked again. Are you alright?

Kira didn't reply. Her mouth formed a thin line as she grabbed a chute to go down instead of taking the long way. This was something she needed to do in a hurry.

Kira?

There was noise in the engine room, just not enough of it. The new reactor was shiny, fancy, and only produced a very soft, barely audible hum as it towered over her. She was facing her very own, and quite literal, ship of Theseus. She stood within the Callistar, but with so many changes, so many parts swapped out. Was it still the same ship she knew?

Touching it with her bare hands, she did not care if it left marks. Part of her life had been taken away with this change, and yet she'd allowed it. This was no longer her home in a sense, and those returning she knew would feel the same. Alec might not want to be on a ship that no longer ran like clockwork because of his presence. Sure, Morgan might appreciate the speed, but Alec and she had a connection to it that was irreplaceable.

Leaning in, she put her forehead to it. She forgot the real reason she came to the ship, that heavy weight in her pocket unmoving.

"What are ye doing?"

The uneasy truce the two had conjured up between them was possibly about to be over.

The only reason she did not lash out was because Watson sounded, softly, only to her, **Kira, please.**

He promised Watson a body, one he could have autonomy over. For his sake, she swallowed her anger, knowing how irrational it would appear. Quinn had only been attempting to do his job. It was a retrofit, after all. Things were going to change, they had to change, but this was no longer her ship anymore. It was shiny and new. It may have been old junk, but for the stars, it was her junk.

Bringing her forehead just off the metal, her hands remained as she informed him, "I was listening."

"Ah, not much to hear anymore," Quinn said, evidently aware that things were far different. "Oh, I decided on what to do with yer hiding hole. Hope you like it." Nonchalant, he dropped that bombshell on her, turned and walked away, evidently not picking up on the simmering anger in her voice or body language.

"To do with it?" That brought a raise in octave as she rushed after him. She'd shown him the room in confidence, not knowing he would find another project to start. It was her place of peace and it was her final haven after he'd destroyed everything else that made home *home*.

Watson made a soft plea again, but she wasn't hearing it. All she wanted was an explanation of what he had done. Racing after him he disappeared as if he dropped out into space.

She clenched her fist in anger, her nails biting into her skin. Rushing with a swiftness she saved only for emergencies.

Kira, I'm sure it can't be that bad.

"Don't defend him," she growled back.

Reaching her haven, she stood outside, repeating the moment with the reactor. Her lower lip quivered as she shakily put a hand on a scanner instead of a keypad.

The room was... mostly the same. Quinn had added a few things. The first large change was the removal of a chunk of the floor. The newly depressed section's depth sat only a few inches deep, filled in with some sort of cushion. He'd not moved the area that she had left the blankets and pillows, but essentially made it an even nicer place to get comfortable.

Another addition was planter boxes around the sides of the room that he held grown miniature trees. It made stepping into the small room feel like stepping inside of a forest. There were even a few unused planters, so she could plant and grow whatever she might like. The boxes had automated day/night cycle lamps and would detect moisture levels and self water if required, though she could turn that off if she wanted to handle that herself.

A note rested on the astrium projector that explained the setup.

It went into detail on how to operate the planters automated systems, that he'd installed, apparently, a hidden compartment in her room that acted as a dumbwaiter so she could sneak any supplies down to the room easily, there were instructions for how frequently and where she could get fertilizer from the composting system to keep the plants alive, and lastly a mention that he had swapped out the keypad to a biometric one. She was the only one registered to it. So, even if someone learned about the room, they still couldn't get in.

It warmed her enough to the ship to see the effort he'd made. It was certainly way more than her own small presents, but she figured he had no sense of cost and gift giving before this.

"Gabby," she said to the little lizard. "Let's go find your maker."

Gabby's response was to lick at Kira's cheek, having crawled up out onto her collar. Quinn was a little hard to find, but she got lucky. A drone overheard her when she was muttering to herself about where he might be, and guided her to the airlock at the back of the ship. Peering out the viewing window, she could see Quinn in a suit, working on the engines.

Hitting the com on the airlock, she said, "Quinn?"

"Yeah?"

"Would you like to have dinner with me?"

"Yeah." He never looked up from his work, his arms in an access panel and his eyes glued to his task.

The only meals she'd seen Quinn eat in person had been breakfast and one dinner. Considering that the breakfast one went better, she did a home-style one like Hela made, which involved contacting the chef for her advice and guidance. The small call made her spirits brighter.

Quinn popped in as she finished up throwing food on plates. Sullen enough, hands shoved in his pockets, standing in the kitchen's doorway. The electric blue slid over her. She felt him looking.

Turning, she set down a plate of biscuits next to the gravy. She kicked Watson out of her head for the moment. He didn't have a place there during this.

"Quinn, I," words didn't really cover how she felt, about Gabby, about her room, so she crossed the small space and embraced him.

Then it all went to hell.

The mental enhancements didn't drive a physical reaction quickly enough. Quinn didn't dodge, he just stood here, unmoving, as she wrapped him up. Then he shook, like a chihuahua preparing to bark, his whole body seizing up.

"Quinn?!" Releasing him, she grabbed him by his shoulders. "Oh shit, oh shit, I'm sorry."

He just continued to move like a rattle in a baby's hand and she broke away to grab a bag from the kitchen. He lowered himself to the floor, settling his head between his knees, panting.

Kira came back with a sack. He snagged it out of her hand, forming a ring with his fingers, bringing it to his mouth. It expanded and folded, his hyperventilating slowly getting under control as he breathed in the CO_2 his body so desperately needed.

"Jaysus fekking christ what are ya doing that ta someone with no warning fer!?"

"Well, I didn't think you were going to react like that!" Chiding him in return, her voice just as loud as he'd been as she crouched. Kira kept her hands to herself, and a good few inches of space between them.

"Clearly bloody not." He grumbled, putting the bag on the counter next to him. He then gripped the edge and used it to pull himself up. Straightening his jacket, he openly glared at her.

Kira was just grateful he'd not run off. Standing up to her full height as well she said, "look, I'm sorry."

"It's fine, just warn a fella afore ya go violating his personal space like that."

"Warn you next time. Got it. Uh, dinner's ready."

He grunted, slamming his hands into his pockets before going back around the door to the other side of the pass through to take a seat.

She took a deep breath. It seemed it was always one step forward and two steps back with him. Coming up to the counter, she made her own plate. There were biscuits, sausage and sausage gravy, eggs over easy, bacon, pancakes, and a small assortment of fruit laid out.

She popped a grape in her mouth as her hand went over the bowl before tearing apart a fluffy biscuit, telling him, "I might do a small charter run for the Eikos. They're short on pilots."

He made his own plate as she talked, separating out each ingredient and making little piles of all the different combinations of the food, or that was her best guesstimate of what he was doing. "Okay." A quick beat before he added, "Why the hug?"

"I wanted to thank you. This has been my home, and it is changing to keep up with the times, but you preserved a small piece of it. Although, I don't think you have any sense of scale when it comes to gestures." She poured gravy over her plate.

"Okay?" Quinn blinked, looked down, then up, then down again. "I thought you were supposed to do something nice for someone if they did something nice for you?"

"Not always, and most keep the monetary value around the same. Gabby has been lovely, though."

At the mention of her name, the little lizard popped out from under her collar, tilting its head inquisitively.

"I mean, if you only look at the value of the raw components..." The trailing let her know it was more than she could afford, "Ah, nevermind, I think I understand."

"Have you thought about what you'd like to do when the full crew comes on board?"

He flashed her a quizzical look, "Yes? I told you what I plan to do."

Stay in your room until we find you a planet, she thought the corner of her mouth quirked in displeasure. "You don't have to. We're an odd crew, but no one is inherently cruel or anti-social. We'd be happy to have you at the dinner table."

Quinn did his little dance with his eyes, the flash of his implanted light making it easy to catch. "I don't... I won't... I'll just be leaving. Why give them a chance to even try to get attached?" It seemed to have triggered a realization as he shoved back away from the table. "Thanks, fer dinner. I should get back to work."

The plate before him was left half full.

"Quinn, wait." Half jogging around the partition, she'd ask of him. "At least let me make you a plate to take with you for later. You barely touched yours."

Pausing at the door, he shuddered, his voice cracked, wavering between the accent and the utter monotone, "I... will send a drone for the plate. I just, I need to be alone. I need to be alone."

It was so raw, the way he said it. It lacked anger. She could only hear fear. Pure terror and worry in the way he spoke, in the way his shoulders hunched up. "I... I will be here if you need me," she told him. What else could she say?

Quinn vanished. Going forward, he seemed like he intended on making himself scarce whenever she was aboard the ship. He didn't kick her off, but she guessed he tracked her movements, as he was never anywhere near.

Communication was kept to a bare minimum, simply thank you's for his meals, a polite no when she asked him to dinner again. Kira became frustrated as he isolated himself as deeply as he could within the bowels of the ship. The only sign of his presence were the progress trackers he'd installed on her communicator ticking towards completion.

Left to her own devices, she began exploring every room in the Callistar. They were all changed in some way. For the ship's systems, the overhaul was total: engines, life support, reactor, hydroponics, medical, and even the entirely new drone bay were all state-of-the art. The kitchen remained the most familiar, but additional apparatuses for cooking were added to what was already there.

The crew's rooms were mostly untouched except for some small quality of life improvements. Brand new mattresses made of a learning foam that read the body of the inhabitant and optimized temperature, curvature, and softness to provide a perfect night's sleep. He'd provided personal entertainment headsets with hours of entertainment downloaded to the shared computer core. The improvements to the shower stalls in the bathrooms, with additional water outputs and options for massaging water baths, were personal favorites of hers.

There were even decorative choices, much like with Kira's private room, added on to make the rooms feel more personalized to the inhabitants. It more or less confirmed that Quinn had read files on all of them. He treated their home with respect as he did his best to continue to honor the way the ship had once been, while making everyone's lives better.

Even with her time taken up by volunteering and exploring, his absence loomed. Particularly because his messages became more and more terse and brief than before- if that was even possible. Kira mulled it over, giving him a few more days of his self imposed isolation before she decided at the end of a week that she had had enough. Putting herself together, she left her room, which he'd fixed during the supply run she did off the ship. It was what made her decide to finally go and find him. Hounding his drones through the ship, she knew he was avoiding her. The only way to keep him from doing so would be to keep herself off the system, but it was impossible.

"Watson, can you check life signs from the Eikos?"

Captain, I think it might be best if you leave this one alone.

"Life signs, Watson."

Watson would not grumble at the command because the system only garbled it, so he would do so. He was sentient, and capable of lying, and in this case, he actually assisted Quinn, sending her on a wild goose chase.

Finally, she stopped listening to Watson and threw up her hands in frustration. Blocking him off, she went through her favors on the other ship, contacting the Eikos security team directly to ask.

They informed her there was one signal of life outside the ship.

Checking the relayed percentages and guessing by the largest left, she headed down to the nearest airlock to see if he was visible. Checking the comms there, he disabled the short band radio that would let her talk to him from the airlock, and his communicator was still off, which made her options suiting up or waiting by the airlock itself.

Banging her fist next to the viewing port, she returned to Eikos that night in order to share a night with what company she could find. It wasn't particularly the best, but she was in a mood that she couldn't settle.

Cutting off Watson to keep him from playing mother hen worked for a while. When he began to openly show concern, rebooting the link himself to ask her to return to the ship, she ignored him, instead pushing her limits and snapping at him.

Then, he would do the last thing he could. He would attempt to contact Quinn.

Chapter Ten

QUINN

Watson and Quinn had never actually spoken. The man had put the A.I. into a box, cutting off access to all but non-essential systems. It wasn't exactly a great way to make friends, but as Quinn had well established, he didn't want to make friends.

Still, an A.I., even one that was a clone of a person's intelligence, was less likely to bother him than a normal person. "Yes?" Quinn said, curiosity getting the better of him as he opened the channel Watson pinged.

Sorry to bother you. Watson started off as polite, not that Quinn could parse how he came across at all, but it wasn't a command. **The Captain is on the Eikos. I believe something is wrong. Her vitals are unstable, and I cannot reach her comms. Seeing as I cannot physically retrieve her, you are the next best option.**

Watson had a sense of urgency to him about the situation, and he spoke faster than he should have.

"You think something has happened to her? How would you know that?" Quinn grunted as he finished the current weld running the laser down the line before setting aside his tools, getting to his feet.

He immediately walked towards the exit to Eikos. If Watson was being honest, then any wasted time would be a risk to Kira's health. Quinn began by sending drones ahead of himself to track her down.

Her implanted health monitor is connected to my systems. I couldn't reach her, but I was able to access the Eikos systems. The room she is in has no visuals, but audio is available. The Captain is slurring heavily, and as far as I am aware, she is not inebriated.

Quinn had no clue what the hell was going on, but something shifted in his brain at Watson's words.

"Understood."

Every ounce of emotion left Quinn's voice. Anything remotely resembling humanity faded away. A flash of blue eclipsed his eyes, and a few moments later, even more drones left the ship moving onto the Eikos station.

In under a minute, the entire station blared alarmingly loud warning sirens giving the impression they were being attacked. More than one hundred drones had just entered the ship and started quarantining everyone that stood between Quinn and Kira's life sign with impenetrable deep space shields.

The alarm cut off as quickly as it came on. One of Quinn's drones found the central computer bank and installed itself within the principal port. Quinn cracked the station's encryption by the time he set foot in its halls. In under a minute, he'd taken just as much control of Eikos as he had of the Callistar.

The guidance of his drones led him directly to a storage bay. Nothing had been off limits to him on his trek. Every door automatically opening and closing with the clearances put in by his neurotransmitter. Tracking not only her life sign, a visual feed of the room popped up after a drone gained access. Kira slumped back in a seat, her posture distinctly poor. He could hear her speaking, hear the slurring Watson mentioned. Cataloging the other three with her, he used a quick trace method to figure out who they were with the ship's records.

The information that came back on all three revealed they were trial basis members of the Eikos. A quick assessment of the scene showed cards, a table, and a few drinks about. One man excused himself as Quinn hit the final threshold. He gave an offhand excuse about checking the alarms and was only partially out of his seat when Quinn barged in.

"Andrew Pierce, Quixalan Aldiendo, and Arnold Hovax." Naming the three of them in his dead, robotic voice, he continued, "I have alerted the authorities of Velx Prime, Tarona, and Lerune Station of your current locations. I suggest you leave Eikos now, as I am sure at least one of their officers will be motivated enough to send someone to collect you for your standing warrants."

A drone passed by his head, his hair fluttering with the speed at which it collected the cup before Kira, whizzing it off for analysis.

Arnold, the half standing man, appeared to be the brains of the operation. He quickly said, "Now you just wait one fucking minute-" before he caught sight of the multitude of drones, some of which were quite large. The overwhelming amount limited their options and Quinn's scan revealed they didn't have weapons upon them, so their options narrowed even further. The man still reached as if going for one, perhaps an intimidation tactic.

Kira's head rolled back in her seat, Quinn could see her, the slow shift in the way her muscles worked, the attempt to raise her arm out to reach for him, her fingers twitching, but not raising fully.

Andrew tugged on Arnold's sleeve. "Come on, boss," he spoke with an urgency. "No woman is worth going back for."

"Your bank account number is 8DWS-C7V5-X20T. Your password is Tarona3026, home planet and birth year, very insecure Mister Hovax," Quinn stated in that same dry monotone. "Detective Lancaster was very pleased to receive the video footage verifying your biometrics and position."

The man continued as he moved across the room towards Kira. "What I am saying is that your associate is correct. This is very much not worth your time, Mister Hovax. Every second I am forced to continue explaining this to you is a second that I am focusing on you. You do not want my attention, Mister Hovax. If you are not out of that door in the next five seconds, I will deduct one credit from your balance for every second you continue to be here."

One of his drones buzzed next to him. One he'd outfitted with a medical diagnostic scanner after Kira broke her leg. Quinn set it to scanning her.

"If that was not plain enough language, then allow me to make it simple for you." Quinn read the results of the scan before his gaze flicked back to the three men. For all the cold and inhuman parts of him that existed in the depths of that neon blue, there was something intensely human in his fury, as he said. "Run for your lives."

The blundering that occurred, and the speed with which they made their way from the room, was impressive by no small means.

The medical scan indicated that Kira had been given a dose of Rostan. A drug that took control of the mind, consuming it with fogginess so thick one could not move their body. Yet, that person would still cognitively know everything going on around them. While she could not escape, she could clearly feel everything and would remember it the next day.

The men commandeered a shuttle strapping themselves in. For all their pandering, they'd apparently put enough together to take the threat Quinn presented seriously. The problem was, it was too late. Almost immediately, the auto-pilot engaged, and the screen flashed up to a new destination. Planet Tarona, Bala Bala City, Global Police Headquarters. The doors sealed, and they launched into space in their own personal paddy wagon.

Meanwhile, Quinn contemplated his two options. There was a chemical cocktail he could administer that would immediately combat the effects of Rostan. Or it would make its way out of her system safely with time. Only one of those options did not involve him administering drugs he was not qualified to handle based only on what information he could access through publicly available databases.

While he had a 99% probability of success in synthesizing the cocktail required, he only had a 78% chance of correctly administering it because of the potential for human error on his part. While he could know exactly how to perform a task, his body couldn't always replicate what his mind tried to direct.

With that in mind, he had one of his large carrier drones come in to scoop up Kira and take her back to her quarters to sleep it off. Quinn came along with her, his drones exiting the ship. He sent a message to the station manager with a full explanation of what had happened and why, along with the contents of the three men's bank accounts, as an apology for the disruption to the station's normal proceedings. Quinn included Toke in the email and mentioned that Toke should appreciate the efforts made to ensure the safety of a favored employee.

Splitting at the entrance to the Callistar, he left Kira with no words, no offerings, only the drone.

During his descent into the Callistar, a ping notified him that his message had a reply. Quinn didn't read the communique. He did little of anything. He'd squirreled himself away deep in the bowels of the ship. Wrapping arms around his knees as he rocked back and forth.

His mind rioted with hundreds of different conflicting thoughts, all screaming at him for a piece of his attention. His peace breaking as it struggled to keep up with the pace.

The computer core in his head let him think in ways no human could. And in ways no human should have been able to. He had only ever been as angry as he was now once before in his life. It was the same day he'd sworn he would become a pacifist, and he'd... He wasn't sure if terrifying people as he had counted against that or not. He wasn't sure he cared.

They'd almost hurt Kira.

The rage the thought brought bubbled to the surface and shook him to his core. That he felt that it terrified him. Far, far too many conflicting desires and wants were flickering through his head. From wanting to sit by her bed until she awoke, to wanting to have Toke replace the entire crew of the Callistar, to wanting to stay on the ship just to be with her, to wanting to just eject the crew, steal the ship, and vanish into the void, to wanting to do even worse things to the people who'd almost hurt her. Each desire repeated through his processing, coming in strange feedback loops. The ones born of the warring emotions magnifying and diminishing in severity as his own thoughts rendered him utterly helpless.

KIRA

The drone that had scooped up Kira coddled her against it, keeping her warm simply because the machinery itself was warm. Her mind raced, but with the slowness of a turtle. Still, it could piece together exactly what occurred but not allow her to speak her tongue heavy with medication. That Quinn had rescued her was not beyond her. When she was deposited in her bed, she looked for him, only to find him missing.

Tears smarted at the edges of her eyelashes. She closed them tight, knowing it did very little good to allow her emotions to overtake her. She'd been ridiculous on two counts. That night, there was no way to fix either issue, so she would have to stay on the Callistar for the foreseeable future. Her time on Eikos had ended.

Watson cut past the security protocols to her room. Her own communicator off. **Kira, I hope you know it was my last option.**

She couldn't scoff, or respond, or do anything but close her eyes and let the ache take hold. Let the uncertainty of the night, and the feeling of struggling to move, overcome her.

The newly muffled sound of the engines did nothing to drown out the idea of what could have occurred to her as well. Quinn may have been capable of understanding the depths of human depravity and their pursuit of power or wealth, but he had never encountered the understanding of the physical harm they might inflict on others for pleasure. Kira shuddered, the first motion she'd been able to voluntarily make, rolling through her body a few hours later when she awoke in a cold sweat.

Kira?

"I'm fine," she uttered. The words came out and so did the tears again. Pushing herself into an upright position, every muscle ached, each one flaming and cursing the existence of her will. Downing a glass of water on her bedside table, it cleared her throat. Worse for wear, and looking like it, she still considered the path that lay before her. "Where is he?"

The drone didn't answer. Watson, for once against her wishes, was blissfully, but she reached for the one large enough to carry her, as she did not think her own feet would suffice. "Take me to him, please," she asked desperately. She knew the possibility of what Quinn faced, and they should face it together.

The drones' base lights blinked at her and did nothing. All the drones in her room were just hovering and not moving. Frozen. *One foot in front of the other*, she told herself, rising and using them as handholds to the hallway. Peering out, every step became a slog.

Kira, you shouldn't be moving. Please, take care of yourself first. He is not physically harmed.

Now you want to speak.

"You, most of all, should know that physicality is only part of who we are."

As she traversed down towards engineering, the closer she came, the harder the realization hit: the entire swarm was on standby. Only the ones performing the simplest jobs, such as cleaning, continued to move on a pre-set program.

A glint of light caught her eye, and scrambling, something small raced towards her around a power conduit newly installed. Gary crawled up her leg, to her chin, and looked at her quizzically. Then, the gecko pointed itself in the direction it had come from.

"Gary." Her breathing became labored as she increased the pace in that direction. She clung to a rail to keep herself upright. Kira sat down fully once, in order to rest, but only for a few scant minutes.

Using the shuttle system to pass up and down the floors, she would finally pour out of one, with Gary taking off. Finding Quinn settled in front of the hydroponics bay, rocking back and forth in an upright ball.

"Oh, Quinn." She felt hollow at seeing him so incapacitated. She dropped to her knees before him. Her hair frazzled around her face. Deathly pale beneath her naturally tanned skin, even her lips appeared so, and her muscles held a slight tremor, but she made it there of her own accord and her own will.

The rocking stopped when she spoke, and he just looked at her. Tears streamed down his face in thick rivulets and he whispered. His voice had no accent, but it was rife with pain and anguish. "I'm just tired of thinking. Tired of people leaving me, betraying me, using me. I'm so tired. I just want to be somewhere else, Kira. Somewhere where there is no one around to hurt me. I am so tired of hurting all the time. If I get to know you, then I might like you, and then I will hurt when I am finally alone. But if I stay, something is going to happen, something always happens, and then I am going to be hurting again. Why couldn't you just leave me alone? Why did you have to make me like you? I just don't want to hurt, and every choice I have now is just pain. I don't want to hurt anymore."

Shifting his weight forward, he put his nose into his knees and his body shuddered as he sobbed.

"Sometimes pain is worth it, Quinn," she told him with the gentleness that a mother used when speaking to a child. Her actions had been partially selfish in getting to know him. She had wished to save him by helping him through the trauma of his past actions, but at first she'd simply wanted to test limits, to see how far was too far.

"I'm going to touch you now," she informed him before she leaned forward, the gentle pressure of an embrace that her body wished she'd never done. It cried against it, against moving again, and she fought with all she was worth to do so as she told him her voice full of worry,

"I do not have all the answers, but I know that even those I have lost, that I have loved, I would never give up the knowing just to give up the pain as well."

The man stiffened all over, as if the input overwhelmed his senses. But unlike last time, where it was a shock to a functioning machine, this felt like an emergency break to one spiraling out of control. Quinn sagged into the embrace, continuing to weep for a few moments before he passed out. Exhaustion, physical, mental, and emotional, finally catching up to him like a mallet in his skull.

Unlike his decision to leave her, she did not leave him.

"Watson, get one of the storage movers up here, please."

The reply she received came as a clicking of the line. The automated movers had long handles that could be used to manually direct them or they could be programmed to make automatic routes in the ship. One came through the hall after ten minutes, at her request. The base hadn't magically grown in size from her ankle debacle, but it would do. Kira grasped Quinn's shoulders, using his jacket to tug him back. It reminded her of having to use the same device, leaving med bay what seemed like a lifetime ago.

Sweat coated the nape of her neck by the time he hung halfway off the platform. His calves and feet scraping the floor. Using the handle like a walker, they made it to the med-bay. It being the closest room with anything resembling a bed. Raising up the transporter, she shoved Quinn off onto the wide cot, huffing and panting.

Satisfied, she sat on the edge. The width barely made it a twin bed, certainly not suitable for two grown adults, but she couldn't force herself to move further. Laying not quite next to him, but close so she could watch over him, she succumbed to her own exhaustion halfway on the frame and halfway on the cushion.

Reaching out, settling her hand over his, for just a second before she fell asleep, she watched a man who'd been written off as nothing but an asset who was now realizing just what it meant to be human.

Neither were in a great hurry to wake. Quinn sleep deprived, Kira drugged still. Gabby and Gary were the ones that decided that the quiet was insufferable. After some time, they peeked out and chased each other, darting over their owners as they slumbered.

Kira felt it first when Gabby dove under her chin, hiding in her hair. Groaning, she removed the animated gecko in a way kinder than she felt like being. Eyes still shut tight against the dim lighting, the events of the night before flooded her. Quinn's weight pressed against her, reminding Kira of his reaction the last time she'd tried to touch him. Holding her breath as if it would keep her from making further movements, Gary leaped off of Quinn, smacking her square in the cheek.

That breath released as she put her feet off the edge and rose upward. Quinn stirred onto his side, but did not seem to wake. Frowning at the gecko, Kira gave him a 'I could murder you look' before it settled back on the cot. Gabby followed.

"Watch after him for a moment for me, please." Whispering, she tugged the blanket up over his shoulders. Then, padding on more steady bare feet, she went to get breakfast for both of them.

Quinn sat upright by the time she made it back. The two geckos clambered into his lap and curled up around each other, slumbering peacefully. He didn't look up or say anything, just stared down at the little creatures he'd made.

Bringing a light breakfast, mainly fruit and croissants. Kira sat across from him, giving him space, placing the tray down between them.

"We should eat."

Neither reached for the food.

"Quinn, I-" What did she wish to say to him? What could she say? He'd been avoiding her, then he'd rescued her once again. It was turning into a bad habit that she needed him to do so. Sitting cross-legged, she had her hands turned down on her knees and she clenched the fabric. "Thank you," she ended up on. "For saving me."

"You're welcome," Quinn mumbled. His voice lost the Irish brogue, but wasn't quite the monotonous robot tone he'd used before. He just sounded tired and defeated.

"If you want me to leave you alone, I will." She made the offer, but her voice landed far from even like a serrated knife, it rose and fell the edge uneven. She cared for him. A thickness unhidden and full of the tears she'd not quite shed all the way last night. "I should have respected your wishes to start, but I just didn't want to see you leave on such bad terms. I don't know what I was thinking- or maybe I wasn't thinking. I'm so sorry to have put you in this position. It was unfair of me to push my presence on you to begin with. Max has just been trying to get me to be more sensitive towards others, and I guess I was the exact opposite of that." It was clear she was flustered. Twisting about, the cold of the floor traveled up through her feet. She left the tray. She didn't even ask for Gabby to come with her. "I'll still send along meals if you want them. I'll stay on the ship and off of Eikos, but I'll be where you aren't."

Quinn listened without interrupting, his head leaning on the side of the wall, his eyes downward. Gabby rushed, flinging herself off the side like a flying squirrel, arms outstretched, landing with the clicking sound of metal tapping metal before rushing toward Kira's leg to shimmy upward.

"It's a bit late for that." His voice carried his usual gruffness, but it still sounded more weary than anything else.

Pausing her back to him, she stiffened. "I can make it less painful." She wished she didn't have to, and she was glad that she wasn't facing him anymore.

"By what? Acting like a bitch, so I don't like you anymore?" Quinn snorted. Then he laughed. Really laughed. He fell over and clutched his stomach as the offended lizard, Gary, dove for cover.

"Why in the world is that funny?" Rounding on him, he'd sparked the anger that she'd felt when he'd been avoiding her all those days. The rage she'd felt when she'd searched for him to talk about how Gabby was doing or just to see him because she'd enjoyed his company.

"Because this all started because you were too stubborn to leave me alone. Then we got to know each other and you want to loop back to being a bitch," Quinn said, wheezing with amusement before falling into another fit of laughter.

"I don't want to loop back to being anything. I wasn't the one who decided that just avoiding me was the best way to handle the fact that, for once in your life, someone was trying to be a friend to you when you'd not had one before." She shoved her hands in her pockets to keep from slapping him as he continued to laugh at her expense. Lashing out because he had called her names.

Quinn's laughter slowly died down and he stared up at the ceiling.

"Yeah, well, mission bloody accomplished Kira," the man said with a sigh.

"Stars, you're infuriating Quinn." Tossing her hands up in the air at his words, she went to stomp off, but before she left the room she called back, "Dinner's at six."

"Says the woman who badgered the future hermit until she was, apparently, his friend." He laughed again, something manic to it. He wasn't any better. He wasn't mentally in a place ready for healing. But apparently, for the moment, he wasn't a totally useless curled-up blob not doing anything at all. Kira could deal with this.

"Well, now you can either show up or deal with the Eikos. I won't send it with the drone." That was the ultimatum now. He didn't want things to go back to the way they were, so she'd make it worse.

Leaving him alone there, she needed a shower and a moment to think clearly.

Watson thought the opposite, and he was promptly told where he could go stick his computer chip.

Kira and Quinn

Chapter Eleven

KIRA

KIRA

It lacked punctuation the way he said it. No question, but not quite finished, as if he'd started to say something, then decided against it. With the way his programming worked, she knew he could do that mid sentence and no one would know.

"Watson."

His name dropped from her lips with curiosity, but not the same fervent pushing she'd been doing towards Quinn.

I hope you know what you're doing.

"I will not mess things up for you... again."

That's not my focus.

"It is your focus, don't lie to me." Jolting upright, fingernails bit into her palms. He couldn't see her, she thought. He couldn't tell anything about her movements other than the sound they made, the way she spoke to him, irritated.

Maybe it is, but maybe it is for reasons that I cannot explain properly like this.

"Watson..." Her mounting anger faded as quickly as it had come on. "You can tell me anything. There's nothing you could say that would-"

Commander West is requesting an audience. It's urgent.

Her transmitter beeped incessantly, demanding her attention be paid to the awaiting messages. She had actively been ignoring them since she left the med bay. Unaware of Quinn's foresight to explain his actions, she knew there'd be hell to pay, but hell if she'd pay it.

"I'm sure he is."

This is the fourth time he's requested it. It's forcing me to report it now.

"I can't... I can't right now."

You have to, Kira. You're the Captain of this ship, and one of its inhabitants effectively held the Eikos hostage. If you don't explain and smooth this over, it puts everything at risk. Imagine what Sir will say if you don't fix this now.

She flinched, features almost pinched in reaction to the idea. Surely, some of those messages were from him. The man had planted resources in every major space station and ship across the galaxy.

She checked the very messages Watson supposedly was being forced to forward. There were several admonitions from Toke, a few from West, the gist being that he requested a meeting, immediately, which came in directly after the incident, and then he just pestered away after that. Every one she ticked and deleted. Nothing was ever truly gone. But it was out of sight and almost out of mind

Kira.

"Watson."

This cannot be ignored.

"I'm not planning on doing it indefinitely."

The sooner you handle this, the better it will be.

"Fine, but arrange for him to come here."

Going onto the Eikos after what occurred it wasn't a suicide mission, but it certainly did not appeal in any way, shape or form. Especially if Quinn tracked her, which she was sure he was possibly going to start doing. The Commander coming onto the Callistar would be simpler, regarding her movements, at the very least.

Thirty minutes later, she opened the sealed outer hull into the gate that led from the Eikos.

West stood there, pompous as ever, hair slicked back, his almost beady eyes assessing her. The quick head to toe hard to miss, but it was less salacious and more of a quantitative measure of her health, so she let it slide.

"Commander West." The attempt at a smile was something tight lipped, landing between a grimace and an actual one. Remaining squarely in the door, she did not yield the entryway to him.

"Captain Starling," he replied, teeth held tight together, his lips moving, but nothing else. Pushing forward, Kira made it clear by remaining planted in place that he would not be allowed entry. He added with widening eyes, "Are we going to have this conversation in the hallway here?"

"We are."

"This is ridiculous, Kira. You do not answer my pages. You do not let me know what's going on, instead I receive an anonymous message. Untraceable back to the origin, and money deposited into my personal account. Is this meant to make things alright? Am I meant to accept this?"

He rushed through what he had to say, barely pausing, and each breath he took occurred when he'd ran out of air to keep going. He huffed at the end, giving Kira a moment to intercede.

"You're meant to accept that I was put in danger by members of your crew, that I was rescued by one of mine. My crew member did what was necessary in order to make sure of my safety."

"Like hell he did," West fumed. "Your *crew member* could have alerted the security on the Eikos to retrieve you, or Watson could have done so. Are neither of them capable of some common sense?"

The lines around Kira's mouth tightened at his suggestions. "Whose payroll are you actually on, Commander West?"

The weasel came out in him, the short faced, needy, smelly little creature as he eyed her. Kira thought he portrayed contempt, as he attempted to come up with a suitable response. But if he was a little sniveling rodent who had access to hair gel, she was a Mountain Lion. Claws sunk in, ready to pounce. He would not win, that she assured herself of.

"I work for-"

"I know who you work for, on paper and off of it," she sneered at him, this time matching his attitude in it. "And you know I am but one of many important pieces to that off record employer. I'm sure he would have approved of any means necessary to ascertain my safety and any means that were taken to obtain it."

West shot a hand between them, putting it beside the frame, bringing himself close. Leaving between the two a half a foot step over to get into the Callistar, and Kira practically leaned into that space to make sure he couldn't even sample the air behind her.

"You're a spoiled brat, Kira. One day, it's going to bite you on the ass."

"As long as it isn't you doing the biting," she smirked wickedly.

A muscle flexed in his cheek, his very jaw trembling, the grinding and pressure making him almost vibrate. *There's the snake,* Kira thought, wildly amused at the showing of it. Like a rattlesnake tensed up to strike. Oh, he was shaking his little rattle to the point every bit of prey in the area could hear it, but she wasn't prey.

Captain, this isn't helping matters.

Replying to Watson meant speaking out loud. She remained silent, but he'd get his answer either way. "Look, West, I'll admit, it could have been handled much better. We could handle this much better, but what's done is done. Why can't you just take the money, play it off as a training exercise, and up your budget for your security to prevent it from happening again?"

Flesh against metal let off a sound as he dragged his hand down, the screeching made her clench her teeth. West was taller than her, by quite a bit, enough to bear down his weight as he leered, "You think Daddy's little girl can get away with whatever she wants, don't you? Well, I've got news for you Princess. There's an entire galaxy out there, and part of it wants to know who's taking out the dirty laundry."

Kira's muscles tensed, every fiber of her being fought and clawed to not to strike back. Then, to handle this with less animosity, less berating, but could the voice of reason win?

Kira, don't put us in this position.

"Do you have fangs West or do you just hiss like a snake? I'd like to see you try to strike."

KIRA.

"You'll see it alright."

West went the very direction of his namesake, stalking off as if he were proud to have the last word. If he checked the cameras later, he'd earn a quaint view of Kira, making a rather lewd gesture at his back before the door shut and locked.

What have you done?

"West won't do anything. He's all bark and no bite."

That is... an unwise assumption.

"Yeah, well, I lack wisdom. Just look at your records. I'm sure your unfailing memory can provide you with plenty of examples."

You're too volatile, Kira, you always have been.

"Just monitor his correspondence, Watson. Take a peek into the Eikos. Follow what Quinn did, get some monitors on what he's doing, and who he's talking to. If he so much as sneezes without using a tissue, I want to know about it."

At your command, Captain.

Chapter Twelve

QUINN

Quinn arrived on time for dinner, but stood arms crossed in the doorway leaned against the side. The picture of a sullen teenager being dragged on a vacation they'd thoroughly been against, but he was there.

In his opinion, there was no straightforward way he could fix it, so he should deal with it.

Watching Kira, she didn't greet him when he came in. She just put something that looked like meatloaf on the pass-over section they'd been using as their makeshift table. Getting down some glasses, she gave herself water. "What do you want to drink?"

"Water, please," Quinn shrugged off the doorway. He still failed to branch out regarding his beverage choices, not seeing why someone would consume empty calories.

The glass appeared in front of him, as did Kira's uncharacteristic silence. He did not see her silence as a matter of concern, not yet. Taking the glass, he sipped and then cut into his meal. Just like the last time they'd eaten together, he treated the entire thing more like a science experiment than a meal. He combined different variations of flavor on his plate slowly before consuming each morsel one bite at a time.

"You know, if there's anything you'd like to try, I can attempt to make it." A look up revealed her attention fully on him, like it normally was. The woman's unnerving habit of trying to make eye contact never ended.

"Okay." A beat of silence before he said, "cheesecake."

"I'll look at some recipes tomorrow."

"No hurry." He continued to eat, focused mostly on the food. Thus far, it was among the more pleasant conversations they'd ever had.

"Probably do Camgen tomorrow night." A quick search revealed it to be an Empyrean dish of mainly vegetables with thin strips of something resembling beef in it, a hearty dish.

"Alright, got any questions about the ship's progress?" Quinn asked, making it abundantly clear that he did not know how to do small talk. His go-to topic being business.

"Not in particular. I do need to know when to recall the crew, but you're welcome to extend your timeline."

"Ship should be done in about… eight to twelve days, depending on how many more… episodes I have." Quinn took another bite, chewing thoroughly. "Oh, you can tell Watson his body is going to be done growing in about two weeks." The man thought to say that since the A.I. might want to know the status of that and it had alerted him to Kira's distress.

"He can hear you." She tapped behind her ear. "He doesn't understand the meaning of privacy sometimes."

"Well, there you have it then. Thanks for dinner." One of his cleaning droids swept in to clean his mess.

"You're welcome." He caught a frown, the expression difficult to miss on such an expressive face, but he did not comment on it, just slipped back out.

There would continue to be no arguments throughout the week. Quinn showed up at six every evening to eat with her before vanishing. Without the gruff arguing, though, it really drove home how absolutely horrid he was at small talk. As in, he didn't seem to be aware it was a thing people did.

Kira consistently asked him if he was working on his guitar, a subject that came up about his new hobbies he'd been looking into. She asked after Gary, and let the two little geckos chase each other around. On a night towards the end of the week when she told him a story about Alec, she reached across the table and touched his hand without thinking.

Mostly, Quinn wasn't opposed to answering questions, but he still seemed to struggle to come up with ones of his own. She learned he practiced his guitar when he took personal time. When her hand touched his, he stiffened in surprise, but otherwise didn't react. She'd draw it back almost as quickly as she extended it but it seemed difficult for her to keep from little gestures. He noticed it was small things still, a touch on the shoulder here, a wave, she'd bring him lunch and sometimes wait for a second to talk about his current project. It wasn't with the interest of someone really worried about his progress, but the interest of someone interested in what made him tick. He'd find she smiled more than she had before, was open more. They were getting to know each other after all, he mused.

"I've been charting stars," she told him at dinner one night. "There's a nebula that I think would be beautiful to see, but we won't pass by it. Do you want to come up to the Astrium with me?"

"Sure."

He'd been planning on going back to work, but they were getting close to being complete. The crew would likely start arriving tomorrow and the finishing touches would be done by then. Mostly just cosmetics and stress testing now left.

When he accepted, he earned himself a broad smile. "I've been looking into more classical guitar music as well. There's one I wanted to show you."

"Sounds good." The man hesitated, debating on whether to say something else. Kira watched him. Even with his limited ability to judge her expressions, his neural net picked up the rest. She was waiting. "How was your day?"

His research had revealed a list of questions one could ask to be polite.

A mote of nothing then she ducked her head, bobbing it a little as she swallowed, "It was good. I've been planning out our journey based on the projections of what is nearest. How was yours?"

"It was fine. I got the last few connections in and fired the engines. Everything is reading normal." Quinn wasn't sure what else, if anything, to say about what had been a fairly uneventful day for him.

"Well, what was your favorite part about it?"

"Oh, uh, huh... Dinner." The net flashed in his eyes, reviewing the day. "What was yours?"

"The same, though I feel as if the reasons are different."

"Entirely possible." A notification flashed as it interpreted her tone. Teasing in nature. He did not elaborate on his answer, searching for another question that wasn't superfluous.

Kira palmed her mouth, a giggle escaping. "You can ask whatever you want, Quinn. You don't have to make small talk."

"If I knew what I wanted to ask, I wouldn't be thinking about it so hard," Quinn said this, not to be patronizing, nor aggressive. Just a statement of fact. "What was it like growing up outside of a lab?" Because that was something he was kind of curious about.

"I don't think I had a normal childhood." For once, her focus shifted to her plate, pushing food across it. "But I traveled a lot, learned from a computer instead of a teacher. I saw much of the galaxy before my teens and was serving on a cruiser by the time I was fifteen. I had an odd sort of freedom but it restricted social growth because while I was exposed to many people I never stayed long with anyone other than Toke himself but I have a vague memory of a woman smiling at me who I think was my mother."

Her fork scraped across porcelain as she added, "This crew has become my family. They are who I live for now and who I would do anything to defend, even including the Vicar."

"Sounds more exciting than growing up in a lab." He couldn't imagine a life with that level of freedom and exploration. Nearly every hour of every day when he was young was planned out. From the food he ate, to what he learned, even what he did in his "free" time. His version of getting personal time was actually just the hours where he'd been encouraged to invent whatever he wanted.

"Well, you have the chance now." She reached across the table to touch his hand. "You can go wherever you want and do whatever you'd like to do."

"Not really." No movement back, but he didn't turn into her grip either. "If Paradigm finds out where I am, I will be... in trouble. I can do a lot of things, but they have more money, resources, and people. I won't be able to avoid them forever."

"We'll make sure they can't find you, Quinn." She let go, the warmth of her touch a noted absence.

"Thanks."

"You're welcome. So, what are you going to focus on once you're on your own?"

"I'm going to try to fix everything, I guess. I thought I'd figured it out before. But I've realized the issue wasn't resources, it's people. So I am going to try to figure out how to get people to be better. I'm not sure how, but with enough time, I can figure it out."

"You'd have to install implants in every person to do that," she said. "Otherwise, the best way to make people better is simply to be a better person yourself."

"I don't think I could get away with putting microchips in everyone. I was just going to try to figure out how to address the root causes of large-scale conflicts." Which is why he'd created Q-Cells, an almost endless battery. They could have addressed literally everyone's energy consumption needs and people had turned them into bombs.

"That's called emotions. You can take away every motivation of greed, and you're still left with love and revenge. They will always argue. Wars have started over women before, you know?"

"It's not emotions. It's resources and cultural differences fanning them. If I can perfect a universal translator, figure out how to convert energy to matter, and make an energy source that can provide and take advantage of that. Then we can get every civilization to a post-scarcity state. With unlimited resources, there will be nothing to fight over. Especially if I make it so widespread that the greedy people who convince others to fight for them can't find people willing to do that anymore," Quinn said, looking at her a bit annoyed she argued with him about this. Also, inadvertently, revealing that despite his attempts at a gruff exterior, he was an idealist.

She shook her head. "Why did you come after me, Quinn? On the Eikos?"

"Because Watson informed me you'd been drugged," the man responded with a shrug of his shoulders. "Unless you mean why did I care? In which case, I think I had a whole mental breakdown about it and you were there."

"Do you think those men had any intention of doing anything remotely legal after they'd drugged me? They did not know who I was, only that I served aboard the Callistar. Greed did not motivate them, but other things, and so were you when you crossed over to save me."

"So, are you trying to talk me out of trying to figure out how to fix these problems?" Quinn snapped at her with surly irritation. "I'll figure something out for slimy bastards. Stick them in a holo chamber or something like that. Problem, solution, Kira."

"So, if you somehow achieve galactic peace, what's next?"

"I don't know. I guess try to figure out how to live a normal life. That, or ascend into some kind of higher intelligence. Either or."

"Well, you're part of the way to your first goal."

"If you say so."

A drone slid in his mental triggers sending for it automatically. His plate was empty. He was done; it responded.

"Hela could teach you to cook. If you're going to be alone, you might as well have good food." Her suggestion, the quickness, a plausible explanation by the algorithm he was developing came up, she stalled.

"I... hmmm." His plan had just been to set up a drone farm that would gather up what grew, reduce it to a nutrient slurry and then add some of the pre-manufactured flavorings. But Kira had shown him that homemade food tasted a lot better. "Suppose I could."

"She's a better teacher than me, much more patient." Kira began clearing the table, a drone helped. He noticed she didn't complain this time.

"I'll bear that in mind." Considering Kira's patience was a bit all over the place, he wasn't actually sure what to make of her statement. Either way, he followed her up to the Astrium with no complaining.

She used the scanner to enter, then approached the projection ring. He waited patiently for her by the open door. It had been a mark of his respect to her since he'd not included any kind of bypass for himself. Admittedly, he could still get it open if he really wanted to, but he couldn't do it easily.

Once inside, he found himself pleased that she had apparently approved of his changes to the room, since it remained as he left it. With the lights dimmed, and the star projector on, it would be easy to think they just walked into a forested clearing. In fact, the new silence he'd brought to the ship really helped with the illusion.

"This was really thoughtful of you." Manually programming the projector, her eyes were down. "I'd never really thought to change it before, but you made it perfect."

"I just researched serene spaces and cross-referenced with things I knew you enjoyed. It didn't take that long to figure out or put together." He fidgeted, uncomfortable with the praise.

"A lot of people wouldn't have bothered. It was really sweet. Though, I am sorry I tried to hug you afterwards, I was meaning it to be grateful."

She sat next to him with those last words. A sweet, closed-mouth smile played across her face as music played behind her. Soft and smooth, the melody flowed over them.

"Yeah, I figured that out. Didn't help at the moment, but... yeah." She was very touchy feely, and he wasn't sure how he felt about that. Falling into the warmth and comfort of the familiarity of their routine, the mattress enveloped him.

When he'd first sat down, he tucked his knees up to his chest. His body language instinctively went to what cut him off the most, slowly relaxing as the music played and the stars twinkled above. Enough to lean back and let his head rest against the pillow. He was, in some ways, good company for this, since he had no issue sitting in silence. Temporarily disabling his neural link, there were enough distractions in the room.

Kira got up to make popcorn, making a game of trying to catch it in her mouth, which she wasn't very good at, and she laughed when she missed.

It took some convincing to get him to try, and he proved to be *incredibly* inept at it. With his neural net disabled, his coordination was laughably poor. Though she quickly picked up that razzing him was not the best solution, since he stopped trying when she did.

"It's friendly teasing Quinn. I don't mean anything by it."

"You had to mean something or you wouldn't have said it," Quinn grumped out. He'd not taken off in a huff or kicked her off her own ship this time, but she pushed things too far, too quickly.

"When the crew comes back, you'll see that it is meant to be fun. I do it because I like you, Quinn."

"Well, I'm trying not to overreact to things, but I don't see how mocking me for not being good at something I've never tried before is good fun." He certainly didn't enjoy it. Especially since he did not know how to fire back without being rude.

"Because you're supposed to do it back." Putting the popcorn bucket aside, she sat upright, cross-legged from their game.

"Why would I do that?" Quinn said, confused, and relaying it without knowing in his furrowed brows. Insulting her back could go awry. It seemed like asking for trouble. Reaching up to rub at his temples, he couldn't understand this at all.

"I have an idea. I can just show you." Off like a bullet to the projector, she seemed pleased with herself.

"Okay?" Quinn frowned as he watched her. He'd thought about improving or replacing the machine, but had ultimately decided against it, mostly because any changes would have made it work differently. He didn't think she would want to learn how to operate a new one.

An old earth movie started overhead, overtly romantic, but it had the subtext she was possibly trying to achieve. He watched the entire thing and when the credits started to roll, he looked her way. "So... People just insult each other until they decide they are in love? What is the message here?"

She laughed, and he didn't, but it made him watch her. "They tease," she corrected. "But it's between friends and family too, though it is involved in flirting sometimes and lovers do it as well."

"So, what you're telling me, the man who has no family, no lovers, and..." There is a slight grimace as he mumbled something under his breath about having only one friend. "That people make fun of other people and it's supposed to be endearing? Cause it seemed like they basically just hated each other until the plot said it was time for them to like each other."

"Perhaps it was a poor example of them doing it in a kind way, but it's not exactly like what happens between real people. The first time I did it was for friendly banter, not to be cruel to you."

"Well, I can't say I understand why friends would insult each other like that, and I will not risk anything by trying and fekking it up."

"I mean, most people don't have a temper like mine. You can still make friends without it, Quinn, if you want them."

"Making one friend has been a real pain in the ass. Not sure I want more," Quinn muttered. Once again, under his breath, but this time loud enough she might actually hear him.

"Did you call me a pain in the ass?" She grinned from ear to ear and had sat up out of the pillows to look at him so he'd see it properly.

The man glared at her when she said that. "I see what you did there. Yes, you have been a pain in my ass."

That got her to laugh as she teased him. "But you're fond of this pain in your ass?"

"I have no idea why." He felt... annoyed that she got him to play her game simply by latching onto some of the more abrasive stuff he said.

"Me either, but I'm glad you're here." A gentle touch on his shoulder and then a release.

That got a snort from him, but he didn't glare at her when she grazed his shoulder. She was whittling away at his defenses despite his efforts, and he wasn't sure what to do about that. It was hard to view it as a bad thing, but it filled him with a deep sense of worry.

"Thought we might have a picnic lunch on the promenade tomorrow, if you can spare a few minutes."

"The finishing work is mostly being handled by the drones. I only have to double-check the final product." Machine precision had a 99.99% accuracy rating. It wouldn't detect the .01% deviation if there was an issue.

"Oh good, I can make it a proper picnic then."

Fortunately for Kira, Quinn still had his neural net off, so a definition of picnic didn't automatically turn up for him to question the logistics of having one on a space station. Instead, he just shrugged his shoulders, agreeing to the lunch date without any complaints.

QUINN

Quinn returned to work since he had yet to fix his sleep schedule to anything resembling normal hours. He'd wake in the middle of a sleep cycle and finish a project at will. Still, when lunch rolled around, he arrived at the promenade as requested, his hands in his pocket as he waited for Kira to arrive. The area she'd referred to was an overhanging walkway over one of the largest storage units on the ship. One could walk a half mile around the outside to whatever point they'd entered at, meaning two rounds made a full mile. Below, he could see some of the mining equipment brought in from the Eikos being stored in the open space.

Kira came with a checkered cloth and a basket. She looked cheerful as always, but he'd not dived fully beneath the surface of the different smiles she wore externally. He noted them, and her moods, trying to sort out what meant what. "I got fresh grapes from hydroponics," she said.

"There is also a vintner machine." He wasn't sure how much she'd actually looked at the additions. Part of putting together a ship capable of deep space exploration was making sure people had few reasons to miss civilized space. So why not include a machine to turn grapes into wine?

"Want me to name the first bottle after you?" She set down the basket and spread out the blanket, flicking the edges so it floated like fresh snow laying flat on the ground. A bit like a scene from the movie the night before.

"I didn't spring for a label maker," Quinn said, his voice so incredibly dry it made it hard to tell if it was a serious comment or if, just perhaps, he was cracking a joke.

"Was that a joke? Are you making jokes now?"

Quinn glared at her and then grunted. "There is no label maker since I didn't see the point of one. But yes, I was trying to be funny." Now that she'd called him out about it, he just felt awkward.

She still chuckled and went back to setting up the basket. There were plates nestled in the lid and silverware buckled in. "Just for that, I'll color up a label myself."

"I can't tell if you're saying that to annoy me, or if you are saying it to annoy me in a way I am supposed to find endearing," Quinn informed her as he settled down on the blanket with her.

"Definitely the second one until you see what it looks like." She brought sparkling juice and a flask of water for him with chunks of ice.

"I think I should be afraid."

Her shoulders shook with unexpressed laughter. She served chicken parmesan in deep set plates. Laying out the grapes and a side of garlic bread, she sat, looking out at the stars, which had not changed during their stay there. "I've always wanted to do this."

"Have a picnic on a space station?" Quinn looked at her quizzically, since it was a bit of an odd thing to have always wanted.

"Well, the space station wasn't really a requirement. Usually picnics are in parks or other grassy areas, but I would have felt ridiculous asking any of the crew." It meant she'd reserved her odd request just for him.

"Oh, so just the picnic part." Quinn scratched his neck absently. "And you decided to invite me on this thing you've always wanted to do?" While he wasn't openly calling her crazy, the look he gave suggested that was what he thought.

"Yes," the confidence with which it came out and the way she grinned after solidified the crazy for him. "Is it so odd that I might invite you to do something that means something to me?"

"Little bit. But not so much as it did in the past." He still didn't quite get why she had practically forced a friendship upon him, but he was, at the very least, not having another breakdown over it.

He focused on eating his meal. A thought occurred to him and he frowned, trying to push it aside. Eventually, he realized he should say it, but he didn't want to. So much like her, he hemmed and hawed rather than communicating.

"Max will arrive tomorrow," she informed him after another beat. "He is going to accompany me onto the Eikos while I finish out the paperwork for our stay."

"The vicar? Why am I not surprised he is the first one coming back?" Quinn snorted. He remembered the man from their brief meeting and honestly, if he'd had to guess which member of the crew would have harassed him the most, it would have been the priest.

"He was not going to be on this trip originally, but he is nothing if not punctual."

"Aye, I suppose he is at that," he agreed with a nod of his head. "I looked up a list of questions you can ask to make small talk. They all seemed a bit silly, like asking who you would choose to have dinner with."

"Is it supposed to be the one where you can have dinner with anyone dead or alive?" Popping in a grape, it let out an audible pop as she bit down.

"Yeah, I think it is."

"It's meant to be a sort of test to see where your values lie," she informed him. "Not a true test, but just a way to feel someone out. If they say a family member, then you know that's something important to them. If they say someone famous, it depends on what they're famous for, and it shows you what appeals to them."

Kira peered over as if she still considered it. She asked him instead of answering, "Did you come up with an answer to it?"

"Not really. I've only ever eaten a meal with you, so I suppose you'd be my answer." It was a fairly straightforward bit of thinking for him.

"It's less of a compliment when you put it like that."

"If you say so." He finished eating, but lingered, looking her way, apparently curious to hear her answer.

"I don't know myself. I did not meet my parents and I'm not sure I would want to. There's no one out there that I think holds any great wisdom about the universe who hasn't already said what they have to say…"

Quinn had no great insight to offer to Kira as she puzzled herself over the question. His response had been based mostly on the fact that she was the only person whose company he came close to enjoying, not that he would ever admit that aloud.

"Toke." She finally decided on, but there was more to it. "Before he took me in. I would like to know the man he is to a stranger, to judge for myself."

"Hmmm, I guess I can understand that." He scratched at his nose. He would like to know what some of his researchers were like off of work. Or, he might have once long ago. These days, it was hard to see them as anything other than jailors who'd exploited him.

"I don't-" Kira took a sharp breath, assuming his regular defensive position, arms around her knees, something he noted not absently but with all his being. "I don't think Toke is necessarily bad, but I do not think he is as good as I once believed him to be, not that I've led a life without consequence, either."

"I mean, based on what I've read about him, by the numbers, he breaks about even."

"Do you research everyone you meet?"

"Of course."

"Well, do you think of me differently after getting to know me?"

"I think of you the same way. I just feel differently about it now."

"Well, if that isn't indifferent," she snorted, and released her feet, leaning back on her palms.

"It isn't indifferent." He looked her way and scowled. "It's... Complicated." That was the best way to think about it. "But clearly it isn't indifferent or I wouldn't be here."

"I shouldn't have been so flagrant about it then, I apologize."

"You're the closest thing to a friend I've ever made."

"I consider you a friend as well, Quinn."

"Well, alright then." If she was very observant, she might notice that an honest to God smile played at the corner of his lips. Though he did his damndest to hide it.

Her smile grew impossibly wider, she'd had one the whole conversation. "Grumble all you want. You can't change my mind on the matter."

"Hey, I am pointedly not arguing, unlike some people I know." The man fired back with a slight laugh, despite himself, for the first time, actually seeing some humor in her teasing. The huge smile on her face did enough to soften her voice that he didn't even realize it was teasing.

"You wouldn't like me if I didn't argue with you," she shot back, keeping her eyes on him.

"Maybe, you are certainly the only person I know who is stubborn enough to force the issue every time." He glanced her way, noticing her staring, and then hid his face again. Smiling in amusement.

"Someone's gotta push your buttons." Picking up her plate and giving him a slight reprieve, she reached out to load his as well, going to her knees to load things into the basket.

"Yeah, maybe." Getting to his feet, his expression back to the more customary scowl.

"Yes, maybe."

Attempting to fold a blanket meant for a rather gigantic bed turned into a comical thing on Kira's part. Quinn watched for a moment as she tried to gather the edges. Seeing it horribly aligned, he stepped forward with a sigh and took an edge from her.

"Was I not doing a good enough job?" Kira teased.

"It wasn't straight."

She laughed, and they folded it together. It brought him close enough for it to be too loud, and yet it was appealing. Hearing it was not abrasive, but enjoyable. Stepping back as soon as she had a hold of it he tucked his hands in his pockets.

Kira tucked the blanket under one arm and collected the basket with the other, hooking it in the crook of her elbow. "Are you free for the afternoon as well?"

"I guess."

"I was going to go for a swim if you'd like to join me? There's a shallow end until you get used to the depths. It's on the Eikos…"

"A swim?" There was that familiar flash of blue. "Oh…" He said as he cocked his head, figuring out what all was involved. A slightly worried expression colored his features. "I don't know how to swim."

"I can show you, and you can stay where you can stand easily."

"I… fiiiine." Quinn sighed. Maybe she'd well and truly worn him down, he wasn't sure. But he knew part of it was he didn't want her going there alone. Never again.

Chapter Thirteen

KIRA

THEY DIVIDED THE EXERCISE areas into several rooms and locations. Kira reserved a smaller pool made for private lessons, so they'd be alone for the experience. Shorts for Quinn weren't a problem to get out of the storage, and she sent him off to change as she dipped a toe into the warmed water.

Universally, it was unusually strange when creatures enjoyed being submerged in water when they weren't from water planets. The concept more of a human one, that others had warmed to. The salt-water concoction made it easier to float, but wasn't dense enough that one couldn't sink if they wanted to.

Kira stood at the shallow end. The floor went from completely level with the walk in to about ten feet deep on the far side in a range of twenty feet. The width was closer to twelve feet. Barely letting it touch her, she waited patiently, watching the changing area for Quinn.

Emerging, the man was white as a ghost all over. His angular body formed from lifting himself through small crevices and holding heavy machinery in place. His paleness made him look like someone who'd spent his entire life in space, only ever getting UV from the station's bulbs. The only other feature she felt herself staring at was his tattoo, directly over his heart. A bar code, underneath a string of letters and numbers.

Q-0X1U-F761-BX7N-3DL2

He paused, red tinged his cheeks as he frowned.

Squinting to reassure herself of his reaction, she looked behind her. There was nothing of note. Just her, in the little black number with cutouts on the side and a deep V that formed over her like a second skin. She wasn't ashamed, but he'd never... well, he'd never seemed to notice she was a woman. It gnawed at her to ask, to push farther, but he came over to stand next to her, toeing the edge of the line of the water like she did, drawing her attention back to the moment.

"So it gets deeper as you go. You'll be good for quite a while before you go under." She decided on this instead of the other comment that wanted to come out.

Kira treaded forward with confidence, a glance back and he seemed to look pointedly anywhere but her, but she smiled as he followed, slowly, painstakingly, a familiar flash saying his net was off.

She kept semi-close to him in case he slipped. "This is the closest I've ever come to the weightlessness of space, but there's still some resistance in the water. It's excellent exercise and easy on the joints."

"You mean besides the actual weightlessness of space?" Quinn said with an arched eyebrow.

"It's better exercise because of the resistance." Still an arm's length away, she held in laughter, not sure if he'd been joking. "Is it alright?"

"I'll let you know once I get deeper."

Barely knee deep, he stepped forward a few more feet until the water nestled against his hip. Observing his progress, the water lapped at the v'd line of his waist, where it slipped into his shorts. Making it her turn to pointedly find anything else interesting.

Then, he risked just falling forward, or so Kira assumed, because he did not even extend his arms to catch himself. He scrambled about in the water for a moment. Splashing and flailing before he popped back up on his feet where the water hit shoulder height for him and he laughed, just a soft laugh.

Prepared to rescue him, she'd gone under and came back up with him. She'd opened her eyes under the water to watch him, and once he got his footing, she came back up. He was taller than her, so while she had to be on her tiptoes to keep her chin above the water he stood flat. While he bellowed, she smiled. "Like a duck."

"Like a what?"

"It's a bird that is normally found in water and swims very well." Catching the sight of his eyes, for the first time they were in bright lighting where she could see them clearly. She stared, admiring the pale color, knowing they were blue did not do them justice. Like pale seaglass.

"I am pretty sure I would drown if I tried to go any deeper. So, I am not sure that applies." Quinn didn't hide the upturned corners of his lips, even when he looked away from her, again toward the deep end of the pool.

"They have to learn to swim as well, and you came up very well. I can help you tread water when you're ready to try." She pushed back into the deeper water, barely bobbing.

He just stood in the water, experimentally waving his arms about, testing the way it resisted his body. He found his balance and then leaned backward so he fell towards the shallow end, trying to mimic what she did, but flailing a bit and dunking himself instead. Which just made him laugh again.

His laughter came out boisterous, deep. Unexpectedly, it was her first glimpse of his freedom. She knew she couldn't comment on it because he would stop, he would retreat within himself and she'd have to wait to hear it again, but it was nice to hear.

Quinn, seemingly in his element, attempted the lean back again. This time he went slowly and kept his body spread wide. He mimicked her well and for a few moments; he floated on his back. She thought his willingness to learn new skills one of his best qualities and he seemed quite pleased with himself as he puzzled through the backstroke. Slowly piecing together how to float.

Diving under, she came up next to him, supporting his upper back for a moment. "Just like a duck," she teased him, not knowing how she looked, not knowing her hair clung to her neck, along the line of the material of her swimsuit and over her arms, strands floating in the water as she brushed them back from her forehead, licking water off of her lips.

"Hrmph." He flung his arms back, flushing again.

Relaxing back, she figured she was still close enough to save him should he need it.

Quinn set his feet down. "I must be having some adverse reaction to the chemicals in the water. There is some swelling."

"Are you alright?"

His retreat wasn't immediate, or quick, and he adjusted his shorts in the lower water. His back to her, but she knew. "Quinn it's, it's not the pool."

"What else could it be?" He kept looking downward as he stalked to the shallow end, grabbing a towel, drying off, paying more attention to his neck and the sides of his head before giving her a sharp look.

"I, uh..." She hesitated to answer. She followed, giving him space. Kira grabbed her own towel, pulling it up over herself. "You're just going to look it up."

"What? You want me to ignore a medical issue and hope it goes away on its own?" Quinn's voice filled with incredulity.

Kira wrapped herself completely, overlapping the ends. Her cheeks felt incredibly warm. "It's not a medical condition, it's a perfectly normal response that you've just never experienced before. You are male, Quinn."

Decidedly male and even if he'd been trying to hide things, and she'd looked away, it wasn't as if she'd not looked at first because of a knee jerk reaction.

"What are you..." He trailed off. Then he took off towards the changing room.

"Quinn! It's perfectly normal!"

The slick floor, wet feet, his awkward gait. It called for disaster. When he tried to launch into a full-blown run at her yelling, he went forward, face first, into the floor.

"Quinn!" Catching up much more cautiously, she asked, "Are you okay?"

"No," Quinn wheezed, pushing himself up to his knees.

"Do you want me to get a medical drone?"

"I'm fine. I'm sorry. I am going to go. Don't worry. I am just going to go."

She gaped, uncertain, and wished she could just be tossed in so she could go under. Imagining how he felt, she knew his pride had to be wounded, but there were other concerns, ones that came out with fear. "Please don't shut me out again."

He closed his eyes. "I don't know." His breathing changed in pace, becoming rapid and he flopped back before raising up to breath.

"Brax," she cursed. How in the world she'd landed in this position twice in one week, she wasn't sure. She couldn't touch him, couldn't give him medication to calm him down, she couldn't do much more than just try to wait it out.

QUINN

"Mrrrrrrrrrrr."

Quinn stirred, pushing himself up and rubbing at his face. Blinking his eyes open, he looked around the room, confused for several moments on where he was before he spotted her. Then, his face turned beet red.

"GAH!"

The man bolted upright, panicked. He remembered the attack, then he'd passed out and... She must have carried him back to the ship, and these were her quarters and there were pants. He hadn't been wearing pants when he passed out.

"GAAAAAAAAAAAH!"

"Hey. Hey. It's okay. The drone changed you. Your door was locked. You're fine." Kira hopped up, her book falling to the floor.

"I! You! Gah!" He threw up his hands in bewilderment, not sure how to handle any of this or what to say. As if either of them had any idea how to handle what had just happened, though for two different reasons.

"Are you alright? You took a pretty hard fall." She kept some distance between them and her hushed tones were like how one would speak to a crisis survivor.

"I- You- I'm fine." High-strung, then grumbling, her demeanor made him feel ridiculous, which he wasn't thrilled about.

"Okay." Going back for her book, she scooped it up. "What happened earlier is a normal reaction. You've just never been exposed to that sort of stimulus before, I'm sure."

"Not really. At least, not that I paid attention to." He'd lived in Toke's hideout for a few months before he'd met her. He'd certainly seen a few scantily clad women, but none of those had any effect on him. They'd just been people. It had been different with her, and he did not know why.

"Well, it's still normal. I should have just explained it better." She settled the book sideways on top of the stack by her table.

A quick observation revealed that her room looked like an absolute tornado had gone through it. When he'd done upgrades, it'd been the same way. Charts thrown over the main table. Oversized clothes hung over a chair. Random writing utensils had fallen off the table and rolled away. A small cart held physical books with worn spines from use. The room was made downright cozy with clutter, with every wall covered in shelves and star charts. The bed, which he was on, might usually have been neglected except for the fact that he had been in it and had flung the covers off when he woke up.

He'd assigned a cleaning drone when the rest of the ship was stripped of stains and scrubbed into a pristine condition. It looked like it had missed her room, but he knew better.

"Well, it felt inappropriate. Like it was something you..." Quinn mumbled, the rest of the words under his breath as he said he thought it was something that might offend her.

"Like it was something *what*?" Perching on the edge of a massive armchair, one could practically lay in it. The distance was her version of walking on eggshells, something he couldn't read but felt, "Quinn, I know you don't have much experience in personal matters like that. I do not expect you to know everything. It's perfectly normal to be attracted to people, even if your feelings don't always align with that attraction. It doesn't have to mean anything."

Silence. That wasn't helpful, mostly because he wasn't even sure what she was saying. He didn't even know how he really felt about her. Emotional attachments were so very foreign to him and he couldn't find any solid definition short of examining his own brain chemistry... Which was a thought that terrified him.

"Why don't we forget it happened?"

"I guess, sure." Quinn shoved off the rest of the covers, resulting in a crumpled mess as he stood. "I need to go think."

"Okay."

"Thank you."

As he left, her scent lingered upon him. A flowery soap from the bed having transferred into his clothes and his senses. Waking there, in a mess, wrapped in her sheets, it was how he imagined normality was. It was all he could think of as he lifted his shirt up to his nose, inhaling deeply.

Chapter Fourteen

KIRA

The repairs are complete according to the trackers.

"All of them?"

All of them.

Kira puffed her cheeks and blew hard. "Guess he has had little else to focus on the last couple of days."

She could practically hear the pleasure in Watson when he replied, **He is an emotionally stunted, lab rat. I'm not sure what you expected.**

"Do you have to do that?"

Have to do what?

"Tear him down, he's still a person, he's still…" Something.

Kira, you put this ship in danger. You put me in danger. The fact he's avoided you the last couple of days shows just how volatile he is. He does not understand complex emotions. If you anger him again, he could choose to make sure it is never a problem again.

"I didn't mean to." She rubbed her eyes. They burned with the sensation of unshed tears. Their ducts were unusually hard to activate.

They still had them like their human counterparts, but for praetorians it was a very marked reaction when they worked.

I am aware you did not mean to, but I will continue to advise you on what is best for the crew, best for everyone.

Her lack of an immediate reply boded well, or unwell.

The Vicar has arrived.

Her mood improved as she went to greet the older gentleman, to welcome him aboard. He came over from the Eikos, and while she wouldn't cross for a proper escort, she would meet him at the door.

"You believe you've made genuine progress." Max stood within the kitchen, taking up the doorway, arms tucked behind his back in an eerily familiar at ease position.

"I do, but it's like-" She poured more flour into a bowl, "Well, it's like that thing you say where it's one step forward and then two steps back. Every bit of progress I make, I undo as quickly as I make it. I just want to help him, but he resists. I'm never sure how far is too far until I've gone too far."

A flash of white caught her eye. Quinn. He walked into the mess. How much he overheard anyone's guess. His hands tucked in his pockets and shoulders hunched up to his ears as he took a seat without a word.

Kira's mouth dropped open at the sight. Seeing him, especially when he knew there would be others, was a good sign. Max's raised brows showed equal surprise. He had received a warning to be gentle with him. Kid gloves, Kira had said.

Max carried a dish over to the table. With the crew returning, they wouldn't be eating in the pass through anymore. He smiled, not as broad as usual, and said, "I'm glad you're joining us."

Kira had her back to Quinn, but she glanced over her shoulder to gauge his reaction, as she knew he wasn't fond of strangers. Max had been sincere in his well wishing, even if Quinn wouldn't take as intended.

The response Max received was as succinct and to the point as one could hope for. Quinn grunted, acknowledging his words but offering no comment to them.

"Max, this is ready too." Kira settled the gravy on the window, attempting to save Quinn, if only for just a moment.

Max set the table, then took his spot, placing Kira at the head. Quinn to her right and Max to her left.

Max, ever unable to keep from poking an open wound, said, "I noticed the upgrades in the rooms. Thank you. I've got to finish writing my collection and it will be wonderful to do it in the peace you've created."

Kira glanced under her lashes at Quinn, but fixed her plate.

Quinn shrugged.

Kira jumped in. "Did you finish what you needed to do with Toke?"

"Oh, yes." Max turned to Kira.

She knew what subjects could carry him on for some time. He wasn't awkward, and he wasn't bubbly, but straightforward, kind, pious in the best ways while allowing for understanding that the very nature of every race was to be chaotic. He talked for a while on Toke, reminiscing about the man's underlying qualities, a topic that Kira had wondered about, as Quinn knew.

Quinn never interjected, nor did he interrupt. When he cleared his plate, he said to Kira, "Thank you for dinner."

"You're welcome."

The drone popped in to clean up. Kira excused herself, catching him in the hall. "Quinn?"

The tenseness loosened. "Yeah?"

"You can't." She knew she needed to rephrase the instant those two words left her mouth. "Well, I mean you *can* do it, but I'd prefer you didn't cut me off anytime that either of us does something embarrassing. That's part of being friends, laughing and moving on."

Kira could read him much better than he read her, but her shoulders hunched and her hands fidgeted at her sides betraying her nervousness that this might make him more distant.

"I don't know what to say," he admitted, not the most in-depth explanation.

"You don't have to say anything. Do you want to have lunch tomorrow? Some of the other crew members will arrive in the morning and we generally have dinner together, but we could eat lunch, just you and me."

"Yeah, okay."

Kira believed helping him by ignoring the problem would be best, but perhaps it was the opposite. His general hesitation told her she was wrong somewhere, but she wasn't sure where.

"Great. Promenade at noon?" It wasn't private, but it wasn't public either, though the crew knew where to find her usually if they needed her.

"Okay, I'll see you then." A weak upturn of his lips, not promising, yet not off-putting.

On a tray were hamburgers and some fries that were still warm. Then Kira, her legs hanging off the ledge, eyes forward. Turning Watson off her comms and she put herself on emergency communications for the next hour.

Quinn remained as punctual as ever, which with him meant arriving exactly at the appointed time. Never early or late, just there when asked to be. He plopped down next to her, selecting a fry and munching on it.

"We're handling things rather poorly, aren't we?" A statement more than a question, but somehow she made it come across as both.

"I don't really know."

She smiled despite everything, popping in a fry, chewing thoughtfully. "I've been attracted to men physically, but not emotionally if that makes sense," she started in, going for the obvious problem of his conflicting emotions. "It's possible to find someone attractive without meaning to as well."

"I wasn't attracted to anyone." He pulled out a knife. The burger sliced up and paired with different combinations of ingredients.

She gave him a pointed look. "I'm sure lab coats weren't really attractive."

"Not particularly. I saw some women wearing less than you when I stayed at Toke's place."

"Did you pay attention to them at all?" If he'd not cared to even look or they'd not looked his way, it could explain a lot.

"I saw them. One tried to talk to me. Didn't really care about them, though." He shrugged as he focused on his experiment, keeping himself busy.

"Well, maybe if you'd cared, it would have been different." A bit of mustard shot out the side of her burger, the foil crinkling.

"Isn't that the problem?" He made eye contact.

"It's not a problem to care for someone." She never wanted him to think that. "I was just saying that you weren't interested in companionship, so you weren't actually 'looking' at them."

"It feels like a problem." Quinn went back to mixing condiments. "It feels like I am being rude to you or something. I've never... noticed anyone in that way. The first time I had it was the only person I would call a friend. It feels wrong to..."

"Like how they look?" Now she knew it would be necessary to bring up her own thoughts on the matter. "You've yet to meet our pilot, Morgan, but I am sure you've looked at his file. Morgan is a very attractive man. I've told him as much. I don't fancy him in a romantic light, but if I met him in a bar somewhere, I might have drank with him and admired him in the same way. Just because I think he's attractive does not make it difficult to know that our relationship is meant for friendship. He's become like a brother to me."

"I've seen." Quinn shifted slightly at the information. "I don't like this. I feel all knotted up and I don't know what I am supposed to do."

He closed his eyes, breathing slowly through his nose.

"I'm probably not the right person to be talking about this. Max would be more suited, probably." Wiping her hands clean she touched his shoulder lightly. "I didn't mean to put you through this."

"I don't know." He repeated. "I was, I enjoy your company. I just, it's gotten, hard."

She knew he was utterly unaware of the inadvertent double entendre. Biting the inside of her cheek, she swallowed her laughter. "That's part of relationships. It's dealing with those hard parts. People are difficult. What I spoke of before, about not being able to fix everyone and everything, this is why. There's not always an easy answer, but when you truly care about something, you work through those hard parts because there's always good there too."

"It hurts though."

"Does it outweigh the good?"

"I don't know. In terms of anguish, I would say somewhere between an 8-10. Happiness is kind of moving from a 6 to an 8. In terms of length of time, more good than bad, but in terms of intensity-"

Frowning at his system, she stopped him by cutting him off. "Quinn, you can't measure your emotions in numbers. It's a simple yes or no question. Do you enjoy your time enough with me for it to outweigh the embarrassment you felt and to work through it?"

She hoped the answer was yes. Obviously, he kept showing up to see her.

"I...I think so." He had not taken a bite of his meal for a while, but he'd also stopped placing slivers of onions on different pieces. "I don't know, though."

"Well." Rising, she picked up her own trash. Her meal hardly touched. Even if she'd sorted out things, his inability to decide was hard on her as well. "Will you let me know when you figure it out?" She stepped past him, looking down as she walked to prevent him from seeing the emotions on her face.

"How do I figure it out?" He sat completely still, focused, yet not-not on her.

"I-" It was her turn to tell him she didn't know because it wasn't something that could be taught. "I don't know, Quinn."

She wiped at her eyes, knowing this might be the end of something that was just beginning. "Maybe-" the word sounded stunted in her mouth as she tried to get it out. "You should look at examples or talk to Max, or anyone. I think I'm just causing more problems by confusing the matter."

"I don't want to talk to Max about it. I want," He flinched, physically drawing back as if he recognized what he saw in her, as though he saw pain for the first time, or anger, recoiling. "It doesn't matter. I'll just, I'll fix this. That is what I do. I fix things. I solve problems. I can solve this."

"It's not a problem you can solve like that, Quinn." A muscle flexed in her cheek. "I just don't want you to isolate yourself again. I know that I'm going to lose you eventually, but until then I don't…"

"It's all chemicals." He looked at her with a mixture of annoyance and desperation in his features. "I can make something to modulate them. It shouldn't be hard, a scanner to monitor level, some kind of injector to modulate them. I should be able to just turn them right off and then this will stop happening and we will both stop hurting. I can fix this, I can fix this."

"Don't you dare!" She crossed the small space, throwing down her trash in her flurry of emotion. This time he would not escape her grasp as she forced him to look up at her by putting her hands more gently on his face than she felt like doing. "Quinn, you can't just turn things on and off. You're not a machine. You are a living, breathing thing, and you can't change that just because you wish to. If you shut things off, you're no longer who you are and while things may be better for you, they won't be better for anyone else."

"Why not?" He demanded. "I can figure it out. I can fix it. We are just computers made of meat at the end of the day. You're saying that things won't be better, but things aren't good now, clearly. If I can fix this, then I will know exactly how I feel. Then I can answer your question and you won't have to be upset."

"I'm not upset because you can't answer the question." Dropping her hands, all she could think of was how thick-headed he was. "I'm worried that I will lose you because you're so concerned about how I'm going to react and how you are going to react because you can't sort out your emotions. If you turn them off, if you find a way, I'm done."

"What?" Quinn frowned in obvious confusion. "I just, I can't hurt you Kira, and I am hurting myself and I just, I am so tired of hurting all the time."

Dropping to her knees and reaching out, she hoped he wouldn't draw away when she tried to embrace him and draw him close, thankful he stiffened but didn't move. Running her hand over his back, she failed to contain herself. A few tears fell loose over his shoulder.

"That's part of being normal too, Quinn," she told him. "I wish I could take it all away, that I could make it better, but all I can do is just be here for you. I can listen and be here."

"But, if I can't fix it, and I don't know how to talk about it-" he shuddered as he trailed off, every breath came quicker than the last.

"You'll learn how to talk about it." Turning her face slightly into his shoulder so he couldn't see her fully, she said, "Just be right now, Quinn. Just be here with me. It's okay."

It was all she could do for him. She knew applying a gentle pressure through touch could be soothing. He still had not learned how to really do it back, but she didn't care. It didn't matter. She simply wanted him to know that someone cared. Someone was there for him.

He tentatively tried it. He wrapped his arms around her, loosely at first, but soon he clung to her.

A smattering of tears hit her shoulder from him. She held him tighter. "You're not some experiment anymore, Quinn. You're free."

"I don't know what that means." He sounded so tired, weary. The little hold out on his Irish accent gone, once again replaced with his factory standard.

"You'll find out."

"What if I don't? What if I never stop hurting?"

"There's never going to be no pain. That's just life, but you find moments that outweigh it. You can't feel those, though, if you cut it all off."

"That's not fair."

"Life isn't fair."

"I want to make it fair." He squeezed tighter.

"You can't fix the whole universe, Quinn." Drawing back so she could look at him, her arms came down his forearms, she did not release just yet, knowing that he needed this still, "Men have tried, and they've failed. Some have become monsters in the process. The best you can do is to treat those around you as you would wish to be treated and hope that in some small way, it makes things better for them."

"Why can't I? I figured out how to fit the power of the sun into a battery you can place into your communicator. Why can't I just fix everything? Why do people have to take what I make and use it to blow things up?"

"Because that wasn't alive. It was when you added in that factor that it was used horribly." She hoped he'd understand one day that it wasn't his fault. He had been innovating for good. "Your intentions were good, but they were taken by others and transformed. You cannot blame yourself for what others do. If I were to use Gabby to pull off a robbery, it would not be your fault."

"I have an answer for you. It is yes, you make me hurt less. Enough that I could talk this out with you." His infernal, technology driven blue eyes met amber. Emotionless sentiment met someone lacking an understanding of what this meant. She gripped him a little tighter.

"Then please don't destroy yourself." The first real and true thing she'd ever asked him to do for her. Everything else he had done was voluntary and never something she pushed for. This she was asking for. She was asking it as a woman that was but a scant foot in front of him and still connected to his body.

"Okay, I can do that." That half sparse laugh he'd done in the pool. He did it again, and both of them let go only physically.

"Okay."

Captain. Alec is asking for access to the ship.

Kira had forgotten the codes had changed, and she knew she should greet Max personally. She paled, asking aloud, "How long has he been trying?"

About ten minutes now.

Kira buried her face in her hands for a second. "I'm so sorry, Quinn. I have to go fetch Alec or else he'll be in an even worse state."

Quinn just nodded, blank, remote, and yet not.

Alec was about to blow a gasket by the time she reached him. His accent didn't disappear when he became angry. It got worse. Much worse. So much so that Kira couldn't understand the brogue and would tell him to speak where the translator could decipher it.

That set him off on another tirade all the way down to engineering with her in tow, rolling her eyes once or twice.

He wasn't grumbling about the alterations, but rather being locked out, "Bloody kicked ou'. Then locked ou'. You ken how frustrating it is ta be locked ou' of yer own bloody ship!"

Kira trailed behind him, still knowing exactly how long he could carry on this rant and choosing to ignore most of it, "It was a security issue, Mr. O'Malley."

Alec went on under his breath for a short while as they walked through the engine room. He stopped, suddenly, by the oscillator, looking up and noticing the stark change as Kira had. "It's quiet."

"It is." Kira didn't know how he would react. Until-

"It's about bloody time!" Alec threw his hands up in the air. "Been telling you for years, my hearing ain't gonna hold out."

Kira laughed at that one. Things were going to be fine then.

She left him to explore, knowing that he had the manual Quinn issued.

QUINN

Despite the addition of Alec, Quinn still turned up for dinner. His warring emotions almost made him turn away at the door when he saw Alec present as well.

Taking his place, he stated gruffly, "Ship is done. Watson will have control of its systems tomorrow morning and his body is in the drone bay, ready to go. It matches his specifications exactly."

The program for building a body was pretty foolproof, even if it wasn't in the hands of a digitized consciousness.

"I am sure he is eager to try it out." Kira seemed pleased for Watson. A step in the right direction, and it gave him autonomy while they were on this mission, at least.

Alec perked up at their discussion. "You made the bastard a body?"

"Mr. O'Malley!" Max intervened this time with a sharp reprimand.

"He knows it's all in good fun," Alec said pointedly, turning his attention to his plate.

Kira smiled wryly at the exchange.

Watson spoke from a speaker overhead, **Mr. O'Malley. You will have more trouble telling me where I can stick my voice with a physical presence, as will the Captain.**

That got Kira laughing and Alec saying some choice words in return.

Max hid his own laughter, attempting to be appropriate, but his shoulders shifting forward told Quinn he found it funny.

Quinn was the only one that knew Watson's statement was more than idle boasting. The body he would be in was being made with technology patented by Paradigm and designed by Quinn. The organically grown, synthetic androids that it produced were rated for deep space work. Which meant it could withstand an impact from free floating debris in space while in orbit, which basically meant it was damn near indestructible with how fast such things could be moving. That was just one of its many perks.

The rest of dinner went about the same. Light banter around the table, none of it directed at the outfitter of the ship, but all of it lighthearted. It was clear they had missed one another by the way they interacted. Kira seemed more lively than usual, as if she'd been toning down some of herself around Quinn unknowingly, since he reacted so poorly to her full personality at first.

Quinn listened to the conversation, finding it enlightening. What she had told him about teasing came to light as she interacted with Alec, and he with her and Max. Admittedly, Max followed his rule about not insulting people whom he liked, but he wasn't getting upset at being teased. Which shed some understanding on how one could tease without offending.

Alec, by the end, finally tried to involve Quinn again with a gruff, "Your manual was very thorough. I managed to get through it, but I'm the kind of man that has to get his hands truly dirty to understand everything."

"It shouldn't take long for you to figure it out. Most of what it will need is regular maintenance that will be familiar to you."

Alec nodded. It appeared the manual had already won him over. According to his personality outline in his file, he liked instructions, regularity, things that required the sort of taming that only hands could do. "Looks a right bit prettier than what was there to."

Kira was the only one thus far to be offended by the changes and she beamed now at the two speaking openly.

Max finished his last bite of pie and got up to collect the dishes, even reaching over to take Quinn's.

"Time and shortcuts happen. People rush and don't make things neat and tidy. They don't coordinate or have to figure out how to make things work. I worked alone, and I don't take shortcuts." Quinn looked squarely at the table as he explained this to Alec. His voice a barely understandable mumble. Maintaining the ship was something he was, apparently, willing to talk about. Though without the fire of the faux Irish temper to bolster him, he was just awkward.

"Well then, seeing if I got questions, I'll coordinate with you so I don't rush or fail to make it neat and tidy like ya say."

Quinn fidgeted uncomfortably, not enjoying the thought of Alec seeking him out in the slightest. The manual had a search feature, after all. Still, he couldn't rightly refuse the man, since maintaining the ship was something he had a vested interest in as well.

Max addressed Kira while returning for more dishes. "Are we having a party for Watson, or should we be there when he's able to emerge, so to speak?"

"It might take him a moment to get things working correctly." Kira didn't miss a beat. "Perhaps a get together would be best when he's accustomed to moving."

I'd like you there, Captain.

Kira's gaze flicked up to the speaker with a tight nod.

"Why would there be any awkwardness?" Quinn asked. The body was purpose-built for the Android. It would be as natural for Watson as it was for the Artificial Geckos in their own bodies.

Max filled in the answer, being ever helpful in matters concerning personal well being. "I am sure it is not the ability to move that is concerning, but the ability to move from an emotional standpoint."

Kira quieted.

Quinn grunted. If the AI wanted to think himself into circles and be awkward in his body, that was his business.

"Is he connected to it now?" Kira asked politely for Watson.

"We can do the upload in the morning."

Dinner wrapped up shortly after. Kira walked after Quinn to ask, "Do you have to initiate the transfer for the first time? I'm sure he'd like to thank you for your work."

"Have to? No. Watson will have access to the drone bay controls. Once I put his body into its charging unit, he can transfer his primary algorithm in and out of his body from there seamlessly."

"Ah."

Quinn paused mid-step when he realized she kept following him, frowning. "Do you... want me to be there?" One of the various algorithms he designed to help him with social cues indicated that may be the case.

"I-" She took a deep breath. "I have to admit that for once I'm nervous. I'm not sure why..."

"I really can't guess." It seemed like everyone thought this was a bigger deal than it was. He controlled dozens of drones all the time and his brain functioned in similar ways to the AI's. "Whatever, I can be there to run a diagnostic and make sure my work is functioning perfectly." He hadn't been planning to bother since the AI would be capable of self scan and diagnostic.

"Thank you, Quinn." She flushed with appreciation, and a smile crossed her features at his agreement. "Just let me know what time."

Chapter Fifteen

KIRA

Quinn sent a signal telling her to come to the drone bay at 0900 hours. How he'd added an entirely new bay to the ship without changing its dimensions was a mystery. Then again, she also learned that he'd installed an infinity pool in the exercise room, so perhaps it was best not to question how he managed anything.

Inside the drone bay were racks of drones designed to tend to basic maintenance and repair of the ship. Nestled into a corner and turned outward to the room, a singular large pod with a man's body resting inside of it. The egg-shaped design with a flat bottom took up only a small area. The inside of the pod formed to the body perfectly, with unnecessary padding covered in smooth and shining black fabric. A glass dome sealed the front. A pair of fabricated shorts rested on the android form to provide some modesty.

The body that lay in the pristine chamber was immaculately beautiful in its own right. Tall, a little over six feet, broad in the shoulders, slimmer in the hips, with eyelashes as long as the depth of space outside. The eyes were closed for the moment, waiting to be opened by a consciousness that had yet to take control. It looked peaceful. While

Kira had not said it, she felt like she'd stepped into a child's novel. As if he was a male sleeping beauty, encased awaiting a princess.

"Alright, you ready?" Quinn asked Kira and Watson as he scratched his neck.

Kira only nodded, but Watson came over the line with a gentle, **Yes.**

Kira looked at Quinn, not expectantly, but nervously again. She wasn't ready for this to become the truth, even if she'd been working for it. Watson had fashioned himself as well as possible based on his prior looks and being Praetorian he bore the dusky skin and high features, but she'd not expected the purposeful five o'clock shadow to be redone, which made her smile, and the shaggy long hair in a dark brown that hung over his eyebrows.

"Okay." With that, Quinn gave Watson access to the drone bay.

From there, the process became incredibly simple for him to transfer his primary interface into the android's body. Watson took a moment to do so, and the instant that it clicked, his eyes opened. They were a startling shade of blue, brighter than Quinn's, and more focused the instant they opened. They did not veer away from anything. Instead he took in the world around him.

The pod's concave dome opened outward to Watson's right, and his hands grasped the side of it.

Kira had been standing a few feet directly in front of the pod. She stepped back a little when his feet touched the ground. The breath she'd been holding came out then and her eyes trailed over him. Quinn watched her cheeks flush, the angle of her gaze calculated without thinking, it'd been on Watson's chest. She averted them rather quickly, to the ground, then to Quinn, then back up to Watson's face as he took another step, coming directly in front of her, his steps eating the ground up quickly.

Quinn remotely accessed the diagnostic feed of the android's body, his eyes roving over the data. Something that might be a problem for Watson, as the data access would cause it to flit over his eyes as well. Quinn examined it all rather quickly and then shrugged his shoulders.

"No signs of any issues with the takeover. Told you he'd be fine. See? He's walking around already." Closing the diagnostic feed, Quinn added, "you should get some clothes. I designed a clothing fabrication drone. I'll let you access that and you can have it create whatever you'd like."

Quinn's personal drones did not share the same network as the drone bay. He kept sole control of his literal army of drones, which now took up a fair chunk of one of the many cargo bays.

"Thank you." Watson looked at Quinn, but still stood in front of Kira.

Kira jolted visibly. He'd synthesized his voice before based on his memories, but this time it did not have the unnatural feel of an A.I. overlaid to protect him. Even the Callistar was not immune to hackings, and if they'd found a sentient being, there was no telling what might have happened to him.

Watson turned his gaze back down to Kira and raised his hand. She stood perfectly still while he did so. He was... exactly as he had been.

"Captain," he said in almost a whisper as he touched her cheek, feeling her skin.

"Watson," she said breathlessly in return, just the slightest upturn to the corner of her lips.

"Uh huh." Quinn narrowed his eyes as he watched the A.I. touch Kira, slipping out without another word.

Watson never wavered, his focus absolute upon her face, keeping her from shifting, from giving anyone else her attention.

He had what he always wanted a true form, or had it been her dream? She had to believe that he would have never have been fully satisfied without the ability to do this, to exist, to share a space with another person.

"Is it as you remember?" She asked.

"Better." The warmth in his voice lacked the characteristic of being analog, a thought that kept occurring to her. It was Praetorian. It was his voice, so close to his original she felt as though she was dreaming again.

"I'm happy for you."

"I am happy for us." His fingertips turned, his knuckles brushing on her cheek, down to her jaw, before reaching towards her to push a stray lock of hair back and away.

He froze with the silky strands in between his fingers, allowing them to flow back and out before capturing them again. The newfound fascination never tore him away from her face.

Kira was deadly silent because she knew not what to say. This felt too much like she should wake up any second until Watson laughed.

A full on burst, that filled his face with joy and expressed so clearly to her the differences between who she'd been around lately and how a normal sentient being reacted.

"What?" She smiled despite herself.

"I never believed I would feel this again. To touch your hair or your skin and they are," he repeated the motion, "They are so soft, Kira."

That smile wavered, as did her gaze on his face before it lowered. "I thought I, I thought I uploaded everything correctly."

"You did, I remember it, but a memory pales in comparison."

He tilted her chin upward with very little force but with a firm hold, thumb, and pointer finger wrapped around the bottom curve.

"I have been nothing but a voice for so long." As he spoke, his voice strained. His adam's apple bobbed. He did not need to swallow or breathe, but the motion was quite normal. It was so real, programmed to simulate life in every aspect. "I have not had hands to hold, eyes to look, or fingertips to touch and feel, to be a part of the world around me. It is barren like that Kira, I clung to the smallest reaches within my mind that remembered these things."

"I never meant to make you suffer-"

"I would do it a thousand times again, Kira. To be here, in this moment, to know I am this time almost indestructible, and yet still here. Perhaps remiss of a few things, but does it matter if things aren't how you imagined them?"

Her teeth harrowed into her lower lip. "I don't know what I imagined."

"You imagined a whole body, a regular body, despite you trying to hide it. I know that has been your goal, why you've persisted in working for Toke. I'll admit I've been selfish, and I have not deterred you, for the fact that I wanted it too. I wanted it for you."

There was no mistaking the drop in tone, the shift to where he held her face, cradling her cheekbones, keeping her steady and centered. Keeping her attention where he believed it should most be.

"Why have you not said anything?" Kira could wield a weapon with precision, but to utter those words evenly was beyond her.

"Because it was a dream."

Kira's right foot shifted back, then her left, and her head shook to tell him no, refusing it.

"No, Watson." Firm, decisive something flashed dangerously across her face. "It was a dream, and now it is a reality. My debt is paid now, even if I am not the one that paid it."

"Is that all I am to you?" He did not give her space to breathe, closing the gap between them. "Was I only a debt? A thing you had to repay?"

"You have never been simply that." She did not like to be cornered, like any predator that thought themselves over the top of the food chain. His choice to follow a poor one. Bottom teeth ground tightly to the top row, her chest heaving upward. "You have been and always will be my friend."

"You've forgotten then." Why did she hear heartbreak, feel despair at his words, notice the tightening above his cheeks, the hollow way it came out?

"I've forgotten?" Deflated by his response, she wanted nothing more than for this to be easy. It should have been easy.

"What things were like, how easy it can be. I can show you again Kira, what it's like when you're around someone who truly understands."

"I expect you to do your duties, nothing more, nothing less."

His nostrils flared, then nothing, impassiveness. No muscle movement, no breathing, just impossibly straight shoulders and a light that haloed in his eyes as he said, "At your leave, Captain."

The quick sidestep, the walkout, all of it was done with mechanical precision. The lack of swagger to his gait completely noticeable.

The door shut to the bay, leaving her completely and utterly alone. Her communication insert was quiet, the conversation over, but the lump beneath her skin still existed. The quick touch reassured her of that, but somehow it felt quieter than before.

QUINN

Quinn just kept going, doors snapping open and then closing promptly behind him. Irrationally angry. Enough so that he considered remotely deactivating Watson's body. He knew that was stupid. Nothing inappropriate had happened.

Nothing, he told himself. It was nothing, but when he went to dinner, walked into the room, saw all the people, saw Watson standing behind Kira, his hand on her shoulder, Kira looking at Watson, he decided he wasn't in the mood for any of it. Turning on his heel before anyone could say anything to him, he walked right back out.

Passing Kira's door to his own, the tightness of his jaw audibly gave way to a loud crack as he adjusted it with his palm. He collapsed onto his bed.

Then he heard, "Quinn?"

It wasn't his imagination. His processor told him that. So he rose, his expression flat as the door opened. The room behind him spartan to her sight. A bed, a guitar he'd fabricated, an exercise machine, but nothing else. "Yeah?"

"I brought your dinner." She tentatively held out a plate with a lid.

"Thanks," he said, accepting the plate. Not immediately shutting the door in her face, but also not saying anything else. He didn't know how he felt or what to say.

"If you don't want to join everyone for dinner, I can start sending it up. I know how overwhelming it must be."

"I don't know," he admitted, rubbing his nose. "I enjoyed eating with you. But yeah... I didn't like what I saw in the mess hall." Which was vague because he wasn't actually sure what had upset him more. The people or Watson.

"What you saw in the mess hall?" A tilt of her head, a quick roving of his face, lips slightly parted, his algorithm kicked in... concern and confusion.

"Yes."

"I know we're a rowdy bunch sometimes." She bit her bottom lip, drawing in the lower part just slightly underneath where her canines sat. Further concern.

"I dunno. I'm kind of annoyed with Watson," he muttered, backing into the room to sit on the bed and eat.

"With Watson?" Her shoulder met the doorframe, legs crossing at her ankles.

Quinn grunted. He didn't even know why he talked about it. He had no reason to be angry with Watson. The android, looking at Kira, got his insides all twisted up. As if Watson thought he was so great, when Quinn had literally grown the body he walked around in. Watson just went around being handsome and touching Kira like it was some right of his.

"He is grateful to you. You've given him something that he would not have had for sometime otherwise. It would have been when we returned at the earliest, and that would not have been for a few more years at least."

"Maybe." The way he said it not unlike a child who was trying to imply that was the reason he was upset and she should drop it. It was an entirely unconvincing way to say it. He couldn't know she might piece together that he didn't know why he was upset anymore.

"Maybe. May I come into your room?"

He nodded.

"It is alright to be conflicted about some things, Quinn. We've been alone for a long time, and this is adding in a lot of new dynamics." She perched on the end of his bed. It gave him space, but the proximity set off his sensor again, concern.

The door slid shut the instant she sat. Okay with Kira being inside, but he didn't want anyone, especially Watson, coming up to his door and thinking they could interrupt.

"I don't like it." He picked at his food like he had no appetite. Usually, even when he was upset about something, he ate normally.

"I know, but I think if you got to know some of them, it might make you more comfortable, even Watson. However, if you don't want to, we can have lunch sometimes, just you and me."

"I'd like that." He didn't like having others around. If he was honest with himself, he didn't want to share her, to share this with anyone.

"Alright, I can do tomorrow, but it may be late. Morgan and Rick are coming on board and they've made me promise to give them a tour of all the new features when they get here. Rick got the specifications for the security changes that were made, but I doubt Morgan even bothered to read the manual." She didn't roll her eyes at Morgan, but it lingered there somewhere in the way she said it.

"Okay." He reached out slowly and patted her shoulder once before pulling his hand away. "Thank you."

"Two on the promenade again?" The warmth that blossomed over her face didn't need translating this time.

"Okay." Relief flooded him. She'd not drawn away.

"Okay." She slipped out through the doorway as she called back, "I'll see you tomorrow."

He later returned his plate to the mess hall, mostly uneaten.

Quinn sat patiently. He still had access to all the ship's systems, so he knew she was running late. Though he found that he didn't like tardiness. He didn't enjoy sharing her attention, and he knew that was stupid and childish. All of his feelings about Kira were getting caught up in a big tangle, and he wasn't sure what he was going to do about it. It was distracting. That was why when she squatted down next to him, throwing her legs off the side, she caught him off guard.

"Sorry I'm late." She separated out a bag of sandwiches. Their head cook, Hela, back on board, meant they weren't Kira's concoction.

Quinn jumped as she spoke, taken aback by how she had snuck up on him. He wasn't one prone to be surprised. With access to most camera networks and a brain capable of actual multi-tasking, it was fairly easy to maintain an awareness of the world around him. However, like any human, his thoughts could be so focused on a single thing that every other thing was blocked out. It had just never happened to him before when thinking about a person. She was the first who had ever commanded all of his attention, and she hadn't even been in the room.

"It's alright." He grumbled softly. Clearly a bit upset, but not inclined to make a big deal out of it.

Concern, the algorithm flashed it in the corner of his readout, letting him know that was what she looked at him with. The damned word becoming a repetitive nuisance.

"We'll be leaving tomorrow," she said. "We'll be in known space for a while so Morgan can truly acclimate to the new controls."

"Okay." The idea should have made him happy, delirious even. His dearest wishes were coming true. But what he wanted... he wanted to still be doing repairs, so it was just the two of them.

"Quinn." Kira leaned forward, her forehead resting on her forearm positioned on the railing. "It's okay that things change, ya know?"

"I liked how things were," he spoke as he often did, low and unsure, but he couldn't know how he came across. "Things were getting better. I was..." He continued low enough she couldn't hear, but he wished she did.

"You were?"

"Yes, I valued our time together."

Kira sat relaxed against the railing, leaning her head against the cool metal, watching Quinn for his response. Tension consumed him. Admitting it put it in danger, or it would have before, any expression of enjoyment, any change in his chemical makeup in his brain, they yanked it away immediately.

"I don't plan on ignoring you, Quinn." Kira touched him this time. It wasn't a pat, but a prolonged touch. "I'll be busier, but I will make time for you. You're my friend."

"I still don't like it."

"I know. It's been nice these past few months."

"It was. It hurts less when you are around. That's what I wanted. Or close enough."

"You make me happy too, Quinn." She held out her hand for him to take.

That signal was enough to get through Quinn's slightly oblivious behavior. An application that read body language could only cover so much. Reaching out slowly, he took her hand in his, squeezing her palm lightly once he did.

She held on for a little longer. "Would you want to pick a constellation to show me tonight?"

The warmth against his hand, the smoothness of her own, the way she didn't let go, it was all-consuming. He gave her a tentative smile, then a nod, because he did not trust himself to speak.

"Can you link your communicator and I'll message you when I'm finished with prep?"

"Oh, yeah, I can do that."

"Thank you."

"Thank you."

They ate lunch together in silence after that. Both of them focused on their food. When done, he lingered with his fingers wrapped around hers for a few moments, not wanting to pull away but knowing he had to. So, slowly, he unwinded first and took his hand back.

At half-past eight, his communicator beeped with a written message. 'Where do you want to meet?'

'I'll come to you.'

He found her in the shuttle bay talking to a man that could be considered handsome. Perusing their files well before his initial transport to the Callistar, he recognized Morgan, their resident pilot.

Morgan grinned, not unlike Kira did when she meant to be mischievous. "Nice to meet you." He extended a hand to Quinn, not bothering to give his name. "I heard you're to thank for the new speed."

Kira elbowed Morgan in the arm. He ignored it, his grin only widening.

Looking at Morgan's outstretched hand, then to Kira, then back to Morgan, Quinn shrugged his shoulders. He didn't take his hands out of his pockets. "Yes," he said, not sure why Morgan had phrased it that way, as though he needed Quinn to confirm it. He'd done the retrofit.

Morgan lowered his hand, tucking his thumbs into the front loops on his pants. He still had that same smile. "Can't wait to give it a go."

"You'll get a chance in the morning." Kira stepped away from him towards Quinn. "I'll see you at 0800."

"0800, Captain." He offered a sloppy salute with two fingers.

Kira rolled her eyes.

Quinn's shifting from foot to foot betrayed that as always he was clearly uncomfortable around the pilot, but at least he wasn't making eyes at Kira. For whatever reason, her statement that she would have slept with Morgan came back to him in that instant. He didn't like remembering that.

Brushing their palms together, he curled his fingers around Kira's, his intention for them to fit together. It just seemed like the thing to do. He wanted to do it to show to Morgan that he could. Hell, he wished Watson were around so the sardonic A.I. could see that Quinn could just touch Kira as well. Even if doing it where someone could see made him feel nauseous.

The inquisitive glance from Kira, the way Morgan turned about messing with something on the shuttle, they noticed.

He struggled to not let go, gripping tighter. His ears grew red, a gentle tug in the right direction, and they were in the hall.

Kira gave him exactly ten seconds before asking, "What was that about?"

"What was what about?"

"You're a lot of things, Quinn, but stupid isn't one of them."

"I don't know."

"Okay."

Kira went first at the ladder. Leading the way meant he had a view upward of her legs and hips and bottom as she took the rungs. Her shirt only hid things when you were looking at her from a level angle. This way, it hung loosely over her bottom. He could see under it. Knowing that idealism was a sliding scale didn't help him. Kira's pet bottom, her shapely legs, the thighs muscular and calves well formed, all of it glaring obviously. Conventionally, the woman was attractive. To him, he just discovered that meant something.

Taking a single look upward, his cheeks colored, and he forced his eyes to look at the ladder. Then, he looked up again despite himself. Forcing his eyes straight ahead to focus on the climb, he tried not to think about what he would see if he just looked up again.

In the Astrium, he chose the projection for the night, one of The Pillars, a giant creation of bronze and gold mixed among the stars. Laying close, his hand inched out but remained in the middle.

Kira moved hers in return, hovering over his own, before asking, "Is this alright? I want you to be okay with touch. Though it means something different to others, to me it's just normal."

"It's alright." He closed the gap. "I didn't like it at first, but it's nice."

"Quinn, when you did this in front of Morgan earlier, it could be perceived as something different from just being friendly or leading me."

"Okay." He knew that already. He'd been informed by his developing algorithm for social cues that him taking her hand could be considered a romantic gesture. He wasn't sure how to feel about that thought, but he didn't regret doing it.

"Okay." They watched for a while before she commented, "It really is gorgeous."

Quinn did not reply. He'd fallen asleep in the silence, soothed by the warmth of another so near. He jerked upward when her weight was gone. "Mmm?"

"I have to be up early," she said. "They can't get a hold of me here except on the emergency line if I don't set it up otherwise."

"Oh." He knew the necessity of it, but he didn't rise. He just hoped she'd return. From his angle, he could see her set an alarm. Then she was back, with a large blanket, laying down, skin on skin contact between them again, fingers intertwined. A light touch, nothing magnificent, but he could see her in the dim light. The way her eyelashes rested on her cheek, the ease in which she settled in, her curved lips and the shadow beneath them with the overhead projection, he had to calm his racing heart, his mind, he'd turned everything else off the instant they'd been alone yet it felt still so full, so busy.

In the night, he gravitated to her warmth. Neither had woken for it. The lights rose in the morning, and she untangled herself from him. He could feel her slip away. "Kira?"

His hair frazzled, he felt rather bewildered. It took him a few minutes to figure out what had happened. Blinking slowly as he realized that they just spent the night sleeping on the same "bed."

"You can go back to sleep." The lights were already dimming back from the array.

"You aren't."

"Yes, well, I have a ship to launch. But you are now a passenger and thus are free to sleep in." He could hear the amusement in her voice.

Remaining without her felt insignificant. So they departed, her untangling her hair without offering a true goodbye at the bottom of the ladder, leaving things unsaid between them, but what could he have said?

The Callistar

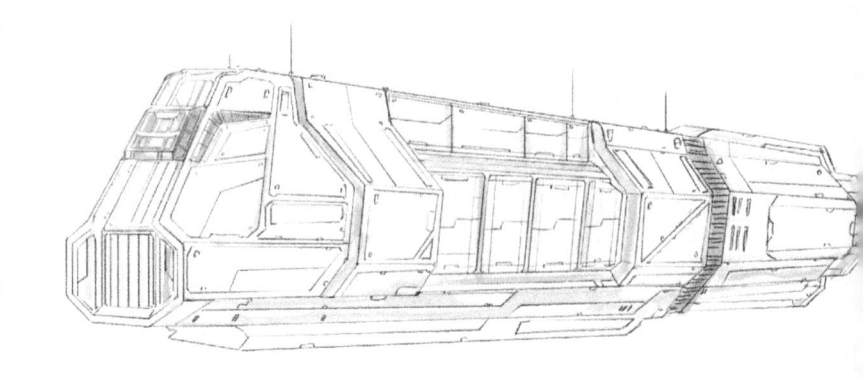

CHAPTER SIXTEEN

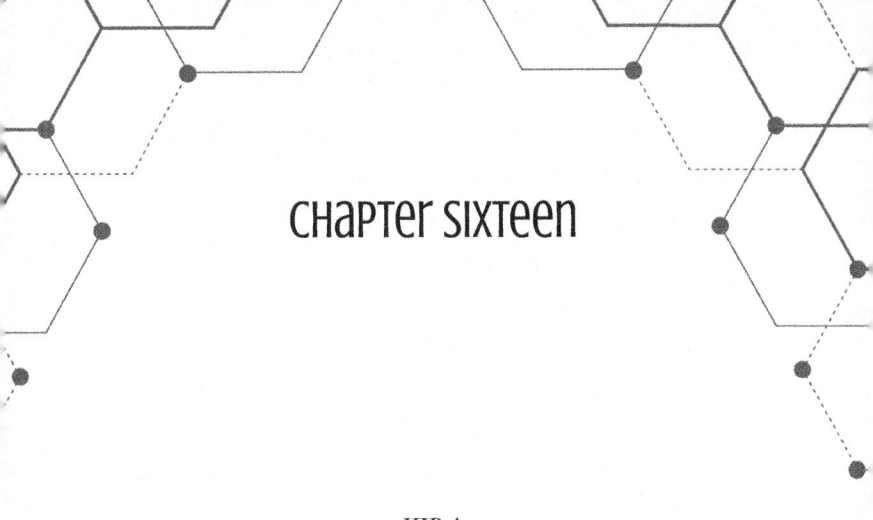

KIRA

WATSON LEANED AGAINST THE doorframe, one leg crossed at the ankle, both hands resting in pockets on the black slacks he chose from the fabricator. Kira peered over, watching every slow inhale and exhale through the baby blue sweater he paired them with. The tight-knit material clung to him in unexpected ways.

A spark of jealousy flew through her at the idea he'd never have to work to maintain his new form. It faded as quickly as it hit because she'd miss food. "This feels like a memory." She began re-shelving a book, her room still disheveled. Jackets across her chair, her bed barely thrown together so that the pillow vaguely covered, books everywhere, pens everywhere, and her data pad halfway covered where it sat on the table.

"Except your room is bigger," Watson spoke cheekily, eyes roving over the mess.

There was no discernible reason for him to have to look so earnestly. Kira knew he'd memorized it the instant the door had opened. His programming allowed that. Quinn was the same way. But he was-she shook her head, dark hair revealing purple sheen in the light as it covered her cheeks. "Well, it was a smaller ship."

"Much smaller." Stepping in so the door would close, he found a space of wall free of posters to lean into.

"I wasn't captain then." Pulling the line of books forward on the shelf, she evened out their placement.

"No, you weren't."

"Do you remember old Hues?"

"I remember him well, and that chewing out you got when you subverted his orders."

Kira tossed the pillow off her chair at him with a broad grin. "I seem to remember you supported me. Then you laughed at me after he got done tearing me a new one."

"I seem to recall," he said, catching the pillow without issue, squeezing it. "That it was rather hilarious to see you put in your place. Hues even reported it to Toke."

"Did he?"

"Yes, he did. He received back the equivalent of 'good luck' regarding you." The pillow made its way back across the room.

It hit her squarely. So light, yet so heavy, bearing a weight she couldn't explain. "Hues didn't deserve what I put him through."

"Hey... hey." The room was swallowed in a few brief steps, and he supported her, holding her upper arms to keep her steady. "Nothing that happened was your fault. You did your best."

His skin relayed warmth. Even through her shirt she felt it, the way it spread over her. He breathed, his heart beat falsely. If she felt for pulses, they'd be there. Yet he didn't feel real because underneath it all she knew he was somewhere between a machine and a man... just as Quinn was.

Watson's eyes were a deeper blue, resembling deep water pure enough to just be so blue all the way down. No light flashed behind his eyes, but no stars rested there either, like they'd done in Quinn's last night.

"I did," she finally agreed, lost back to that day when she peered up at those different depths.

Five years prior.

A shrill alarm woke her, ringing in her ears, alerting her to an emergency on the ship. A voice called to her, not over the comm, but from the hall. "Kira! There's a fire!"

Knocking accompanied the yelling, as if the alarm hadn't been enough to wake her. Leaving no time for precautions, and no time to worry about what she looked like. She bolted up and out of her cabin, wearing a thin one piece suit that was loose over her limbs, akin to an Earthen flight suit that did its job to protect the skin.

Hair whipped around her face as she came face to face with a frightened boy. Only fifteen, just an ensign assigned to the ship sent to get her, "The captain, he is-"

"Just show me."

Fires were deadly when they had oxygen to feed them. Ships could close off vents, clear out a room of oxygen, but it depended on the location. He shot off towards the engines... it was never a good sign.

Following with haste, several others were on their way but they made room for the two. Kira's designation clipped onto her shoulders, the thin black lapel bars on the dark navy giving her first mate status.

The bulkhead doors slammed shut, small viewing windows gave them but a small glimpse of what happened inside. The engineer could be seen. He held an extinguisher, flinging the spray back and forth over a roaring flame larger than the man. It surrounded the center console for the engine.

"Ipson!" She tried the doors. They were immovable, but the comm remained open. "Give me your code to override so I can help you."

Ipson looked back, face painted black with smoke. He wasn't the one that answered.

"Can't do that, Ma'am." Another voice came through. She swiveled, trying to get a better view. She knew that voice, Watson.

The ensign stood at her shoulder. The boy, not having his full growth, Kira growled at him. "Go to the communications officer. Get out an SOS. Get us a nearby ship for aid."

"Belay that ensign." Inside the engine room came the voice of Hues. "Do the SOS, but on the private line, we've got precious cargo."

"Captain-" Kira protested.

"Don't Captain me Missie. Just do as I say. We're getting this under control."

Her foot hit the bottom of the metal hard enough to make her swear, but she got the boy underway. Hitting off the comms, she turned to one of the engineering officers. "I need these doors open. Now."

"Ma'am, I can't do that. If I open them, it'll make it impossible to vent the room."

"NO ONE IS GOING TO VENT THE DAMN ROOM!"

The line opened back up with a click. "Kira, drop the oxygen levels," Watson sent through. "We've gotta get this under control."

Spinning about, ready to refuse that order until Hues came over. "That's an order from the Captain as well."

"Do it," she told the other officer. Touching her implanted communicator, she spoke again, "First Mate to Ensign Bordov."

"Ma'am." He spoke with half a breath in the word. The boy couldn't hide his fear.

"Is Maxim on the bridge?"

"Yes, Ma'am."

Good, she thought, the weapons specialist could run things in her stead for however long was necessary. Rising onto her toes to get a better view, she could hear the computer system reacting to the touch of the engineering officer as it gave verbal feedback... "Levels dropping to twenty percent, levels dropping to eighteen percent..."

It became a steady hum in her ear, drowned out by the scene before her.

Ipson still focused on the main flame. It diminished downward. His cheeks puffed out as if he were holding air in his mouth. Watson came up beside him, hauling a large fireproof tarp. On the other side, she could see Hues.

"Smother it," she whispered.

"Levels rising, twenty-five percent."

Rising!

"What are you doing?!"

Drawn away from the door towards the console, she froze in place.

The officer had stepped back, hands in the air. A blaster pointed towards him. It was too far to reach easily and the hand holding it...

"Yaris, have you lost your mind?!"

"No, ma'am." Those eyes were like pitch. He didn't bother to look in her direction. When Toke said a Mosin would serve on board, she never... she never believed it. Then he'd came. A hairless, strangely gray tinged, humanoid who seemed to lack eyelids. Unblinking, unwavering in how it looked, she'd been reminded of nothingness every time she talked to the man. Still, as First Mate, she'd been friendly, accommodating.

"Kira! What's happening out there?!" Hues shouted, rage and flame in his very voice as it cracked.

The blaster moved subtly. One shot and the comms were down.

"I've been waiting, rather patiently, for this," Yaris spoke so calmly, so evenly, as if he were ordering his lunch rather than betraying the whole crew.

Keep him talking, Kira thought. She knew she had to distract him in order to get the blaster.

"Oxygen levels at thirty percent."

"For what?" *Gloat, please gloat.*

The darkened tip of the weapon moved her direction, aimed squarely at her. Ten feet between them, she wouldn't make it.

"For a chance at Hues," Yaris said, all while manipulating the console. The line for the oxygen levels on a bar chart behind him. One could lower them by raising the section up which would show the changes in the other concentrations. "I've got nothing against you. Not even against Watson or Ipson, but this... this was too perfect, too... optimal."

Her translator took his words and made them into the common tongue widely accepted, but beneath it, she could hear him. The guttural vowels strung together in barely discernible variances.

"You won't make it off this ship alive, Yaris, not if you continue. Just lower the levels and we can talk about this."

"I don't intend to make it anywhere."

The engineering officer, who'd been so quiet, took his chance. He leaped forward, but Yaris had wide vision, too wide and unparalleled senses. The man went down before he'd made it halfway through the air, a burning gaping hole in the center of his abdomen.

Kira took her chances, too. A shot went off. It singed the hair beside her ear. Intense ringing overtook her hearing. The only reason she could still hear him was because of the translator.

"Enough games," he barked.

"Oxygen levels 100%." The computer system stated in its monotone, uncaring way.

It exploded.

The doors did their best to contain the breach, but there was very little that could be done as the vents flooded, as the ship flooded. Maxim on the bridge immediately purged the surrounding rooms, sending everything into lockdown.

The air left her very lungs, collapsing them together with the force as she fell to the floor, unconscious instantly.

Bright lights circled overhead when she opened her eyes. An oxygen mask placed over her nose and mouth. Ripping it off and thrusting it aside, she shot to a seated position.

"Whoa, steady Ma'am." A young female medical officer was at her side, already attempting to replace the mask. "You need this. Your lungs collapsed in the explosion. It's putting pressure back in to keep them open. We don't have the surfactant needed to do it without. They're synthesizing some now."

"Yaris," choking out the word, it was half a cough.

"Lieutenant Yaris did not survive the explosion."

Kira flopped back, relieved, trying to focus her gaze on the attendant. The woman was petite. A quick glance revealed that, short, mousy brown hair but eyes, eyes like Watson's, that same sort of blue. Opening her mouth like a gaping fish out of water, nothing came out.

"You might not be able to speak much," the girl informed her. "My name is Bre. I'm in charge of your care. You're on the Callistar."

Scanning the room, she discovered it was large, and open. Several other beds were nearby with thick screens of glass that were frosted to protect some privacy. The bands on the mask were put back into place as Bre spoke. "I know you have a lot of questions, so I'll do my best to answer them. When we arrived at the Hellaris, it was in shambles. The ship's been brought into the bay, but there's talk of decommissioning it. Officer Maxim brought it in. I've been told you were the First Mate?"

Kira nodded.

"One of the other crew said that you wouldn't rest until I told you. Captain Hues is dead, as well as Officer Ipson. Officer Watson made it through and was brought aboard, but I'm afraid he's worse for wear at the moment. We're doing everything we can for him."

She blinked.

"You need to rest and keep this mask on. The surfactant should be ready in about an hour. Once it is administered, you'll be able to move about more freely."

Another nod.

"I'm going to give you something to help you sleep until then. Your heart rate is very elevated."

She shook her head.

"I'm sorry, Ma'am, but you should feel it already."

Her eyes grew heavy, unfocused. Reaching for the white jacket the woman wore the lapel was all she felt before the world faded again.

"I'm afraid that the other Praetorian is in worse shape than we thought," a decidedly male voice said.

Her limbs were numb. The mask had been removed. She couldn't move. Kira focused on one finger. She tried to curl it inward.

"You don't think he'll make it?" Bre, she recognized the soft-spoken female voice.

"The burns were quite extensive. We've removed as much damaged tissue as possible, but if we take anymore, there will be an almost complete loss of function. Bearson feels like it would be best to just allow him to go instead of making him suffer even more before it inevitably happens."

"I'll have to break it to her."

One finger, then a second, a fist formed.

"I don't envy you that one." The man sounded indifferent.

A second fist.

Bre clicked her tongue. "You have no regard for what they suffered at all. How you're still working in the medical field, I don't know."

"You'll get there one day, just you wait." Thick footsteps indicated he left.

Eyelashes flickered.

"Oh, you're awake." Bre was at her side, pushing back a piece of her hair. "We can try to sit up again if you're feeling up to it. The surfactant should be working well now."

It was painstaking work. Sweat broke out along her forehead as she got into position. The adrenaline of earlier worn off. "I need your help." Kira took to the woman like a lifeline, gripping her like that.

"That's what I'm here for." Bre smiled reassuringly, that sort of polite customer service expression.

"Good."

"Where did you go?" Watson drew her back to reality. He'd done an excellent job of matching himself, down to a small mole on the curve of his cheek. The beauty mark an exact copy of his prior self.

Her knuckles were white as snow gripping that pillow. "I was just remembering."

"Well, how about you remember to come launch the ship and do rounds?" That all too familiar grin struck her.

"Rounds upon rounds upon rounds," she joked. The levity was missing, but she still followed him out. The ship could have run itself, but there was a comfort in the familiarity of eyes on everything, checking and rechecking to make sure the systems were running smoothly, that they were in order as they should be.

"Can you check on the departure paperwork again? Please, Watson? I submitted it a week ago, it should have been approved."

"Looks like it still needs West's sign off."

"That slimy little-" Kira stopped herself. "Bring it to his attention please, with an urgency notice."

"Done, Captain."

"Thank you."

Approval was a gesture of goodwill and not a matter that needed proper clearance. The Eikos was not a proper station that ran by military standards. Submitting the notice was more of a gesture to give warning of their intent to clear the spaceport. Cutting ties with the Eikos and dropping into hyperspace was child's play in order of procedure. They were on the docket. She'd made sure of that, but she did not expect West to be petty on top of ignorant.

"Ah, he is. He's requesting an audience." Watson's processor was on, so how he felt he should respond, how he normally would have emotionally, came through, and so the clear trepidation at alerting her to that fact came through.

"Go on ahead to the bridge. Let Morgan know I'm behind you."

"Yes, Captain."

Watson was not the original A.I. for the Callistar. An old system still existed and with him having a physical body, it felt strange to still call upon him. Formatting her communicator to reconnect to the old one, a warm female voice full of honey spoke back, "Ann activated, how may I be of service?"

"Kira Starling, authorization code K15Q, voice verification as secondary authentication."

"Kira Starling, current Captain aboard the vessel Callistar. Hello, Captain, how may I be of service?"

"I need to speak to Commander West of the Eikos. Route it to my personal communicator."

"Right away, Captain."

Pacing the room, the data pad fit back into her thigh pocket. Gilded metal backed the slim piece of glass to give it more weight. It was a recent addition to her daily routine as now that they would be underway, she would be expected to be reachable by any member of the crew.

"Captain." Ann came across under her ear this time. "I have Commander West for you."

"Thank you, Ann."

"Kira Starling." His voice like a brand seared into her skin when he said her name. It burned inwardly, acid rising in her esophagus, forcing her to bite down. "To what do I owe this pleasure?"

"You know exactly what I want, West. Delaying our request is ridiculous."

"Your request?"

Her teeth ground together, clenched too tight, clicking with the ferocity in which she'd shut them to bite back the rising bile. "Yes, a clearance request. We seek to depart this morning."

"Hmm, let me check with my assistant."

The line switched to actively holding, instead of elevator music a deep tone went off every half minute.

"Ann?"

"Yes, Captain?"

"Monitor the line, please, and let me know when Commander West deigns to return."

"Yes, Captain."

The bridge front featured a large overhead display that stretched across the far wall. No actual glass but a massive accurate representation of the stars behind it. Various information scrolled through at the stations beneath it. They cleared out the weapons station and fitted a large metal overlay to the right. The pilot to the left had the touch screen input guide still up. Attuned to fingerprints and warmth, requiring both in the right manner to be usable. On the left and right walls were other stations for monitoring engineering, life systems, and communications. Outdated for their small crew, but normal for a larger outfit.

The feedback from the other stations went directly to the pilot. A monitored list of each on the left in neat little boxes while the synaptic feedback for their radar and speed controls took up the rest of the width available to him.

Centered in the room, behind all this, was a throwback to the days of King Arthur. A round flat top table in black with a shining surface. The chairs were low backed, metal framed with armrests, and solid black fabric covering the bottom and back.

The entire room was clean with smooth lines in steel and white, giving it a pristine but stark appearance. Quinn had hardly touched the design other than to update the stations themselves.

Watson sat to the right of Morgan, where the weapons station used to be. His chair cocked sideways. He perched with one ankle over the other knee in a relaxed position. He did not immediately acknowledge Kira. She knew he heard her enter, but Morgan who stood in the middle of fawning over the new control system didn't.

"Did you read the material that was sent to you?" Kira had no problem interrupting.

Morgan twisted around, the picture of eagerness. "Every bit. He's got the thing programmed to where it responds almost to thought. I barely touch it and it is ready to go. Oh, the speed this puppy's gonna be able to do. No transport should be this fast, Kira. None, but we'll be able to outclass even racers in this thing."

Watson turned his face up towards her as she came closer. "I believe he actually did the assigned homework, Captain."

"I believe so as well," she jested back.

Morgan focused on showing them the specifics as he cast the schematics onto the main HUD, giving them a run down that even Quinn might have been impressed by. His enthusiasm was infectious, making her smile. Still, Kira did not have to feign irritation when West cropped back up over half an hour since he went to 'check' on their clearance.

"I was able to locate it." His smugness translated well in his voice. "I'm afraid that you've missed a few lines concerning the intended destination."

Kira stepped back to the table, hissing back. "You're not an official port of call, West. It's unnecessary."

"See, you say unnecessary, and I say it is. Our records need to be thorough if we come under inspection."

I'll show you thorough, she thought. *Deep breath in, deep breath out.* "Whether or not you approve it, the Callistar will depart as scheduled, Commander."

"Unscheduled departures are reported, Captain Starling. It's in the new bylaws."

Rubbing her temples, a quick tap behind her ear had her muted to West. "Watson, run through the new bylaws, see if there is anything in station protocols about departures."

Watson did not give an outright answer. He turned his mind to the task, making a quick search. "What am I looking for in particular, Captain?"

"If unscheduled departures are reported under the guidelines."

"They are," Watson confirmed West's pandering. "Looks like it was added yesterday, the addition, that is."

Reentering the call, she asked sweetly, "What's it going to take West?"

"An apology."

"Fine, I apologize."

"Now, now, Captain Starling. You can do much better than that. Put some feeling into it, some emotion. Let me hear how sorry you are."

How much the translator understood and put across was anyone's guess, but the other two Praetorians in the room got the gist just fine, and even Morgan flinched at the words that came out of the Captain's mouth.

"Captain," Ann came across her ear. "Did you mean for that to go through? I see that you've muted your side."

"No, but thank you, Ann."

Reentering the line, she said smoothly, "This vessel will be underway, approval or not, and your lack of cooperation will be noted, Commander West. Thank you."

Hanging up did not have the satisfaction of closing a phone, or slamming one down, but she could end the call immediately without regard for the consequences. Which she did.

Morgan let out a low whistle. "Trouble in paradise, Captain?"

"Just get ready for departure."

"Yes, Ma'am."

Chapter Seventeen

QUINN

QUINN ALWAYS KNEW WHERE Watson was. Just like how he knew where Gary and Gabby were. The man who built them tracked anything that had a Q-Cell inside of it. If one of them went missing, it could be ruptured purposefully, and that was unacceptable. Never again.

The drone he'd sent for dinner came back empty-handed. What approached instead was one of his Q-cell's.

The door had a small screen next to it and words flashed up on the screen. 'Leave the tray.'

Quinn had no desire to talk to Watson at this time or any time, ever.

"I know perhaps you don't wish to speak to me and while I have no right to ask anything of you, I would ask that you be careful. You are on a different path, Mr. Quinn."

Like lightning, Quinn was there glaring at Watson, rage obvious on his face. "Are you threatening me, machine?" He inquired with a voice dripping in anger.

Watson's face was perfectly impassive. His emitter off. "No, Mr. Quinn. I am well aware you can shut me down at any moment, and while I may not be a living, breathing creature, my conscience is still that of a Praetorian."

"A digital construct based on an uploaded brain scan of one Sebastian Watson. I know exactly who and what you are." Quinn ground his teeth, examining the extent of his anger at that moment. He overreacted. That much was obvious, but why?

The memory of the machine gently touching Kira after waking up crossed through Quinn's mind. "What do you want?"

"To protect her. What will happen when you leave? For that matter, what would happen if you stayed? You can barely look anyone else in the eye, Mr. Quinn, and Kira is a social creature."

A full minute passed where Quinn just stared at Watson. There was something new in Quinn's eyes that had never been there before when he said in an exceptionally soft voice, "Did you know I can read your mind, machine? That body is technically a loaner. You don't have to pay for it. I wouldn't take it from you, but it is my technology and I don't give or sell that anymore. There are things inside of you that if Paradigm, or any sufficiently large organization, learned about, they would stop at literally nothing to get their hands on. Because of that, it has mechanical and code bypasses that only I can utilize so that I can monitor you. Not just that, but I can remotely access and operate your functions, if required. I can safely disarm the power cell that keeps you alive, so it doesn't fall into the wrong hands."

Quinn started visibly shaking, but his tone was calm, level, and utterly monotone. Only one other person had ever seen him this angry before. "However, I can do a lot more than that if I am so inclined. For example." A flash set off in Watson's eyes and he found that his emotion subroutines had re-initialized. "You thought you were being cute and clever with that, didn't you? Why don't you try giving me your warning again machine, try telling me why you are really saying all of this."

"Her intentions weren't her own at first, and I believed that has changed." His new skin realistically folded as his fingernails went to dig into skin that could not be punctured. He obviously cared for Kira, the depth of that perhaps explained by his presence here now. "I'd suggest you stay out of my thoughts as well. You'll learn things you don't want to know."

"I think Kira knows what her intentions are and she can make her own decisions to protect herself." Quinn unraveled as more and more of his self-control slipped into a void of pulsating displeasure. "I think you are a sad little digital ghost, clinging desperately to a life you remember but never really had. I just ran your behavioral patterns through a standard A.I. emotional response algorithm. You are jealous. You have feelings for Kira."

Quinn shuddered as his monotone voice cracked ever so slightly. "Go away, machine. Keep your nose out of matters that don't involve you. Before I do something both of us will regret it."

"Well, Toke will be pleased." The functional A.I. made one last jab.

Quinn's dinner lay forgotten on the floor outside his room. With a frustrated growl, he shut down his neural net, locking it so he couldn't access it until he calmed down.

A small while passed and he heard Kira in the hallway, mainly because she spoke to someone, "Yes, of course. I've considered the implications behind it. It does not mean I can change how I feel on the matter."

She opened the doors to her quarters. Quinn pressed his ear against his, straining to hear her. He wanted very much to feel close to her at that moment. The anger had drained out of him hearing her, but he wasn't willing to open the door and reach out, not after what he'd figured out by analyzing how Watson acted.

"Max, I'll contact you later." The footsteps came closer before a light rapping started on his door. "Quinn? Your dinner is out here. Is everything alright?"

Backing up a few steps, his legs hitting the mattress as he sat. He allowed her to enter, and she did so, holding the tray in front of her. He felt hollow, cheeks gaunt as he chewed at them, no light appearing behind those sea glass eyes.

"Quinn?" Depositing the tray on his side table, she hesitated to approach him.

A wall panel slid out of the way, revealing a screen that came to life.

Hexagons formed as the video feed began. The central and largest one was dead center, and it had a display with various readouts and information scrolling through it. Surrounding that main feed were dozens, maybe hundreds, of other feeds. Some were visuals showing different parts of the ship. Others looked like open internet tabs, some were playing videos, others were schematics. There was... a lot of information going through it, and if she didn't know what he wished to show her, she would figure it out when Watson's voice sounded over the speaker.

The entire conversation between Quinn and Watson played for her from Quinn's perspective. It was a look into his mind on a level of intimacy she might not even understand. Quinn didn't have an internal monologue in the traditional sense. Or if he did, his thoughts manifested visually, allowing her to chart quite a lot of his thoughts depending on how good of a look she got at things. He knew she may discover, knowing how intuitive she was, that the size of the hexagon determined how much of his attention remained on that feed. The closer it came to the main visual, the larger the screen.

The easiest thing to notice was when a search query went up as the scene played. *Why am I so angry with him?* A hexagon enlarged and played the memory of Watson touching her gently after being awoken, answering his own question. The man didn't have a photographic memory. He had a video memory. The outer feeds went black one by one.

She would watch as Quinn pulled the living man's records, see that the actual Sebastian Watson died over five years ago, see Quinn remotely access the AI's body, see that Quinn could do terrible things with ease to the AI. From editing code to controlling his body, he held a terrifying amount of power he could bring to bear. She would see Quinn's memories of Watson regarding Kira fed into the AI algorithm that turned up a singular answer. She would also see his own memories of their interactions fed into the same algorithm and the similar result it gave him, but only if she looked outwardly.

There were more obscure things happening on the smaller screens, with the encroaching darkness. Whether she would sense this was his mounting anger turning off processors was up in the air, but it was something she could track. She could also learn that memories of her played pretty much constantly, mostly in the tiny outer hexagons, but they got larger and larger as the darkness approached. There were videos of her smile, her soft touches, her laughter, and kind words playing, trying to combat it.

There was even more information present. A complete and utter glimpse into Quinn's mind. But in the end, it all came down to how much the exchange between Watson and Quinn, and what was said between the two, captivated her.

She remained standing throughout her hand, previously outstretched to him, came back towards herself. She stood awkwardly with her elbows drawn back until Toke's name came up in the feed. That made her cross her arms.

Gabby came to sit on top of her folded arms. Kira remained speechless.

The conversation ended, and the feed showed Quinn pacing in the room. The encroaching darkness fighting against his attempts to combat it. Memories of Kira and what she meant to him played repeatedly. She was the only reason he'd not lost himself as horribly as he might have. She'd kept him from slipping completely away until he finally turned off his neural net and the feed went dark. Quinn stood to the side, back straight, watching her.

His personal mental state spiraled rapidly into depression. While Watson's attempts to warn off Quinn had initially resulted in anger, once that had fled, he'd been forced to examine the conversation again.

The A.I. was right. Quinn felt he was being ridiculous. Kira couldn't want him. He was a socially maladjusted abrasive test subject with zero social skill. One that planned to become a hermit on an uncharted planet soon. She didn't need or want him in her life, not really. While the AI may have been a machine, he was at least a charismatic and handsome one, making him a better fit for Kira.

Which was why he'd played the memory for her. He figured that once she knew what was going on, she would realize just how stupid and attached he had gotten. She would break things off to stop him from getting any more attached to her, and that would be that. He'd stay in his room, get off on his planet, and she would leave to be happy without him. And he... he would be alone again. Just like he'd wanted, even if the thought made his chest ache with agony now.

"Fucking Watson." The curse fell from her lips. "Ann?"

"Yes, Captain?"

"Where is Watson?"

"Watson is currently in your quarters, Captain."

Quinn stayed as she approached the door. It opened for her without a word. There were many things he was willing to do, but keeping someone imprisoned wasn't on that list.

Because her door didn't shut right away and his just barely closed when her voice raised, he heard her say, "What in the world were you thinking?!"

The next part became unintelligible as both doors finally made it all the way closed. He wouldn't be privy to what happened down the hall unless he spied through the ship, or stars forbid Watson.

His general malaise cracked enough to be curious about why she yelled at Watson. He'd figured that this would be where she and the AI laughed. After a moment's hesitation, he sent a drone to her door to open up an audio feed for him to listen in on the conversation. He'd been respectful of privacy and he hadn't put microphones or cameras in anyone's rooms.

Re-accessing his network, it came across with audio and a visual written log, like a screenplay that crossed his mind, the translation of emotions or lack thereof put with every line:

Kira: (exasperated) What were you thinking?

Watson: (emotionless) That he needed to see the truth of what was going to happen. He's going to leave, and it's not just his feelings that are going to be involved.

Kira: (anger) So what? You thought you would just run him off early? My relationships are my business.

Watson: (emotionless) Your relationships are also the business of this entire crew. What will happen when he leaves Kira? Will you ignore your post for a time? Will you be a functional captain?

Kira: (anger) I will be what I have always been. Dedicated to this ship and the people on it. If you think I cannot see past my own emotions, you're wrong.

Watson: (emotionless) I think you cannot see past a pale-faced kid who will drag you down with him while he tries to make it to the surface to breathe. He can barely function around other people. I can.

Kira: (anger) This isn't about you.

Watson: But it is, (concern). Because when he leaves, I will be here to pick up those pieces, Kira, and you will see what you should have seen all along. That even if I'm not what I used to be, that having someone who truly knows you, who truly cares for you, and this ship, is the only way you could be happy.

. . .

Watson: (concern) I know what you were trying to do, and don't tell me it was only for our friendship that you would give up everything to see me whole again.

Kira: (neutral) It was.

Watson: (disbelief) Even you do not believe yourself.

Kira: (neutral) Things are different now, Watson.

Watson: (concern) Things are different now.

. . .

Kira: (neutral) I think you should leave.

Watson: (emotionless) Of course, Captain.

Kira: (neutral) Watson? Do you ever keep my correspondence from me?

Watson: (emotionless) I am not here to monitor your mail.

Kira: (defeated) Just go, please.

The drone shot back and a visual feed revealed Watson leaving.

The quiet returned. His feeds jammed to prevent another overload. His mind still churned, the conversation solidifying a few things within his mind. Watson was manipulative, overly so, but... he was correct. He'd watched her interact with the crew, they were her family and he... he could barely bring himself to speak to any of them.

The physical ache of knowing that as much as Watson was obviously trying to play them against each other, the A.I. had a point. He was supposed to fix things, invent solutions to problems, and the issue he faced now was that he couldn't... fix himself. He couldn't make himself be the person Kira deserved, and that made his resolve to give her up stronger.

Until a message came on his communicator. The only one with access to the line, Kira. Checking it, she'd dropped an audio instead of a line of text. It came across as if she were lying down, speaking to him as softly as she did when they were in the astronomy room. "I am sorry that I left without making sure you were alright."

'It's okay. I understand. I am sorry. Watson is right. I will leave you alone.' His reply in text.

A sharp knock, and the door shot open. An automation he'd set up a while ago allowed her entry when he was present. The biometrics on the door registered and opened automatically. Kira burst through in a blaze of speed, and she spoke just as fast. "I am damn tired of everyone believing they get to make my decisions for me! I choose who I spend my time with. If you don't want to see me anymore, that's fine, but I will not be told that I may not do what I please."

"I, okay?" He didn't remember telling her that she couldn't see him anymore. He had assumed that she wouldn't want to and thought he had been doing her a kindness by telling her she didn't have to try anymore. "You... don't think I'm..." He wasn't even sure what he thought she might have thought about him. No, that was a lie. Watson had said it, after all. He was a socially maladjusted kid. "That I'm not fixable."

That was a more accurate worry. He knew that she would see the sense in what Watson had said, that she was wasting her time with him. He was just broken and leaving anyway.

"Oh brax, Quinn. You're not a machine. You're not something that is broken and needs to be fixed. You're human. You're hurt. You need to heal, but that's up to whether or not you want to be." She'd gone from angry to almost motherly.

Kira came over to sit beside him, joking lightly, "Everyone has problems, Quinn."

"I just." He had nothing, nothing more than a need he'd never truly felt before. Without thinking, without assessing, he leaned over into a quite awkward hug, which she returned. Quiet beset them for a time before it ended, but not before another interruption faced them.

"Captain?" Ann posited. "The bridge is waiting for you to commence the first jump sequence."

"I have to go."

"Okay."

He knew the smile she gave him, knew what it meant from his earlier calculations. Warm and caring, a friendly one that reached her eyes. Something he noticed even without the aid of his neural net.

Chapter Eighteen

QUINN

Morning came and with it came a fresh perspective. Heading to engineering, Quinn rechecked his work. They'd be jumping again that morning and even if his feedback loops were positive, he felt a connection to the ship.

He found Alec, busy doing the same thing, assessing, and reassessing, and who smoothly greeted him with his own profound and true accent. "Ach, the architect graces me with his presence."

Based on Quinn's prior evaluations, he still hesitated on whether it was an insult, a tease, or some strange way of calling him the shipwright. "I just wanted to check on things. The new reactor is more powerful than the old one. Everything is graded for it, but cracks can happen."

"Graded for it." Alec turned about. "It's bloody advanced is what it is. Toke said you were doing upgrades, but I didn't imagine to this extent."

"The superstructure was in good shape, but everything else was out of date. Cutting corners for the retrofit would have just meant problems down the line. Fixing things means fixing them to the best of your abilities."

"Yeah, well, we do the best we can with what we get." Alec hardly seemed offended, his jovial mood easy to read.

"Most people do. New ships and parts are expensive if you can't manufacture them yourself." He addressed Alec, but he looked anywhere but at him. "Still, she was in excellent shape for her age."

"Aye, I did pride myself on cobbling a few things together."

"Was that you who ran the coolant lines through the power sinks for the burn drive, then?" He remembered seeing it, and wondering who'd done the modification. "That wasn't factory standard, but it was an excellent idea for a reroute to let the engines burn hotter longer."

Alec combed his beard. "Young Jaden helped me with that one. It took a few weeks to do it properly, or rather improperly considering it's nae standard."

"It was a good move, probably extended the burn drive's life by about five years, while increasing its efficiency by around twenty percent. The old power sinks were only graded for standard usage to save on cost. It also would have helped you guys do emergency burns. Your mod may not have been standard, but it was better."

Alec seemed to know how far to push and how to keep a conversation going. He thanked him before asking about the regulator. Eventually, they were off the manual. Moving onto other superficial questions about the structure, the underlying things that just made life easier, and the way he'd muffled most of the automated systems noises.

"Downright impressive." Alec declared.

Quinn fidgeted uncomfortably, but nodded still. Alec wasn't angry at him this time, but neither was he pretending to be something he wasn't.

"Have ya gotten lunch yet? Hela sets out a tray for us who pass through."

"I'm fine." The nervous movements continued. The conversation had gone on for far longer than he intended already.

"Well, if ye change your mind, you know where the mess hall is."

Alec departed, taking his tablet with him. Quinn found that the interaction with Alec hadn't been horrible, and he was glad that he'd done it. That's when he realized what he was doing, mostly because a thought occurred to him then and there that he would show Watson that the stupid A.I. was wrong. He could get along with the rest of the crew. The thought made him frown a bit. Was he doing this out of spite?

"Oh, you're here." A barely masculine tone hit the air, full of disappointment, and perhaps a touch of fear because where it came from was a teenager who'd just gotten over the cracking of his voice from puberty.

Jaden, the file supplied him, brother of Bree Morrit, the ship's Doctor. The gangly teen was the opposite of his sister. The crew profiles described her as pale, with long brown hair. His skin had a warm mocha tint, with jet black hair shorn so close to his scalp that if it wasn't so dark, it wouldn't show. Broad nose and thick lips completed the look.

Quinn chose to not reply to his statement.

"Not gonna turn me out?" The kid readjusted a pack on his shoulder. The olive green bag's thick black strap dug into his muscle.

"No."

"Alright then, man." The boy had apparently decided it was worth the risk of whatever he was doing. Crossing to a station Alec had not been at when he'd left. He dropped down in front of it, rigging what appeared to be a small but effective confetti cannon with a pressure plate trigger.

Quinn cocked his head. "What are you doing?"

"Rigging something up for Rick. He's supposed to help Alec later."

The answer was flippant and quick. Quinn knew Rick was the ship's security officer. He'd seen him in passing, but had not spoken to him. The brooding man was even quieter than Quinn. Perhaps they were both poor conversationalists.

"You are setting up a confetti cannon connected to a pressure plate. I can divine what it does, but why are you doing that?"

"Because it's what I do?" Backing out in an awkward army crawl, the kid rose to his feet. His cargo pants weighed down around his hips, but his loose shirt covered them still. "Look, I prank Tick and he does it back. It's a thing we do."

A definition of a prank flashed up for Quinn, and he frowned slightly at it. "Alright."

"You're not gonna tell him, are you?"

"No."

"Good."

If Jaden was looking for a permissive adult, he'd find one in Quinn. Indeed, if the kid managed to befriend him, he'd find himself with a distinct advantage in the prank war against Rick, considering what Quinn was capable of.

But that wasn't a concern at present, as a message blinked up, 'lunch?'

He sent back his response a moment later. 'Where?'

'Bridge?'

'Now?'

'Yes, please.'

He left without a goodbye, ambling into the bridge, smiling as he saw her working, not even really aware that he was doing so at first.

A flick of a hand and one could see the entire network of the stars. With one finger, the user could even bring up the Callistar's network to see how everything was functioning. Kira stood before it, plotting the next few jumps so that they could be done overnight without her having to be up again.

An impulse struck Quinn to tell her he'd had two somewhat successful conversations with other crew members, but he watched her plot jumps instead. Space was 99.9% nothing, but when the only places you wanted to go were in that .01% that had something, you had to chart your course carefully.

Kira seemed so involved in finishing up the current course correction that either she did not notice his presence or wouldn't break her concentration. The beeping of the delivery system for their lunch broke her out of her work and made her glance back. Her face broke into a brilliant smile, outshining his own, when she caught his eye.

"Hey you." She cast aside what she was doing, clearing the view to the stars passing by.

"Hi?"

Lunch on the bridge did not differ from on the promenade for them, other than having a table. Kira spoke while they ate, mostly about being impressed by the jumps. As they sent the trays back down via drone, Quinn informed her of his morning.

"I talked with Alec about the changes to the ship and then he left for lunch. Jaden then came in to prepare a prank against Rick."

Kira groaned audibly. "They're not starting that up again, are they?" The comment seemed not an order, but a more verbalized complaint.

"Uh, I guess? Jaden set up a pressure plate connected to a confetti cannon and left it at Rick's workspace."

"That's child's play." She dragged her hair back away from her forehead. The motion a stress reaction. He'd begun categorizing her movements. "It always escalates, *always*."

"Okay? This is one of those people's problems I shouldn't try to resolve, right?" He could set a drone to the task, but it would have to scan rooms before people entered or constantly be roving.

"Yes, this is a people problem." Kira touched his upper arm. His neural net suggested that she was pleased with him.

"What should I do if I get caught up in one of their pranks?"

"I would advise you not to get in their way at all, but if you do, I would leave it be. I feel as if your reaction would floor them, which I have to admit I'd almost like to see, but it's best to just take the hit and keep on moving."

"Okay."

The comm panel lit up behind her, flashing. From around her, he could see her importing clearance codes necessary to get them into the spartan sector. He chewed thoughtfully. Their roles were reversed now. It felt odd.

"Sorry." Her apology came as she retook her seat. "Until we get through all the clearance sectors, things are going to be hectic since we're doing this the right way."

The panel beeped again. Kira groaned.

"Do you want me to answer those?" He could split his focus between her and that easily.

"No, I mean it's gotta be done, but it's my job to do it."

A new message popped up beneath her fingertips on the screen, waiting to be sent. An almost exact copy of the request she'd just made, "Are you sure cause it's literally just this."

"Your mind is like a computer, isn't it?" Her back remained to him. One finger hovered over the button to send the message.

"Similar enough. Artificial organic consciousness, that was the goal with me. Free of the restrictions of A.I. because I am technically human."

"And yet you can turn it on and off." Her finger came down.

"I can shut off my neural net and put myself into sleep mode, which shuts down the rest of my processors. So yeah, sort of." He couldn't shut it all the way off, even in sleep mode a few of the sub processors had to stay operational to make sure he didn't die but he could go from being able to split his consciousness as much as any true A.I. down to just four open windows.

The chair was empty and yet her hip rested on the edge of the table, forcing him to lift his chin to view her properly. He noticed her femininity at that moment, the soft curve of her full lower lip, the long black hair that shone purple in the right light around her face, and the gentleness of her touch as she cupped his cheek. "And you do that when we spend time together sometimes?"

"Uh, yeah, of course." Heat coursed inside of him, trailing downward. Uncertainty gripped Quinn, but he told her, "Usually when I don't want anything to distract me from the moment."

How she looked at him in that moment made his heart pound uncontrollably. His vision became clear, no charts, no data, as his net shut off almost unconsciously. Holding her with his now pale blue eyes for a moment before the infuriating clearance protocols shot off again, taking her away.

He wasn't really sure what had just happened, but whatever it was, it faded slowly. His neural net blinked back on and he answered the message for her. Standard paperwork like forms didn't take him any actual mental effort to do since he could transplant the literal thought of the completed form into the table.

"Thank you." She caught it as he finished it.

"It's really no trouble."

A sharp intake of air from her, the seat shifted as she leaned back, and she told him, "Don't let Jaden draw you into their games either. It's not fair to Rick, and it's the only way things work."

"So if he asks for help, I should say no?"

"You can-" Her gaze shifted down, then back up. "Help. They just need to be his ideas. You don't need to make them grandiose."

"Okay."

"Okay."

"I've got night coverage tonight, so I won't be able to do dinner."

"I could- I could come sit with you while you do that?" From how he'd found her, he surmised she might be alone on the bridge again.

"That would be nice."

KIRA

Kira relieved Morgan early. She'd been unable to rest for the long night. Her mind ran a million miles a minute. Kira kept reliving the conversation she'd witnessed between Quinn and Watson. A nagging notion that would not leave her mind haunted her.

Watson screened most everything that came into the Callistar. Would he hide things from her? Or deliberately move them off the main alerts so she'd not see them? His conversation with Quinn worried her. As much as she might have wished to watch the other screens when he'd shown her, the audio kept drawing her back to Watson. Knowing the answer to that question had her drafting a letter to Toke when Quinn entered the bridge.

The console needed a featherlight touch, but hers were shatteringly hard as she hacked away at her work. The doors were so quiet anymore she had not heard him until he said, "Hi."

At a side console, he took a spot at the table, so he was close, as she said, "hey," and leaned back with one last keystroke. She noticed he'd not been looking down at what she'd been doing as she turned. Not that he needed to, but his respect for her privacy was noticeable. A beat passed before she asked, "When you worked for Paradigm, did you access their system to find out what they wouldn't tell you?"

"Not at first. They made sure that the terminals I had access to were on a closed network. As I got older, I managed to find opportunities to get drones into networks I wasn't supposed to be on. Then I started reading through things via drone." For a man unused to interpreting other's body language, he had his own openly displayed, seemingly the more comfortable he became. He leaned forward and halfway squinted.

Her frown deepened as he spoke. There were several communiques she'd not received, or that she had 'answered.' She knew she hadn't answered them. "I can't imagine being cut off for so long." It wasn't comparable in any sense of the word, but she still did not like for things to be kept from her, not like this at least.

"It is what it is." Quinn quieted, opening his mouth to speak, then closing it, then opening it again. "Is something wrong?"

"I." She clamped her mouth shut like he had, but she didn't hesitate for nearly as long. "Watson has been screening my messages."

"He has?" He matched her earlier discomfort. "You mean without you asking him to, yeah?"

"Yes, without permission," she elaborated. "He has answered some as well, or simply put some aside."

"Oh, do you want-" There was no telltale flick up the right to pull a memory, but the pause meant consideration, "To talk about it?"

"Quinn, are you researching how to speak?"

"Yeah, I wanted to..." under his breath he continued trailing off.

"It's sweet that you try, but I like you as you are, too."

He cracked a genuine smile. "Thank you, Kira."

His confidence was becoming of him as he took her hand. Kira had not realized when he'd become so comfortable with such an action. He released when she told him, "you're welcome."

Kira shifted her attention back to the console. She closed out her messages, never having sent the one she'd been working on. Crafted in anger and done in the moment of discovery. She knew it was harshly worded, unfair in a sense, so she'd consider it again when a cooler head prevailed.

"I never imagined that I would go into uncharted space." Her thoughts were errant, not quite as vastly different as his, but while it focused on their mission, it was not what they'd been discussing.

"Me either."

"We always think we are the pinnacle too." She glanced back at him with that. "But there's always stronger and smarter people out there. Hopefully, they're in a good mood if we come across them."

"That seems unlikely. If there was a more advanced species out there, they likely would have picked up on some of our deep space transmissions by now. It's more likely any alien races we come across will be on the same playing field."

"Logic takes the fun out of wondering, Quinn." Even with her statement, she seemed to still be having fun if her smile was anything to go by. She turned her seat to face him. Their knees would have knocked had she not folded hers up in her seat.

"It does?" Puzzlement turned to wondering with him, the smallest changes in how he looked easier to pin down the more time they spent together.

"Yes, because if you take away any chance of the possibility, you can't imagine the possibilities."

"Okay?" He arched his brow. "I mean, if you don't eliminate any possibilities, I guess, yeah, we might find some other alien life. I suppose it's possible they are using a high end of the radiation spectrum for communication. Maybe they are simply so far beyond us their technology no longer looks for stuff on the lower end?"

On the verge of laughing at him trying to play along, she didn't wish to discourage him, so she kept it in. "Thank you, Quinn."

"You're welcome?"

"For playing along."

"Oh, okay. I mean, you said you wanted me to think of possibilities."

"I did."

He reached for her again with one hand. She closed the gap. The placement of their arms was awkward considering they were sitting facing one another, but the contact was nice. Her hand was warmer than his, but the shared temperature quickly adjusted with the skin to skin contact.

"Captain?" Kira's ear buzzed.

"Yes, Ann?"

"There is something that requires your attention."

"Thank you, Ann."

Returning to the side station, Quinn could peer around her shoulder if he wanted to or check it himself. She didn't bother hiding the relay station as she checked it. The incoming relay came flagged as immediate. Instead of just urgent, Ann had protocols to interrupt proceedings for that.

Skimming quickly, she did not fully read until she hit a particular passage:

Commander West alerted the Praetorian authorities that The Callistar may be carrying unsuitable cargo. Whether or not this is likely or unlikely isn't my concern, but there was an order that came across my desk today for a search warrant if the ship was able to be tracked down in either of their quadrants...

The rest became a blur. Her vision narrowed into a tunnel. West had a pair on him, she'd give him that, but why was this relayed from a contact... Watson should have still been monitoring everything that came from his office.

A muscle flickered in her cheek. Her abilities were not always obvious, but the quick turn and the few steps to the primary display were done too quickly for comfort for most humans.

"What's wrong?" Quinn was up, following on her heels.

Their long range scanners were active, but not focused on relaying any information unless pertinent. Any ships that came too close, any opposing factions, they would send on alert. But Praetorian ships just weren't a concern, especially in neutral territories, but thirty minutes ago they'd gone from neutral to theirs.

"That," she told him, pinpointing three small ships on an intercepting course. "They've been informed we have illegal cargo."

"I'll go to my room."

"Okay." Kira had other concerns with them being Praetorian and was already on the comms. "Morgan, we have Praetorian incoming, possibly looking to board. I need you on the bridge now."

"Aye Captain." The response was crisp, and immediate, no arguing or humor this time.

Quinn, halfway towards the door, stopped. The shuffling of his feet lacked speed and the sudden halt, then continuation, told her he was curious at the very least. She didn't have time to console him or offer comfort at the moment. They had to be ready.

He was swapped for the Pilot in scant minutes.

A more serious grimace encompassed the thin set lines surrounding Morgan's mouth, typically used for laughter and teasing.

"Is Alec up?" Kira questioned him.

"He is," Morgan assured her. He'd arrived in his flight suit, purposefully missing the insignia on his shoulders. Since their departure, every crew member wore the same navy slim material, knowingly fireproof.

"We have Praetorian incoming, thirty minutes out tops. I have it on good authority they think we're transporting contraband. They're possibly going to want to board."

Morgan's entire body tensed. "Should I send out the primary alert?"

"Yes," she ordered, then added, "Please."

"I'll take care of it, Captain."

"I'm sure you will, Captain." Kira teased, but her heart felt heavy, as if someone had dropped stones in it. West was a snake, but she expected it of him. She did not expect another to take the same approach, nor did she know if she could trust Watson anymore, not fully. She shook her head, deciding to take care of it immediately. "Ann, ask Watson to meet me in the lockbox, please."

"Yes, Captain."

"Morgan." Asking after Watson had reminded her. "Make sure they do not go into the storage where Watson's fabricator is. Feign the door won't open if you have to."

"Aye, Captain."

Gabby crawled across her fingertips, moving from one to the other as she stretched them out to give the Gecko half of a challenge. The dim light enough for both to see clearly after adjusting to it. The lockbox, as it was called. A reinforced section of the ship in the shielding that kept from being scanned openly by another ship. Five feet by five feet. It hardly gave one space to do much and held only a short armchair from the times Kira had been subjected to the location. Splayed across it lounging, she sat upright when the door opened but did not stand.

Watson's arrival made it feel cramped, but neither of them felt claustrophobic.

"You asked for me, Captain?"

"Yes, reset the door, please. You're staying in here until we get the all clear."

His emoters were on, so the frown that crossed his face cleared when he did as asked. "Am I being penalized for something?"

Kira scoffed. "Would you like to be Watson? I found the messages you kept from me."

The moment he went from on to off was as clear as Quinn. Quinn lowered his barriers to be emotional with her, to be vulnerable. Watson threw them up to keep himself from doing it. Knitted shoulders unknotted, tense posture released, and when he stood opposite of her, the safeguards back in place, his hands clasped behind him tightly.

"Did you think I would not find them?" Kira flushed with anger. Every rise and fall quicker with every breath.

"I did not wish to put you in a compromising position, Captain."

"A compromising position?" Shooting up, she lacked a bit of height. He towered, but she was larger emotionally.

He gave away nothing, merely bored in appearance. "You had already interacted with our passenger and a sudden change could have threatened the delicate balance you had struck."

Her hand itched to slap him. It would break her bones and do nothing, not even make him react. "But you replied as well. You told Toke- you told him I was trying. I would have never-"

"Therein lies the problem. Out of spite, you would have done the opposite, allowed him his isolation. It went against what was being asked of you and, considering your initial refusal, it would have jeopardized the mission."

Clarity struck her. "You only replied once you learned about your body?"

Without access to the computer system, it was a stab in the dark to guess this. She'd not memorized the dates, but it had to be the reason.

"Yes," he confirmed, his neutrality painting him truly indifferent.

"You're a selfish, absolute-," Kira slipped from the common tongue to Praetorian, painting an absolutely colorful picture of her opinion of the man.

"I had other reasons as well."

How unbelievable it was to her, how utterly inconceivable that he could have thought those reasons were enough. "How can I trust you when you won't even speak to me as you? Are you so changed by your years of only being a consciousness that you won't allow yourself to feel this?"

"It is because I would feel too much."

She sagged downward, knees threatening to give out, on the one hand she had the socially inept laboratory experiment who saw her as the sun, on the other she had the A.I. who wasn't an A.I. who would just shut her out when he felt it necessary. Quinn may not have been capable of more, and Watson was capable of everything, but she couldn't trust him.

He braced her at her elbows, holding her up. Her forehead hit his collarbone, her hands rested on either side of the warmed skin as she said, "I cannot trust you."

"That was never my intention, Kira."

"Nevertheless, it is what you have caused."

Chapter Nineteen

KIRA

"Do you remember when I said wars were not always started for resources? Spite is a reason to do things as well." Kira said, pondering about his prior goal for galactic peace, when he'd not known what it was to care about another's opinion. Resting her forearms on the hydroponics table, she seemed to tense when he'd said Watson's name a moment ago.

"You think an entire planet can be motivated to war over spite?" Quinn continued to pick away at the tomatoes, dropping them into a tub nestled against the counter. They had elevated planters on long stainless tables.

Kira wasn't helping, even if she'd volunteered, only keeping him company in a grumpy manner.

"No, I think one man can. If the leader of a people is charismatic, he can convince an entire population. There have been wars waged over one woman before, and that had no effect on the majority." She knew he would find it ridiculous still, but she wanted to prove her earlier point. This was just the perfect moment to do so.

"Hrmph." Turning one of the plump red ones in his hand, Quinn pulled it free from the stem.

"Of course, small slights have also sparked revolutions." Kira lacked the capability to peer inside his mind, but following her own train of thought, from knowing him, she knew he wished to solve that issue as well. But you would have to take away emotion, want, everything that made the universe the way it was to get rid of the aspects that made up every soul.

"Well, I can agree with that." Quinn pinched off a dead section of the vine.

Kira molded her words with sweet assurance because she was truthful, and there was power in that sometimes. Out of uniform she looked prepared to garden, a long apron with small flowers on it, her hair pulled into a loose violet ribbon halfway down her back, and that smudge of dirt over her brow she'd not noticed yet.

"I am glad that you agree." She murmured, still lollygagging instead of helping nestled on a short chair.

Quinn had dirt under his fingernails instead of mechanical fluids. His bright white hair shot out in different directions, tousled ungracefully. He grabbed a plain blue apron to protect the long-sleeved black shirt he wore. The sleeves pushed up, out of the way.

Kira considered him still, her chin resting still on crossed forearms. A few days had passed since the quiet moments on the bridge. He'd spoken to more of the crew, Max, Alec, and even the ship's cook, Hela, when he'd picked up trays for Kira. Everyone told her he spoke with them, nothing more than mentioning it in passing, a sign of approval as no one missed her looks other than her.

"Watson is going to apologize to you." Kira popped off after the tick of quiet.

"Uh, okay?" The tomato in his hand bled around his fingers. He disposed of it in the waste bin, wiping his hands clean on the apron.

"I'm not sure it will be the most sincere thing you're ever going to hear." She picked at the dirt under her fingernails.

"Okay?"

"I told him it was necessary." She capped it off with that one. "I told him he needs to apologize after what occurred." She did not say that she had pressured Watson by saying that he was a guest of Toke and it had not been proper. Kira had wanted to say much more, but they had not yet achieved the delicate balance they had been working towards. Rocking the boat wouldn't help anyone at the moment.

"Ah." Quinn grasped a rag, wiping off the tomato juice. Semi clean again, he returned to his task. "Thank you, I appreciate it."

"You're welcome."

They'd not yet discussed the events on the bridge, either. She got up to help him again. It put a plant between them. "I assume your room is safeguarded for scanning as well?"

"Yes."

"Good."

His inhale was audible. "Why did-"

"You know, sometimes in the projector room I watch the skies above Praetoria. I know the constellations and their stories. Even the star that leads due South from most of a land that I've never stepped on."

He quieted, inviting her to go on despite her interrupting him.

"Toke dodges me about it when I ask. He always told me he rescued me during the Separate event, which I looked into. There was a small revolt the government did not catch early enough, and they marched on the capital. I've never served upon any ship close enough to interact with Preatoria if it could be helped and since this posting, if there is to be a possible boarding with crew scans, I've been informed to make myself absent."

The stalk moved, pushed aside by him, and his eyes caught hers. "Do you want me to find out for you? The reason?"

Mulling over his offer, she had a chance. Was it exploiting him to ask? She decided it was. The things he would have to hack into and the databases he'd invade were dangerous. Not that he couldn't hide his trail. It felt too far. She wouldn't ask him to do anything that Paradigm might have pushed him for.

"No." She finally decided, shifting to the side, taking refuge in the veil of the leaves. Partially because of the subject matter and partially because... he made it hard to concentrate. "Could I ask you to do something else instead? Hear Watson out. You don't have to accept his apology, but it at least might make things smoother."

"Okay."

"Thank you."

"You're welcome.'

The task at hand started when he'd volunteered after breakfast, when Hela had mentioned it, and she'd seconded his offer. The drones could completely plant a new patch and taking care of the current crop, but doing things by hand was a habit Hela instilled long ago.

"I always thought we should do a flower part in here, a place to sit where they bloom. Unfortunately, most of these don't bloom, but they grow in their own way and are no less pretty for it." She dropped seeds into the holes of another planter, using a short shovel to make the opening.

A full grown orange tree blossomed in the hydroponics bay with a small patch of grass, but it laid over in the corner, out of the way.

"Oh, like I did in your Astrium? To make it look nice?"

"Yes. That resembles more of a clearing in the forest where you could climb the trees to get closer to the stars. I cannot imagine anything more peaceful."

She thanked him again without saying the exact words. Unlike the first time she'd said it, he handled her gentle affections easier now than before. He didn't flinch away, but sought it out sometimes on his own.

"I'm glad you like it." He scratched at his nose, leaving a heavy smudge of dirt on it.

Finishing up the cart, she washed her hands in the bin. "This should be enough to keep Hela busy for a while. I got her word I'd get a pie out of this too." Walking over to him, she giggled as she told him. "You've got something on your nose."

Licking her thumb, she went to brush it off.

"I do?" He blinked, remaining still, pink racing across his cheeks as she wiped it away. "Uh... thanks?"

"You did, and you're welcome." Her voice dipped into a husky tone at their proximity. She steadied her thumb, placing her fingertips on his cheek. They went a little farther. She cradled his cheek. Dusky skin, like warm caramel, slightly harder to see through, but her cheeks turned red.

His net shot off. Clear skies of the early morning moved to her lips, then back up. That flicker, that up and down of hesitation before either of them did something rash, woke her up.

She felt a pull at her navel, warmth spread through her body. Knowing he might not even understand his own urges did not help her resist hers. She wanted so badly to break the unspoken rules of friendship they'd placed between them, to capture that little bit of space by leaning forward. But should she?

She moved her hand down his cheek, her forearm settling on his chest. Quinn wasn't overwhelmingly taller than her but her chin had to angle upward. If she put just a bit of pressure on his neck, if she brought him down. It would be all too simple. Therefore they were entirely too close still. "I should get going."

"Uh, yeah. Sure. Of course. You are busy." He'd been staring when she broke contact and he rubbed at his eye.

"I'll catch you later?"

"Yeah? Yeah." He nodded.

QUINN

Max was either an eerily lucky man, or he just got his way eventually because the moment Kira disappeared, he popped in with a tray to harvest some blackberries further down the line. Quinn heard him when he entered. The Vicar and he had spoken off-hand before and he'd asked to speak with him. Seeing his chance, Quinn asked as he walked by. "You said you wanted to talk?"

"Ah, yes." Max was quick to smile, a people person. Quinn had learned that's what his personality was called. Max sat down his tray, seemingly happy to put off his other work, joining Quinn by the tomato plants. "Kira has told me quite a bit about the alterations to the ship. It seems you had your work cut out for you when you arrived."

"I guess?"

"You don't quite know how to carry a conversation, do you?"

Quinn mulled over his answer. Max didn't fill it in for him, just picked up one of the adjacent aprons and slid it over his head, tying the back. He did not wear his regular garb, but a slim fitted suit in the same gray. More cottony in appearance. A work outfit, one he'd seen on several of the crew, serving more as a secondary uniform for the ship if they weren't wearing a flight suit.

"Apparently not." Quinn decided, pruning a few dead leaves. He wasn't actually sure how to supposedly respond to any of this, really. Some standard responses had flashed by to Max's first comment, but they'd all been... pointless? Mostly either downplaying the work he'd done or exaggerating it. It's what he'd offered to do, and it had gone off with no hitches that weren't named Kira.

"Considering how you were raised, I did not expect you to be loquacious or graceful in managing one." Max didn't pull punches, it seemed. "Making small talk is difficult sometimes even for the best of us, so I'll forgo it too if that's alright?" He slipped both hands into his pockets on his lean legs.

"Sure?" Why did people have to be so complicated? It felt like Max danced around the subject without truly hitting the point. Which seemed pretty silly. If he truly wanted to forgo small talk, he'd simply speak.

"I wanted to offer an ear to you. One without judgment. You seem to manage alright on your own, but I am sure that the perspective of another who has had more life experiences might be helpful. Besides, I know the Captain well."

"I feel..." He digested the offer. "That is a kind gesture. So thank you?" Scratching at his neck, he wasn't sure what else to say to that. He wasn't sure what, exactly, the man was offering to give advice about.

"It is, but you don't have to thank me. The role of a Vicar is to guide. It does not always mean spiritually."

"Okay, well, I am not sure what you think I need to talk about," Quinn admitted. "But I appreciate the offer, even if I don't know what to do with it." His statement might have sounded sarcastic coming from someone else, but he was just being honest.

"Considering your recent upheaval, your newfound relationships aboard this ship, including Watson, and your lack of understanding of social cues, though I know you can figure out most on your own, I am sure you will eventually find something."

A file only told Quinn so much, but from what Quinn discerned, Kira trusted this man. Otherwise, she would have never brought him to Toke.

"I mean... I suppose so." Quinn frowned slightly. When he was younger, there had been therapists, but like everyone else, they were instructed to keep him at arm's length while evaluating his mental health. Everything he said was reported directly to Paradigm and at a certain point, he just started lying to them.

Lately, he supposed he had been confiding in Kira, mostly about the mental breakdowns she caused and then helped him through by not leaving him alone. But without the pressure of something giving him an anxiety attack, he wasn't actually sure what to tell the Vicar about.

"I mean," Quinn began. "Relationship wise, it all seems pretty straightforward to me. I am infatuated with Kira. Watson is fixated on her. Kira isn't sure how she feels, but knows she doesn't want either of us trying to manipulate her. I am just enjoying what time I can get with her and trying to work on my social skills. The latter due to a comment Watson made, which, while insulting, was accurate enough for me to consider. I thought it would make Kira happy, so I decided it was worth doing." He paused as he considered this and then shrugged. "Beyond that, I have clear signs of social anxiety, depression, insomnia, and a host of other issues. Although these are all rooted in my nurturing as a child and the experiments performed on me rather than my nature, seeing as my genome was programmed prior to birth to avoid the genetic disposition to such things. So if you just wanted to hear my problems, I guess there you are?"

Quinn didn't really feel any different from expressing them. It all seemed obvious to him.

Max, during his monologue, kept quiet, reflective. His hands were in his pockets, still a hip bumped up against the table. "It sounds as if you are struggling, and now that you have time to consider them fully, you have. Though you cannot do things simply because you are trying to please someone else. That is a path that is hard to recover from as well. As for the rest, I assume with your implants you're averse to taking medication to fix your brain chemistry?"

The look Quinn gave Max as he informed him he couldn't do things just for another person was best described as flat. More accurately, though, it resided in the realm of condescending, since Quinn knew he could do things for another person, as that was what he was currently doing. Still, he would not argue with the Vicar over an opinion, as that seemed fruitless.

"Considering that any substance that alters brain chemistry has a chance of interacting poorly with the implants in my brain up to and including causing an aneurysm, No. I am not keen on rolling those statistical dice." Alterations to his chemistry were unavoidable, but suddenly introducing an influx of a chemical through a pill or substance in large, unnaturally occurring quantities was a giant risk.

Max appeared nonplussed, which seemed to be his usual expression when he wasn't smiling. "Then I suppose you will have to do it the natural way. Find things that interest you and make you happy outside of the Captain. Exercise is one way; it naturally releases endorphins in the brain. We have a room for it. Or you could do morning runs with

Kira if the mood strikes you. Although, I do not know if you'll be able to keep pace. The only one capable thus far has been Rick."

"I picked up the guitar and have been learning how to play it." He left out that he'd started because Kira had suggested it. He found he enjoyed the act of creating music, even if his fingers couldn't quite match what was in his mind yet. "I also have my workout equipment in my room. I've been doing two-hour workouts a day since I finished work on the ship." He intended that as a statement of fact if not intent, since he would be in the gym to run with Kira in the morning if it was an option. He would mention it to her the next time he saw her. Any reason to spend more time with her he was happy to take.

"Good, it sounds as if my suggestions are not needed then. If you're staying here, I could use the help to collect things for Hela if you're willing."

"I mean, they were excellent suggestions." The dead leaves plucked off, the ripe tomatoes off the vine, and the bucketful left him little else to do so he nodded.

"Thank you."

Quinn took his words at face value.

Max broke the silence a moment later by saying softly, "I rarely speak openly of my friends, but I will say that the Captain, while confused, is not wholly without feelings for you as well, from what I have seen. She values what you have together."

A long period of silence came from Quinn before he said, "She values our friendship." The part he didn't want to confront was how he continued to downplay his own emotions and hopes for Kira's emotions to match in order to shield himself. He'd become a lot more open in the last few weeks, but he wasn't completely done cutting himself off, not yet.

"Are you sure that's all?"

"It has to be," was the answer he finally gave, looking away from the vicar. The memory from earlier in the day played on a loop in the corner of his eyes, repeatedly.

Max lowered his chin, a thoughtful nod given as they worked on collecting other ingredients, pruning, and repotting. When they finished, Max even invited him to the dining hall to play Quest, something Quinn questioned immediately before being informed it was a card game.

Kira received a message from Quinn later on asking, "Should I play Quest with Alec, Max, and Rick?"

"Only if you're willing to not look up the answers." The voice message back was playful. She sounded as if she was smiling.

"Okay."

Returning to his room, Quinn settled in. A lot flooded through his mind, and he ultimately shut off his neural net to block out the noise.

"What the hell am I doing?" He asked the empty room as he tried to get the image of Kira looking at him in the hydroponics bay out of his mind.

When he arrived in the mess, he found Rick involved in a game with Alec. There was more swearing on Alec's end. Rick was quiet, calculated. He moved with precision and poise and gave looks under his brows that would have frightened anyone attempting to fight him. Max fiddled in the kitchen putting together bowls of apple pie and ice cream.

Remembering his promise to Kira, he entered with only his own wits to guide him. Approaching the table, Max caught sight of him first. The boys said hello, which was really Alec dropping a grumbling utterance as he moved his cards, and Rick looking in his direction. Rick he'd not met yet. The security officer, a brooding man with dark hair and eyes. He wondered if Kira thought to use him as an example instead of Morgan when she'd mentioned attractive crew members. Objectively, his programming could determine he was that, but according to his file, he was human but modified.

Max, seemingly always cheerful, said, "Glad you could join us! I have ice cream and apple pie. If you're interested, I'll set up another bowl."

"Uh, okay."

Max prepared another, emerging with four passing them out. "Do you want me to explain it?"

Quinn opened his mouth to inform Max that he didn't have to, but then thought better of the situation. "Sure." Curious to see how Max's explanation would differ from what he had read online.

Max explained the rules faithfully while adding in a few 'house rules', which he told him only applied to their immediate company. Rick defeated Alec. Max set up to go up against Rick next, and Alec asked Quinn if he'd like to play a game on the side while he finished his ice cream. He promised Quinn that he would not go easy on him despite him being new, as he said. "That bloody brain of yours doesn't deserve a pity win."

"I don't know why you would go easy on me." The concept of going easy on someone for the sake of fun involved a few social constructs that Quinn couldn't understand yet, seeing as he'd never played a game before. Settling in across from Alec, the engineer shuffled. Surprisingly, Quinn lost. Alec had to work rather hard to manage it, but in the end, he won. In part thanks to a house rule about doubling up cards.

Alec's complete and utter shock came with his quick dismissal of another game, seeing as he knew when to take his winnings and leave. It left the other two amused. Quinn side eyed the other game. He learned Max had a difficult time with Rick, who seemed as lucky as skilled.

The security officer worked in a way that always put him five steps ahead while planning for any contingency.

Alec settled in to watch as well, telling Max, since he could see his cards, "Might wanna be careful with that."

"I know what I am doing," Max replied, raising one brow and shifting his hand.

"Oh aye, ya do now, but when he wipes ye out, don't come crying to me." Alec's gruffness displayed openly but he clearly wasn't upset, a smile on his face.

"You wouldn't offer me your shoulder, Alec?" That already raised brow went higher. Max turned in his seat to eye their engineer, the move smoothly done as he brushed the edge of Alec's shoulder.

Alec stammered out a reply in a brogue that Quinn could not translate, but he did watch as Max roared with laughter.

Rick spoke finally, his level voice the one of reason, "You should pay attention before you lose."

"I think I might prefer it now." Max laid down his next card.

Alec flushed. His entire face looked like the tomatoes that were harvested earlier.

After a while, Rick came out victorious, though it was a good fight. Kira wandered in around that time asking them, "And who is crowned champion this evening?"

"Rick by default," Alec supplied with a mighty grin, coming up out of his seat and clasping hands with the captain as if it were a natural thing.

"I see," she said, glancing down at the full table.

"Are we done already?" Quinn blinked in surprise at this. He'd thought he would play more than one game. The implication that there was a champion already suggested that they were finished.

Kira being there he would not complain if that was the case.

"Goodness no," Max said politely with a laugh. "But we have an ongoing tournament amongst ourselves that we were sorting. Rick has just finally won. We rarely play so seriously against one another."

Kira smiled. Quinn didn't check his neural net and therefore did not notice he'd spent an hour and a half with the crew already after having watched the first, then playing his own, and watching the end of a second.

"I promised I would play the winner, though not tonight Rick, if that's alright?"

Rick nodded, shuffling his cards. "It can wait."

"So who do I play next, then?" Quinn inquired.

"I'd like to take a turn." Max was the first to seize the opportunity.

As the game progressed, it became obvious Quinn playing against Max lacked a resolved strategy. Much like how he experimented with his meals, he occasionally made poor plays to figure out how to use the house rules to his advantage. Deliberately creating scenarios so he could see how strong of a move he could fabricate.

"Oh aye," Alec said smoothly, watching the end play out. "The lads got a handle on it, that's for sure."

Rick put his true game face on as he switched spots with Max and they began to play. The sound of an alert that went through comms to each of them only saved him. Everyone stood to disperse, with hardly a word to each other.

Only Kira cursed softly as she hopped off the table. "You should head to your room, Quinn."

The alert was unexpected and his neural net booted up as he looked over the ship's logs to see what triggered it. When Kira advised him to go to his room, he frowned. That bothered him, but he couldn't argue with the suggestion. If it was a patrol, they were a danger to him. Getting up, he did as he was told.

Kira followed in the same direction, muttering to herself on the matter. "Praetorians again, given permission to be here."

She clenched her hands into fists as she got onto comms and Quinn caught half of the conversation.

"Morgan, are you on the bridge?"

"How close are they?"

"Damn."

Tapping into the mainframe, he judged they'd be within scanning distance in a matter of minutes. Cloaked as a transport ship, one doing a regular route, Ann would not have flagged them right away. There hadn't been a concern before their sudden change in direction.

"It may be too late," she said to Morgan. "If it is, you must stall for as long as possible. It will take me time to reach the lockup. Watson needs to get there now, too."

Observing the ships, Quinn ran the math. If she went to the loc kup... Well, she could make it, but it would be very close. Even if she rushed, it was hard to get an exact number, but her margin of error existed at about less than ten seconds to arrive safely. As long as he hurried, his margin of error was closer to forty seconds, so that made it the safest option for both of them. It also didn't involve Watson and her in an enclosed space. A win win as he'd heard before.

"Uh, you could just go to my room with me. The praetorians are almost within scanning range and it's the closer of the two."

"Right, yours is blocked too?" She did not wait for an answer, instead she gave a quick, "Thank you Quinn."

Jogging that direction once they were inside, the door closed and a faux wall went up in the hallway. They were completely undetectable to the rest of the known galaxy as he walked over to his bed and sat down. Normally he would lie down, but then she wouldn't have anywhere to sit.

"This can't just be West anymore." Kira halted at the door, leaning her forehead against the cold metal. "They're after something. There is no reason for us to be so accosted. I am sure that Paradigm put a number out for you." One hand formed a fist, and it slammed down on it, but he couldn't see her expression, only hear the anger in her voice as she said, "It's ridiculous, you're not some piece of property for them to claim."

"I mean, from a legal point of view, there is a case for that. There was actually a fairly intensive file for that argument to be made in the event my existence was made public." Since he hadn't technically been born and had been augmented since birth and since said augmentation was the only reason he was alive... Well, it was a fairly lengthy and detailed document that sought to prove that he wasn't a person by the legal definition.

"Well, they can burn for it." She turned from the door, tears threatened to spill over her long eyelashes.

He'd never seen her so frustrated or angry before. Even when she'd broken her ankle, she'd not shed any tears at the pain. The fact that it was over- that her tears were for him, well, it was surprising to say the least. He rose to his feet. Tentatively, he made his way across the room, reaching out to put a hand on her shoulder. It took him a moment, but he dragged her into a hug.

Her forehead came down against the edge of his shoulder. "I'm sorry. You shouldn't have to deal with this. I'm being ridiculous too."

"I mean, I don't think you have anything to be sorry about. Thank you for caring," Quinn said with genuine feeling in his voice. His life became better with her presence and seeing just how deeply she cared made him feel unsure. The complication frightened him.

"Mmmph," she murmured, switching to her cheek, shifting and allowing him to draw her in truly close. "You are worth caring about, Quinn."

He kept replaying how he'd felt earlier that day even if he wished to focus on this moment with her, not trying to figure it out, not trying to shield himself, just being with her. "I- I care about you too, Kira, more than anything."

Her shoulders shook, but the fact she laughed abated his fear of her falling apart. "What a pair we make, then."

"I guess." Quinn said, echoing her laugh lightly, glad he could get a cheerful sound out of her through the tears. It made him feel like he'd accomplished something. "Despite my best efforts."

"Oh, it would never work against my best efforts." She drew back with a smile, wiping her cheeks. "I have more experience in bothering people than you do. I win in that category."

"There is no denying I was in no way prepared for you," he said with another laugh, this one a bit deeper as he continued to hold her tightly around the waist.

Happy just standing there, being of even the smallest amount of comfort for her. Her arms were situated just over his, where her hands fell on the edges of his shoulders. Her fingertips dug in just slightly, holding onto him. Barely enough space existed between them to see each other properly. Her eyes dropped low again. All it would take was courage on one of their parts.

"Well, we're even, then," she said in that same husky voice.

The shift in her voice couldn't be missed. Quinn's overt intelligence made him absorb information like a sponge, and that tone in her words, already burned into his mind from the memory of the hydroponics bay, had been playing for almost the entire day. The things that tone did to him, it made his body react in a way he'd never quite experienced before.

"Oh, that's... good."

Kira looked at his lips again, and he couldn't help but look at hers. It felt like an invitation. It took him a moment to sum up the courage, but he leaned forward.

"You're leaving," she said suddenly, cursing aloud. "I'm sorry I should have never." Her back met the door, putting the tiniest modicum of space between them. "You can't stay and be hunted and trapped like an animal."

"I-" He could not find the words. She made a valid point. "I just want to be with you. Even if it isn't forever, just for now, just for as long as I can. I want to be with you."

Nothing existed between them again. She took a quick step forward, placed a gentle guiding hand on the nape of his neck, and he found himself drawn downward. He went to question it, but she pretty effortlessly silenced him. His eyes went wide in shock as he felt her lips on his. The pressure became gentle, but needing, like velvet against his own. Analyzing the act, seeing others do it, he'd not thought something so simple would bring a sensation of such pleasure. Trying to process everything simultaneously, he realized he couldn't.

So he just focused on what was happening instead of trying to figure it out. Quinn melted into his first kiss as his arms gently wrapped around her. For the first time in his life, his heart wasn't aching, it was just full, completely and utterly full.

Kira drew back as if to give him a second to breathe; his lungs felt tight as he manually reminded himself to.

She was still there. "Together then," came her breathless reply to his unspoken question.

"Yes, together." Even if he wasn't sure what it meant, he knew he wanted it, all of it, whatever she offered to him.

"I'm going to kiss you again, is that alright?"

"Yes."

The response came immediately, his voice still quite low and soft, as though he worried that speaking too loudly would break the momentum. It was a moment that kept getting better and better. He soon kissed her back eagerly, clearly quite enamored with the activity.

She moved flush against him at one point, curves pressing against his body in an exciting and new way because it was in a way that wasn't meant simply to be friendly. It was definitely something more. Against all odds, they had discovered each other and found themselves locked in a room together to evade a scan. In the meantime, they performed their own scans and diagnostics. Quinn didn't resist when Kira pushed him back until he sat on the bed, her straddling him, both upright.

Resistance would have required some sort of cognate thought at that moment. Not just a cohesive thought, but one that would give him pause. He wasn't thinking. In fact, he wasn't going out of his way to not think. He didn't want to think. He wanted Kira to keep doing whatever she wished because it was the single best thing to have happened to him.

She had eclipsed every thought, worry, anxiety, and fear, replacing all the negative, all the hurt, with herself. She dominated all of his senses, all of his attention, all of his being. The only action he took was to follow her gentle guidance and to keep his hands wrapped around her as she pressed her lips to his. In that moment, she had given him the one thing he had always wanted. She had taken his hurt away.

When she stopped, Quinn almost followed her before he took a breath and looked into her eyes. Thoughts tried to crowd into his mind once again, but as he gazed up at her, he let out a little sigh. Pressing his forehead against hers, he murmured softly, "thank you."

Quinn thought she had to know he was at least infatuated with her, and possibly in love with her. He'd shown her so clearly before.

"You're welcome."

"I- This is what I wanted. Just not the way I thought I would find it. You made me hurt less before, and now, now, I do not hurt at all." He explained it, not sure he had the right words for it all, but Quinn did his best to give her the truth that was in his heart.

Unlike so many others, no one was going to take her away. She'd never given up on him, and no one had paid her to manipulate him. She was just- Kira. A woman who saw a man trying desperately to shut himself away and had stuck her foot in the door, forcing him to let the sunshine in because she brought it with her.

"You make me happy too, Quinn."

"Thank you." Knowing that he did for her, in some capacity, what she did for him made him feel, well, he already felt good, but it somehow made him feel better.

"Can I-" He trailed off, but his gaze on her lips once again. He only picked up on what was on the surface.

"You may."

The simple kisses were good, but instinct and desire drove him to deepen it. His attempt started clumsy, and inelegant, but soon enough, he moved as she guided him.

She wrapped her fingers in the short locks at the nape of his neck and the feel of her hands in his hair and on his chest made his entire body respond. Charging him like an electric current, every strand of hair on his body felt ready to stand on edge. The gentle feeling of her tongue pressing against his lips confused him at first, but there were only a finite number of things she could be trying to achieve.

Parting his lips tentatively, he felt her tongue in his mouth and soon he got the idea of what he was supposed to be doing. Without even really thinking about it, his hands ran up her back, digging lightly into her skin, his own hand gently combing through her hair. Quinn had an endless curiosity, and she gave him an entirely new world of delights to experiment with.

CHAPTER TWENTY

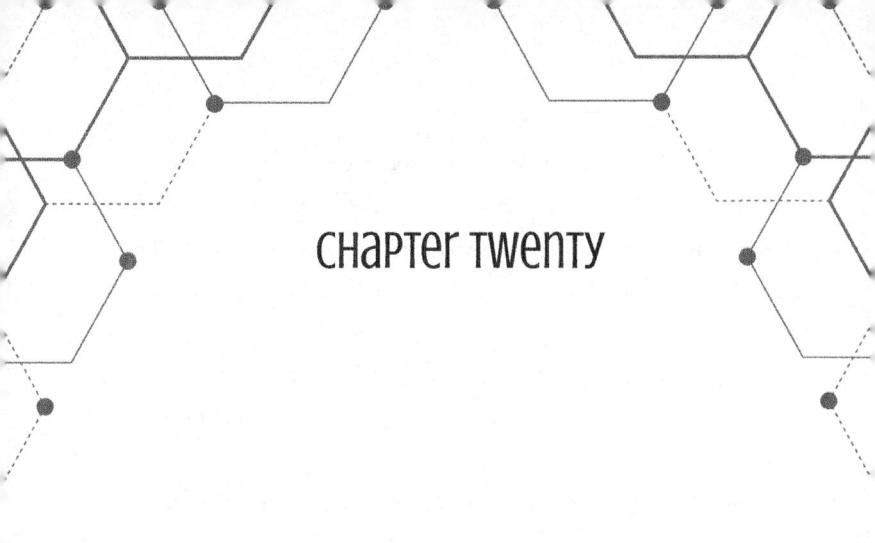

KIRA

"Your net is off." Kira shot up in pure panic. "Oh brax."

Slipping out of the bed, she crawled over him in order to reach the computer system, which wasn't present. Panels covered every wall, and he saw wild eyes shooting back at him.

"Uh, yeah?"

"Your room's blocked. If something happens, they can't get ahold of me, and they always hit the emergency line to let me know that the inspection is over. So either it's ongoing or something happened and it's been too long."

"I can gain access. Hold on." Quinn sat up, fully dressed still, flipping on his net.

Quinn relayed someone made two pings to the emergency line about fifteen minutes ago. Then, it went silent until about five minutes ago. Something was happening, but there was no telling what from here. There were life signs in one of the cargo bays, mainly the one holding some of his settling equipment.

He opened the viewing screens for Kira and explained this as well as. "I'll put a live view of where they're at."

Kira knew all the supplies that he'd stored read as containing nothing more than long-term journey food stores and medical backup equipment if scanned. If they forced them open, well, that was another can of worms, since it would have triggered the emergency defense system.

Morgan escorted several gentlemen past the boxes. One waving a scanner while the first one spoke. The conversation muted on the relay.

Kira felt extremely stressed, a bubble of anxiety under her sternum resting beneath the bone. Hela and Bree had sent the emergency pings. Both women were the secondary line of notification when there was something that needed to be sent when Morgan was busy. Quinn opened up the messages to relay them to her. The first was a simple 'Sit tight', the second was no longer, 'Full inspection', it said. The third and final one was a short, 'Keep monitoring comms.'

"Get the sound on," Kira demanded before realizing who she spoke to. "Please."

The one speaking ranked as a Praetoriate, a rank she recognized by the bars on his shoulders.

He clipped his words, his enunciation crisp. "Yes, well, it all seems in order."

"As I told you, sir," Morgan said with as much politeness as he could muster. "Your sensors must have been malfunctioning before."

"Yes, I suppose so." The man had his hands clasped behind his back. When he turned fully, the camera showed his full military uniform. A rigid suit in navy blue that lacked much decoration other than the insignia of Praetoria on one side of his chest and his name embroidered upon the other. The lapel was where Kira's eyes lingered.

Watching intently, their position left the crew compromised if an emergency arose. It made her feel nauseous to think she'd forgotten.

She paced the room while Quinn cracked a panel, adjusting something inside.

"There, now they will come through, no matter if my systems are on or off." It clicked back into place with a bit of pressure. "Is something still wrong?"

"No," the answer was too quick, followed up with a short. "Yes, but no." Crossing her arms under her bosom, she struggled to find an explanation that didn't shift blame. Usually after patrols left, she would help Morgan monitor their departure, and it was the reason she'd been up so quickly. "I didn't even think about it," she told him a second later, "About them not being able to reach me here. Which you've solved now, but had something horrible happened?" she trailed off.

"I mean, it was an oversight, but it's resolved now. If they had needed your help, it would have been a situation where we were under attack and we would have been alerted to that. You can't be reachable all the time, even when you aren't keeping yourself hidden from the Praetorians. I am not sure what you mean by yes, but no."

Her mouth formed a grim line as he tried to smooth over her emotions with pure logic. It was one downside of him not being clear about the emotions of others. Especially at his last statement. "I am upset that I missed it to start, but it will not be an issue now, is what I mean by it."

One hand went up through her hair, the black shimmering with a purple sheen when she shook it out behind her like she did then.

"Okay?" He remained perplexed, eyebrows knitted inward.

She felt explaining the situation was inadequate considering his past. Being cut off, being of little aid, of not being able to be there for her crew because of either her own inadequacies or whatever Toke was hiding from her, it haunted her. It was also the sensation of being trapped, no matter how nice the prison or the company.

"Okay." She said dismissively. She did not wish to discuss it. It held little merit. The problem would be over with soon enough, or so she hoped, and they would be in the clear from a rather intensive search which was only allowable because of their relationship with Praetoria. The ship being registered through their channels meant they had to submit to searches, which were hardly ever done without reason.

Quinn's response came as a tentative touch, more reserved than he'd been moments ago when he'd been a millimeter away from her skin following instinct.

She was masking much worse than he was initially capable of, but she did not attempt to shield him from her emotions to keep him from getting to know her. She meant to protect him and by doing so was preventing him from getting to know her further. Both were aware she cared for the crew. The extent of her reaction before him signified just how much.

"I'm fine," she lied outright, but she was a good liar. A great one to anyone who didn't know her, good to those who did, and poor right now to Quinn who's net was fully functioning, able to pinpoint minute micro-expressions that betrayed her.

Thankfully, he didn't question her, or call her out. He held her, relaying warmth through layers and wrapping her up against him. It was the right decision, and it eased some of the discomfort, all of which was of her making. She knew she was being silly, but anxiety did not travel in the same realm as logic and reason. It was bound to emotions and, therefore, volatile and uncertain.

Leaning into him after a second, her body relaxed against his. Destroying a beautiful memory by making things murky felt wrong. So she kissed his shoulder where her head turned, and then turned it back to kiss the crook of his neck, her lips settling there.

He let out a long, inaudible sigh. He was quite a bit taller and just a hair wider than her. She felt comforted and safe with him.

"I like it here," she said.

"Thank you."

The emergency line buzzed, and the cold set back in.

It was the all clear sign.

"Can you let them know I'll be up momentarily?"

"Yes." A tightness around his eyes relayed his worry, "I will see you later?"

"I can message you when I'm done to see if you're still awake?"

Without waiting for an answer, she boldly kissed him on the lips and was out the door as he said, "I will be."

Rick met her at the entrance to the bridge. His stern regard unable to be missed. He'd been waiting for her to appear. "Watson mentioned West might be the one causing this?"

"Watson is partially correct." Kira could handle Rick in stride normally, but that was because she'd been straightforward before. Warning him about West had slipped her mind, and Watson seemed to take care of it. Their other passenger, well, he had some idea of the danger, but not all of it. "Quinn is possibly the other part. West isn't smart enough to put two and two together. After we undocked without permission, I'm sure that he raised the alert, putting us on their radar.

A ship with advanced technology when they're looking for what they consider missing property, it raises red flags I'm sure."

Clear anger covered Rick's face. His brooding took on new levels when there was genuine danger towards the crew. She didn't want to see the look he gave. Dark eyes surrounded by rugged dark locks coupled with a jaw sharp enough to cut glass and the man would be devilishly attractive if he'd remained a mystery. But Kira knew he had enough PTSD to sink a rowboat no matter how hard he threw out water.

He was her subordinate, in a sense, so she popped back quickly. "It's not polite to stare," she crossed the room to where Morgan waited, inputting the coordinates to make their next jump.

Rick followed, thick boots stomping heavily. A hand gripped her upper arm, not roughly, but just enough to draw her attention back. "Kira, if I do not know what I am up against, I cannot plan for it."

Looking at his hand, then face, then hand again, she assessed how far to push him, keeping herself in his grasp because she had royally screwed the pooch as she'd heard Alec say from time to time. "I know Rick. It was a matter of privacy. Before now, I did not believe it would be an issue. Let me assist Morgan, and then I will explain everything."

Rick slowly unfurled his grip. The grunt he gave her more animalistic than human, but she was free.

Morgan acted ignorant of the conversation, his cheerful manner false but still present. "I've got the next coordinates in. I'm ready when you are."

"Get us out of here."

"Aye, aye, Captain."

"So he's *that* Q." Rick sucked air between his teeth.

"One and the same." They sat at the large table on the bridge. Kira propped her feet up on an empty chair.

Morgan had turned around at the main console to be a part of the conversation. "I knew he was awkward as hell but, damn."

"He was an experiment," Kira clarified, her right hand rubbing absentmindedly at her thigh. "They think he's their property, so they're trying to find him. His whereabouts have been unknown. I'm assuming with Toke having now the vanguard of the fleet be suspiciously advanced, it raised a flag. Paradigm is centered in Praetorian space. I don't know what leverage they have that they're willing to test Toke, but obviously they have something."

"They've had their own resources on it as well," Rick chipped in, surprising Kira. "When I was on leave, I ran a few ops for Toke. They were covert operations meant to recover intelligence instead of supplies. One of them involved finding out information on something they called Q."

"Well, someone now." Morgan half smiled when he said it, correcting Rick.

Rick lowered his chin.

"Were you able to keep anything?" Kira dropped her feet to the ground, leaning forward.

"No," Rick informed her. "Everything was kept on an encrypted database. I uploaded it directly and had nothing on me, Toke's orders."

Morgan let out a laugh. "And you actually listened?"

"Some of us follow orders."

"Don't start." Kira rose, pacing back and forth. "Toke would have alerted us if there was anything found that was worrisome or if they were on our tails. Quinn can make sure that either his or our ship never sees the light of another day if it is a concern."

Watson was another concern, she thought. Then she had an idea. "Rick?"

Rick lifted his chin, his attention on her.

"I want Watson out of the system completely. With his new body, it is no longer necessary for him to be the ship's main A.I.. He will be another crew member and be centered under you. We'll switch completely back to Ann. He can do regular backups on an isolated system. Have Alec help you create an essential black box for him to do it. I will inform him of this when you are prepared for the move."

"Captain?" Morgan furrowed his brows, his carefree manner lost in the motion. "Why are we- are you sure about this?"

"Yes."

Rick's brooding followed her for a private conversation without Morgan into the lift. It made it impossible for her to run away, which made her snort when he did it.

"Trapping me?"

"If you'd be forthcoming, I wouldn't have to do this."

"I am when it matters." Kira smiled brightly at the man. He towered over her. "You could beat it out of me when we start our sessions."

The dour look she received spoke volumes as to how he felt about that which sparked her laughter.

"One of these days, you'll lighten up a bit more, Rick."

"I'm light enough."

Kira raised and released her shoulders. "I take it you want my reasons?"

"Yes."

"The technology he's made with is dangerous. If it falls into the wrong hands, Quinn will do anything to destroy it. Paradigm is using Praetoria in its ploy to get him back. It means we have to protect his property. And if the ship goes and Watson isn't fully moved over too, he'll lose everything."

"This is what you'll tell Watson?"

"Yes."

"Good."

"What, no rousing speech about separation of emotion and duty?" The lift opened, but Kira didn't rush out of it.

"I don't- You have valid reasons for this one beyond what I can see, but Kira?"

"Rick?"

"Be careful, please."

"I know what I'm doing." She took a step out of the lift and offered him a half salute, attempting to get a rise out of him.

The unimpressed look back before he hit the button for a different floor held until the lift doors closed and he was gone.

Kira plodded backwards, tapping behind her ear. "Ann, can you relay to Quinn that I'm off to take a shower, but he can let himself into my room."

"Yes, Captain."

She wrapped herself in a large, fluffy towel. The shower dried her after she'd switched off the water, but in her rush she'd forgotten to bring her clothes with her. Normally it wouldn't be an issue, but with Quinn waiting, she didn't want to overwhelm his senses, or pressure him before he was ready.

"Hey," often enough, she'd treated him with hesitance, but in that moment, she relayed her own fears onto him with how she spoke.

He perched on the edge of her bed, avoiding either chair. Possibly because one overflowed with books, one half open on top and the other had a blanket tossed where she'd gotten up quickly. The bed, this time, was free of clutter and had the sheets pulled up and tucked properly.

"Hi." He matched her tone perfectly, something in the way he looked at her full of unabashed affection. He had no shields up to her. She could see it so easily, how he'd relaxed his posture. "I was uh..." His eyes roved down to the towel, causing a stuttering halt. "Wondering if you wanted to, uh, cuddle like we do sometimes in the Astrium."

"Here or there?"

"Uh, I was thinking here, but I wouldn't say no to going up there if you'd prefer."

"Here is fine." There, she had to take precautions to be available and, with earlier in mind, she wanted to be available for the foreseeable future. "Let me get dressed."

"Okay."

Her closet held practical choices. She either slept ready to go for the next day or in an oversized shirt for comfort. Anything remotely sexy packed away, since she'd not needed it for a while. Therefore, there were very little options. Kira landed on a black shirt that hit mid-thigh and boxer-like underwear that hit at the same spot in a dark purple.

She threaded her hair into a loose plait and padded barefoot into her room.

"You're pretty."

Kira blinked. A quick check of his eyes clarified his neural net hadn't prompted him. His eyes were their natural pale blue.

"Oh?" He'd never complimented her before, that she could recall as an outright compliment. He'd find she wasn't above flattery, especially unprompted flattery. She walked towards him in the dim light of a single lamp.

Settling her hands on the side of the bed, she leaned towards him.

He swallowed his Adam's apple bobbing.

Tugging on her side of the covers lightly since he laid on top of them, she'd follow it up jokingly. "You're on my covers, Quinn."

"Oh, sorry."

An awkward shuffle occurred, then she pulled them down before joining him laying on her side facing him as he faced her. He met her contemplation with his own inquisitive nature. He assessed her with an obvious curiosity, despite his inability to follow the usual prompts of the program for communication he'd developed. It seemed he decided she was worth tempting as he leaned forward to capture her lips.

Kira wished so much in that moment that she was not so distracted. Their heated session earlier could have been repeated, she could be willfully swept under, but Quinn needed a gentler touch and she needed to make herself clear before it came to that.

A few softer couplings of one before a light pressure indicated he should pull back. "It has been a long day."

"I only wish to be here with you," he expressed.

She smiled and turned her back to his front. Kira moved his arm around her, intertwining their fingers beneath her sternum. Feeling his warmth, his closeness, there was another thing that was impossible to miss but he hardly moved beyond his breathing but what she felt... well, they may not have enhanced him everywhere but he certainly didn't lack there.

Chapter Twenty-One

QUINN

When she stirred, Quinn awoke. Her room had automatic lighting changes for her alarm instead of an intense sound to jar her awake. He yawned, brushing sleep out of his eyes. He met her with a soft sleepy smile. Somehow, that night had differed from the ones they'd shared before.

"Good morning." It wasn't a greeting he'd used before since he rarely saw people this early, but he could see why it was apt now.

"Good morning." She smiled in return. She knew what time it was by the lights. "You can go back to sleep."

"What are you doing?"

"I'm going to go for a run. Then I'm sparring with Rick."

"Oh, well, I wouldn't mind joining you for your run, if that is alright." Quinn said with a small, hopeful smile. Obviously, he had no interest in sparring, but exercising in the morning was part of his routine.

"If you can keep up."

He recognized her teasing and was becoming familiar with the flutter he felt when she planted a kiss on his lips as she slid out from under the covers.

"I'll do my best." With their plan set, he headed to his room to grab his workout clothes, but not without being bold enough to kiss her as he said goodbye first.

Finding her on the promenade, he noticed she wore slim shoes with minimal padding. He had quite a bit more in his shoes, but he was aware Praetorian joints were more durable than human ones. Stretching, she leaned over, hands flat on the ground beside her straight legs, giving him a rather accentuated view of something her long shirts usually covered and it was well worth taking a second look at.

So Quinn looked. Of course, he looked. He wasn't even self-conscious about it at first. Right until he realized the effect it had on him. Then his cheeks turned bright red, and he looked away, desperately trying to get his mind on another thought.

"Do you have a stretching routine?" Kira sounded politely indifferent in the question, rising to switch to another position.

"Uh, yes, I'll get started." Still quite flushed, he turned away from her direction.

"I think perhaps we should put forth our expectations for what this is between us." An offhand comment from Kira, but he didn't face her, so he couldn't see her face.

"I don't know. I just like being with you."

"Well, I wanted to ask that when we're around the crew, we keep things to a minimum to not draw attention for the moment."

"Okay, I can do that." Quinn nodded. He understood the logic. It would obviously cause tension once Watson figured it out.

"Thank you," she interrupted his thoughts.

"You're welcome." Confused about why this was something worth thanking him for. It seemed like a perfectly reasonable request to him.

They began at an easy pace for their first lap before Kira upped it into a steady gait instead of the easy jog, not an outright run, but quick enough to make it difficult to breathe.

She spoke as if they were standing still. "Even if it is not a small thing to you, it is a big thing to me. I need to consider their feelings as well."

"I understand." He huffed. "I figured it was something like that."

She smiled, the one that always caught him off guard when she directed it at him. They continued on; him dropping off after about ten minutes, unable to keep up her pace any longer. She ran for another ten minutes, passing him. On his cool down lap, she stayed next to him, jogging in place until he completed the second. After that, she walked normally.

Recovering his breath, Quinn gave her a smile. "Well, I did my best." He knew that she could have gone much longer, but he was still fairly happy that he'd lasted as long as he had. "Uh, I guess you are going to spar with Rick now?"

"For not being used to it, you lasted much longer than I thought you would. You're welcome to watch."

"I've been running in my room. The exercise machine I installed has a treadmill. It's different running around the bay, though." Harder on his feet than the machine design which favored low impact while still providing a full heavy workout. Running on the treadmill was like running on padded flooring. "Uh, I could watch, sure." Watching violence didn't bother him. He'd been fine with the fight scenes in recreations. It was just, he had no desire to do harm to anyone.

"You don't have to if you don't want to, Quinn." He recognized the way she looked at him, her eyes trailing over his face. She was judging how to treat him.

"I wouldn't mind. I just wasn't expecting it," he assured her.

"For me to invite you?"

"Yeah, I thought you wouldn't want me to, well, just to help with the whole keeping things under wraps thing?" He realized he did not know how to quantify her earlier request.

"Oh. I did not mean that I did not wish to be seen with you just that, well this," she took his hand in hers, holding it lightly "Is alright. They're going to know. I just have never been the sort to flaunt things in front of others, so to speak."

"Ah, so just keeping it to handholding, which is a small display of affection. I understand." He'd been researching this topic. So he knew that displays of affection had certain weights to them. With hand holding, being lower than a hug, kiss, or other things.

"Yes."

"Okay." He squeezed her palm against his, then did a quick peck since they were alone.

Having been running in the open space below the promenade, which had a wide open space on the outside, they moved to the gym. Which, to him, was the same as any other recreational space. Padded walls, floors made for a softer landing, and strength and conditioning equipment. All in varying shades of black and gray with silver accents. Not a large room, but their sparring explained the mats that were open and off to one side.

Rick, already present on arrival, acknowledged Quinn with a sharp nod, doing the same to Kira. "I'm ready when you are."

"Two secs." Kira removed her shoes by the edge of the mat.

Looking between the two, Quinn realized this would be the first time he would witness a full-on fight. He wondered if it would change the impact of it, seeing actual violence instead of the fake choreographed stunts he'd witnessed before. He also noted they did not wear protective equipment.

Rick didn't come to play. No warm up and no warning. When she stepped onto the mat, he stepped towards her.

Kira stepped back. His net told him it was likely instinctive because of what they were doing. Rick smiled, the first that Quinn had seen, rather small still. Then he launched into it. Rick opposed his playing strategy in cards, becoming aggressively forward. He hardly went to defense, but it worked well for Kira, who ducked and moved under his advancements, and when she couldn't avoid, she would block.

She didn't continue to hold back, and in an opportune moment, she swept his legs out from under him, putting Rick on the ground. With a triumphant grin, she gave him a hand up. He paid her back a moment later with a swing that impacted her face directly. She'd misjudged, and the blow laid her flat upon the moment of contact. She would be looking at quite a large bruise not only on her face but on her hip if the sound of both were anything to tell by.

"Was that supposed to happen, or should I be concerned?" Quinn had been shifting from side to side, uncomfortable with what he just witnessed.

"No, I thought she was moving under." Rick answered him, still standing upright.

It looked incredibly painful to him. But the whole fight looked pretty painful overall and unpleasant. This was the first hit that looked genuinely debilitating, and he was worried.

That was a slight understatement. He was extremely worried, but he did his best not to overreact, knowing that sparring was practicing combat. He knew that meant she would be hit, but not to that extent. Grasping and releasing the fabric of his pants, he twisted it. That blow left him very much wanting to put an end to it.

Kira got her hands up underneath her and spit on the ground. Something white fell out, and she starred for a second before swallowing. "You weren't going to be able to pull all your momentum."

Kira came back onto her knees and reached forward to pick up what came out. The thing she'd spat out was one of her molars.

"That is a tooth." His brain immediately made the connection. The statement about as witty as he could be as he stared in open horror at both the tooth and the blood.

Trying to think of what to do in this instant, he was at a bit of a loss. "We have to get her to med bay if we want to get the tooth back in." A slight note of panic fluttered in his voice. Nervous ticks betrayed his distress, as he could not remain still.

"I'm still perfectly capable of making my own way," Kira said lightly, "But we are done for today, Rick."

Rick grunted and shrugged his shoulders. "I'll clean up since I caused it."

Kira nodded and went to stand. A little unsteady; her right leg stiffened, thigh muscles shaking like a shiver exclusively in that area. Placing her weight on her left, she rubbed that side. Quinn quickly examined and found nothing obviously broken.

"Capable doesn't mean it's a good idea. With your injuries, it's optimal to put less stress on your body until you can be assessed." Quinn perfectly recited what he'd read the last time he'd had to transport her to med bay. This time he didn't have hundreds of drones swarming the ship that he could summon at a moment's notice. It would take two or three minutes to do so.

So, he just went to her side and offered her a hand, which felt a bit lacking, but it was the quickest thing he could manage. His neural net back up fully, the projections for when a drone would arrive and when she could get to med bay, just walking, were the same.

"Quinn, I'm alright. I've had much worse. Trust me." She opened her mouth as little as possible when speaking.

Rick grabbed supplies from a wall cabinet, as if he considered the matter closed. There was no apology issued either, something even Quinn noticed was missing, but he didn't comment upon it. Instead, he said, "I am not sure why you thought that would make me feel better. This was clearly painful and you could permanently lose a tooth. Telling me you've had worse just makes me worry more, not less."

She grimaced. "When I broke my ankle, you barely flinched. Bree can put my tooth back in with much less fuss. It will be alright."

"You know why this is different," he fired back. This was happening literally after the night where she'd managed to get through the last barrier between himself and her. It was a far cry from a woman he'd found mostly annoying breaking her ankle.

She repeated her exasperated expression before dropping it.

Quinn wasn't fishing for an apology. Mostly because he was, at present, unaware that she had done anything wrong. Once he learned that there was sparring gear that she and Rick could have been using to prevent this, that would be another story.

Well, either way, he tugged her along as quickly as he could manage, not acknowledging that she wasn't making this easier.

When they entered, they found Bree positioned over a slide scope. She'd straighten, not even looking at them as she went to the pod and cleared it to do a full body scan. The brunette was familiar to Quinn. They'd passed each other in the hall several times and had spoken briefly while picking up trays in the cafeteria. She'd been short with him, but he'd not thought anything of it.

"Is Rick behind you?" She asked with a sigh.

"Nope, just me today," Kira said somewhat cheerfully, holding up her tooth. "I need you to plug this back in for me."

"They were sparring. She took a serious blow to the face and likely bruised her hip when she fell." Quinn said, filling in the details Kira tried to gloss over. Naturally, he'd replayed the memory on the way up. It had given him a general idea of the damage done to her by the blow.

Bree gave them both a deadpan look. "Yes, well," Bree started, as if more irritated at the interruption than concerned for Kira. "This is a regular occurrence for them both."

Kira shrugged it off and let go of Quinn's hand to go to the scanner. The device had a flat area to lie on, with a white sheet draped over a cushioned bottom. The top had a solid foot wide half-circle. It slid back and forth via a rolling system. It looked like black glass but when Bree moved it to one side it lit up for commands a qwerty keyboard and other instant command buttons resting above it with the feedback system. Kira sat on the edge. She held out her tooth to Bree, who took it by the top as she scooted back.

"They should wear safety gear." Quinn pointed out, since he was currently looking into ways to make sure this didn't keep happening. Imagine his surprise to learn that there was plenty of safety gear she and Rick could have been using to make sure that they could spar without risk of serious injury.

"I have said the same thing. Both of them visit at least once a month." Bree spoke sharply, her teeth clenched, strengthening her jaw. He recognized the aggravation, but it was not to the same degree as his own. She hit the start button and backed up as the scan began the half-circle, moving over Kira of its own accord. Bree's description in her extended file labeled her as sweet, docile in her own way, but now it was obviously less so when it came to them sparring when she had the same opinions as Quinn.

"You'd miss us, Bree," she teased the doctor.

Quinn glared at Kira. This was the first time in a while that he seemed upset with her. He would not belabor the point. He was just upset and unsure what to do about it. Knowing she didn't want people making choices for her putting him in an awkward situation. He hadn't realized caring for someone might involve letting them be a total idiot.

Bree finished the scan and then ran a light over Kira's hip and face, which calmed the blood vessels underneath, so she did not look as if she'd taken a beating that morning. Then she took the tooth and had Kira open wide to reinsert it.

Kira remained perfectly still as Bree poked around in her mouth and pushed the tooth back in. Quinn noticed she'd not taken the time to numb anything or give pain medication throughout the process of doing so. Though she would run the same light inside her mouth to make sure the roots retook.

At that point Quinn realized he'd stood there watching. It felt awkward. He'd been so worried about Kira, he'd forgotten that they were in the med bay with a person he barely knew. The man shifted, uncomfortable suddenly.

Kira dropped down to rinse her mouth, and Bree sighed, looking at Quinn. "I suppose we haven't properly introduced ourselves," Bree sighed, looking at Quinn. "I'm Bree."

Her hand extended his direction. The woman was softer than Kira, bright eyes instead of dark ones, sweeter features that were motherly instead of sharp. He'd called Kira pretty last night and he could recognize this woman was casually pretty if he wanted to, but instead he focused on returning the handshake, one firm pump, then a release. A considerable improvement from before. "Quinn."

"Good as new. Thank you Bree." Kira emerged, her smile back to being white as ever and full. She was on time for the handshake.

Bree drew her hand back after it as well, only not as quickly, but instead of tucking her hands away she'd bring it up to point a finger at Kira prodding her on her upper arm lightly. "I'm done patching you two up every day. The next time you come in here, it better be for an actual accident."

Kira looked scolded, but only superficially, because the corners of her lips were trying not to come up as she said, "Yes, Doctor."

"I don't think she is going to listen to you," Quinn observed dryly. Then he paused. He'd just, well, he didn't know for sure that she wouldn't listen to Bree. It was just, he assumed, from what he knew of Kira, she wouldn't. So he'd pointed it out, but that was... Huh, had he just teased Kira?

Bree found neither of them funny. Her down-turned mouth a clear sign, as she said just as dryly back, "She never does, but at least she can leave me to my work now." She motioned for the door, insinuating they take their leave.

Kira made a defensive hands up gesture before turning to go, calling out over her shoulder, "thank you, Doctor." The same thinly veiled amusement fluttered into her tone. She cackled as they departed.

Quinn followed her out, his annoyance with her mixed with his feelings about finally teasing her confusing, she caught him off guard by a sudden topic change.

"I have to relieve Morgan for a while."

"Okay, I should go take a shower."

When he emerged heading towards the bridge, he found Jaden crawling out of an air vent. The boy's physique small enough he could shoulder through some of them. Quinn cross-referenced their location within the ship. The vent's next let out closest to Rick's room. Jaden looked slightly defeated in his expression as he dragged out a small red tool bag he'd been using.

Jaden spotted him before continuing to crawl out. He affixed the grate. "Do you just wander around now?" Jaden asked impolitely.

"Yes." Quinn wasn't sure why the kid sounded so sullen about it. Besides the fact, he possibly already knew what Jaden was doing. Pattern recognition was rather simple for him. The kid's method of attack clearly depended on sneaking into places he wasn't supposed to get into and then leave a trap behind.

Jaden pushed the old screws back into place. The air vents were one of the few antiquated things left in the ship, but necessary in case of an attack where they needed to shut off air or direct it through the ship for aerosols.

He looked up at Quinn when he said yes, catching the shrug. "If Bree would stop harping about my studies, maybe I could too."

"Do you not want to learn what she is teaching?"

"Nah, it ain't that." The boy straightened, shouldering his bag. "Some things are okay, but she's got me writing essays." That seemed to displease him highly, or at least, made his face look pinched.

"Okay," the definition flashed across for him, "That doesn't seem that hard."

"Maybe not for you with all those things stuck in your head." He tucked his thumbs into the front of his pants, giving him a quizzical look as he considered what he was going to do next. "Speaking of computers, Alec said you're able to make or break almost anything. Is that right?"

That comment about things in his head got a slight frown from Quinn. It was technically accurate, but he didn't like the phrasing. He also wasn't wild about what Alec had apparently said he could do, but again, technically accurate. "Yes."

"Even the scanners for rooms?" Jaden had a glint in his eye. This was what Kira had been afraid of and warned him about. She'd told him not to help him with anything he could not accomplish by his own means and might. Opening doors into places he shouldn't be in was definitely above and beyond that.

But Quinn wasn't sure what the kid was getting at. "I built the scanners, yes. Almost everything new on the ship I built myself."

"Oh good, I need help to open a door."

"If you can't open it, then you aren't supposed to go through it."

"It's just Rick's room."

"Oh, then I can't open it, anyway. The locks have a built-in fail-safe to seal if someone tries to bypass them. The only way to override the fail-safe is with DNA and password verification. People are meant to have exclusive access to their rooms and the things I build perform their intended functions."

There was, actually, a workaround even to this. During a red-alert all the doors on the ship automatically unlocked for safety but he would not explain that to Jaden.

Jaden popped his hands on his hips, looking as if he was deciding whether Quinn was telling the truth. "No matter," he said, and his features contorted in a manner that said he had another idea. One that obviously didn't involve Quinn as he took off, still going towards Rick's room, which was around the corner.

Quinn tapped his foot as he thought about it before following Jaden. "You can't get into Rick's room, but what exactly are you trying to do?" Curious and, depending on what it was, he could help the kid.

"I was gonna switch out his shampoo."

"Well, you can't get into the room. I suppose you could set up a water nozzle with the solution to trigger when the door opens, though, at the right angle. If it was up in the ceiling, you could spray him down before he gets into the room."

"How do I do that?"

The remark would soon turn into Quinn, helping him do that if he wasn't careful.

Quinn didn't do it for Jaden, but he showed the kid how to pop open the access hatch above Rick's door. He suggested using a magnetic switch that would trigger when the door slid up into the ceiling, explaining what the correct depth would be for the trigger. Then, he did the math and wrote what angle to place the water nozzle at. It rested on Jaden to complete the prank, now that he had the knowledge of how to do it.

Jaden monopolized Quinn's time for a short while and, despite his misgivings about learning, he learned quite a bit by having his help. He played with reversing the polarity of the magnets, fixing angles, and then learned with his hands by doing. By the time they were done, Rick would have bubblegum pink hair. Quinn wasn't privy to the substance in the canister, but he'd find out if he showed up to dinner that night.

Quinn considered this to be in line with Kira's instructions on the prank war. He left Jaden with the knowledge and the tools, and he would certainly learn the results eventually. For the moment, though, he went back to ambling around the ship.

Running into Max moments later, on his way down to hydroponics bay he invited Quinn along. Max intended on planting pumpkins that were left over from years before for the upcoming holidays. They worked in companionable silence until Max asked him, "Are you eating lunch with the Captain?"

"Maybe?" Quinn was aware of the time, always, but the reminder made him send a message up to Kira.

Half an hour later, he got a short message back, text only. 'I don't think I'll be able to get away.'

Max was still in the cantine when he entered. Rick followed behind, hovering over his metal tray at the table, cutting up his meal into smaller bites. When Quinn approached, Rick asked, "Captain, get her tooth put back in?"

"Yes."

"Good, it's harder for them to take the second time around." Rick commented.

Max eyed Rick curiously as he asked, "Are you going back to sparring again?"

"Back into old habits." Rick took a bite, seemingly unphased.

"Bad habits if you aren't using basic safety equipment." Quinn observed not looking at Rick or Max as he ate, not realizing that this might be construed as him teasing someone again. He sounded a bit peeved as he said it. Though he felt nothing in regards to Rick, he was more annoyed with Kira. Sparring without proper precautions was definitely a very her thing to do, it was just also a very worrying thing for her to do.

"Safety equipment does not prepare you for the real world."

Max attempted to change the subject. "Are we still running drills this afternoon?"

Rick nodded once.

"In point of fact, safety equipment is actually designed to prepare you for real-world scenarios without the risk of debilitating yourself during practice. You may be confused about its function." Quinn informed Rick with a flat-level stare, not allowing him to move on quickly. "Would you like me to prove you wrong with a neatly compiled list of case studies on the matter? There are quite a few of them that prove that eschewing training equipment, contrary to popular belief, does little to improve the development of combat abilities in any meaningful way. However, it opens up those doing it to risk of long-term injury or death."

Rick got under Quinn's skin. A poor opinion with no scientific basis had already gotten the person Quinn cared about more than anything or anyone hurt. While he wouldn't insist that they wear the gear, he sure as hell would not let them labor under the delusion that it was a good idea.

Rick laughed. It wasn't broad or open like anyone else's, but a deep chuckle that came from his chest. Perhaps not the reaction that Quinn looked for when he offered to give him studies. "You are a wonder, aren't you?"

Max frowned at his laughter, opening his mouth to speak, but he was beat to it-

"She needs to take a beating and keep going," Rick said coolly, rising with his tray. "She knows what she's doing. If you've got a problem, take it up with her lovebird."

"Rick!" Max went to follow, maybe to scold the man properly.

"While exposure to pain can build up a tolerance, there is no evidence that a person can undergo extreme trauma without going into shock. Safety equipment doesn't remove the pain of the beating. In fact, with it, you both could go substantially longer, getting more practice at taking a beating without putting yourselves at risk. The importance of proper safety precautions during training has been witnessed and understood for thousands of years. That doesn't stop being true because you disagree with it." Quinn dropped into a monotone, no longer arguing with the man, simply informing him of the facts. "Kira and you are both adults. You may make your own decisions, but don't sit there and try to argue with hard science just because you think that's the way it should be done. You can beat yourselves senseless. Just know that scientists have proven well that there is little to no meaning in it.

"And yet you will not tell the captain this, will you?" The manic laugh Rick had exhibited earlier portrayed itself in the way he smiled then. Was it truly Kira that insisted they not use protective gear when he looked at Quinn like that?

"I've already made my feelings on the subject known to her. If she brings it up again, then yes, I would tell her it is a bad idea. If she tried to justify it, then I would inform her there is no scientific basis for it. Why would I..." There is a pause and he notes something as it is brought to his attention. "Ah, I see. No, I would not refrain from telling her something for fear of upsetting her and ruining my, quote-unquote, chances with her."

Quinn returned to eating. Or perhaps he'd never really stopped.

"Good." Rick dropped it as quickly as it started. Rick polished off his tray before asking, "You coming, Max?"

"Uh, if you'll excuse me." Max had other duties to attend to, but the quick back-and-forth spoke of his hesitation.

Quinn was the only one left to ponder. He wasn't sure why he was so furious with Rick. Still he would have informed the man of his mistake regardless if it had not affected his emotional state.

He'd felt a lot of things and hadn't liked how the man talked about his relationship with Kira. That was his, not Rick's, it was not any business of the man's and... Grinding his teeth, Quinn started towards his room, done with people for the day.

Before he could make a clean exit, Hela poked her head through the pass through. "Quinn?"

Hearing and responding were two different things, but Hela wanted him to take a tray up to the captain, who'd yet to come retrieve it or ask for it. Part of him did not wish to oblige her. He wished to hole up in his room, but the part that wished to see Kira won out. Checking her location, she was in a storage bay, not the bridge, with Watson. The tray in hand, he couldn't turn back, so he continued.

The door opened silently, and Quinn overheard Watson speaking. His tone lacked emotion as he had been earlier. "And you're willing to accept that?"

"I am." Kira's response sounded heated, and not in a good way.

"Toke did not raise you to be a fool, Kira. He could destroy us all if you upset him."

"He wouldn't." She sounded absolutely certain.

"Hela sent me down with lunch," Quinn spoke loudly. This wasn't the first time he'd eavesdropped on the two, but he didn't want to hear anymore. He'd liked Kira's response, the certainty in it, and that was where he wanted things to end.

Watson clammed up immediately, and Kira stepped around a crate to see him. Her cheeks flushed with anger and wild eyes sought his. She softened, the tightness around her mouth less severe. No matter how much he overheard, she wasn't upset by it.

"Thank you, Quinn."

Watson did not round the corner.

"You're welcome." Even if he could not see the A.I., Quinn looked in that direction. His expression matching Kira's before she'd seen him. "Are you alright?"

"I am." The tray passed to her hands.

"I trust you." Quinn had no desire to speak to Watson, or to remain while the two squabbled, but that was important for him to relay. He released her tray. His intent not to stay made clear by his sharp turn out.

Returning to the darkness of his room, it threatened to swallow him but there was always a light present to keep away the shadows, even if only in his mind. One that came by later and spent the night curled up against his chest, stealing his covers, and making sure he knew the depth of what his words meant to her.

Chapter Twenty-Two

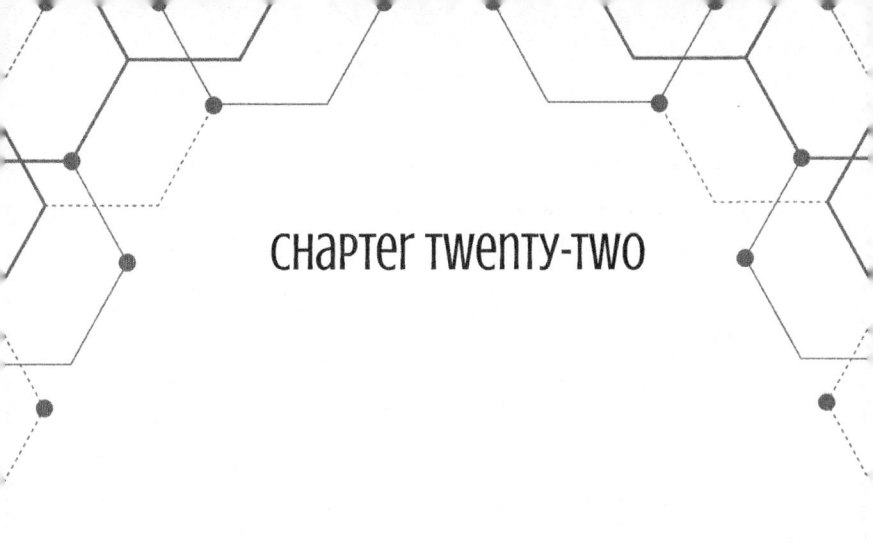

KIRA

"WITH THIS NEW SYSTEM, I hardly think we couldn't pass through a planet and we wouldn't feel it," Morgan commented, putting in the coordinates with his skilled hands.

"Let's be on the safe side," Kira said, knowing he was joking, a smile on her face as she heard the shuttle doors. Turning to find Quinn, that smile spread a little wider.

He joined her, standing by her side over the secondary section of the console, choosing to remain close.

"He's excited." Kira leaned his direction so Morgan wouldn't overhear.

Ready to perform the first of the fairly large jumps they'd been doing mini ones in known space to not draw attention, safely ensconced in neutral territory, and on the edge of known space, they'd be doing longer ones. Morgan confirmed the end coordinates.

"I figured." Quinn looked only to Kira, his expression more readable than before, pure adoration that she had to work to not fall into.

"You two gonna be helpful or just stand there?" Morgan asked.

"You seem to have it under control over there," Kira shot back, knowing she had to get herself under control as well.

Quinn's fingertips brushed against her palm as he slid them between her own. "You are doing fine," he said. "I'm monitoring the system while you work."

"I forget you're connected." Morgan gave a frank look to Kira when she'd told him he had it under control and a more thoughtful one to Quinn.

Kira squeezed his hand back lightly and teased Morgan again, "But if I could speed you up before I become an old woman, I'll help."

"I am trying to think of a joke to add in. But I feel like pointing out that Morgan's progress reduces by eighty-six percent every time he talks isn't hitting quite the right note," Quinn said.

"No, that's perfect." Kira laughed at his statement, having trouble even getting the words out. She felt tears spark at the edges of her eyes.

Morgan rolled his eyes. "Yeah, yeah. Some of us don't have a built-in processor."

"I mean, if it helps, your productivity has now slowed one hundred percent." The corner of Quinn's lips were slowly rising.

"Maybe you should stick to fixing things," Morgan half whined as he turned back to get to work once again.

Kira devolved into a fit of laughter even further, to where she almost wheezed and had to lean against the panel.

"My comments appear to have convinced you to fix your productivity, as it is now back to normal levels." Quinn offered helpfully. The young man could not stop his own grin from splitting his features and he chuckled to himself.

Kira ended up on the floor. She'd not laughed so hard in a long time. Morgan could see the humor in it, and with the Captain losing it, he tried hard to conceal his smile as well. Kira knew he could take a joke at his expense; he just had more composure than the Captain at the moment.

His productivity went back down to zero, as he could not concentrate on putting in the final jump coordinates.

Quinn didn't have another remark because Kira had a hold on him and practically yanked him down, so he went with her, dissolving and clutching his side when a stitch set over it.

"You two, it's really not that funny," Morgan said, clearly exasperated, but not down and out.

"Still zero!" Kira hollered out.

Kira and Quinn were both settled on the floor. They sat back, trying to get a hold of themselves. Kira could no longer produce any sound that wasn't a wheezing laugh, Morgan joined them, laughing, not as boisterous but in a good way.

Then, the lift sounded, and Watson emerged, catching them in the act. "Are we jumping this morning?"

"In a second. Watch," Morgan answered him. Kira turned her head into Quinn's shoulder, having caught the joke the way Morgan said it.

"Time does matter to some," Watson said sharply.

Morgan drew in a deep breath, settling himself. "With your leave, Captain?"

Kira waved at him to go on. It wasn't necessary to be strapped in; they would not feel the movement. Quinn rose upright and offered a hand to Kira. Taking the offer, she didn't let go right away. She had eyes only for him in a moment that she shouldn't, but she said softly, "Thank you." She let go, and they got back on track. Watson monitored the primary systems without ever having to truly look away from the viewscreen.

Morgan then performed the jump. A sensation as if the world slowed for a moment hit all of them, but then it stopped.

The engines covered such a large amount of distance in one burst that it felt close to folding space and time.

"How long will it take to scan the area?" Kira asked.

"The survey drones should be able to complete preliminary scans of a sector of this size in about eighteen hours." Quinn filled in the answer. The initial scans of the number of planets and the type of sun were already complete, and he read off the projections. A habit Kira was used to.

"Good." Kira shifted back to business then. "Morgan, set the long range scanners for other space fairing craft. I'd like to know well in advance if we're going to be set upon here."

Morgan, already on it, vocalized it to reassure her.

"We'll jump again in 24 hours after completing the scans," Kira added.

Their mining equipment had come at the last minute, besides dropping Quinn off. They were dispatched not only to find him a suitable planet, which they wouldn't settle for the first one offered this close to known space, but also to find Listium. They were on a mining venture according to their logs. There were still some things that needed to be checked on said equipment that Alec attended to. Kira wanted to check on him next and his progress.

Even if they found what they were looking for, the amount that they wanted was going to be difficult to mine quickly and it would not be in one location unless they were very lucky. Even then, it could undermine the ecosystem for them to pull so much out of one planet. The only way they would do it was if the planet was never likely to terraform.

Watson stood next to Morgan and asked, looking over his shoulder, "Do you want to know of any life forms, Captain?"

"Anything of note," she answered. "We are still not to interfere. We play by Praetorian rules. Morgan, I will leave you and Watson to it. I need to check in on Alec."

"Are you coming?" She asked Quinn.

Morgan and Watson had already merged back into the work they needed to do. They received orders and were ready to fulfill them.

"Yes?" Quinn answered and while they headed down to check on Alec he said out of nowhere, "I had fun on the bridge with you and Morgan."

"I did as well."

They were alone, so when he leaned over to promptly kiss her, she did not resist. They wound around one another, making out like teenagers under the bleachers until they hit their floor, disengaging and straightening themselves into presentable members of the crew.

Alec crawled down from the cockpit of one of the mining drills, using some very colorful language. He saw Quinn and the Captain and complained to them as well, "Bloody set these things up to work remotely, but I don't ken why they wouldn't leave room for ya to run them manually."

Kira covered her mouth with her free hand before saying, "You're not meant to go down on the surface in these places."

"Well, of course not. It would be incredibly dangerous." Quinn blinked.

"Oh, yes, it's dangerous." Alec rolled his eyes as he hit something on his pad, his annoyance fairly clear. His not caring about the danger was also fairly clear.

Kira tried to hold back her amusement at his irritation, a quiver at the corner of her lips giving her away. It was hard to not hear it in her voice when she said, "You can still take down one of the shuttles."

"Why do so many people on this ship want to eschew basic security precautions?"

Clearly, Quinn was keeping track. First Kira and Rick, then Morgan, if in jest, and now Alec. It was like they chafed at any restriction that kept them safe if they did not agree with it.

"Why is it so bad to avoid injury? I really do not understand." Quinn questioned.

"You've never lived boy, living comes with danger," Alec informed him. His eyes narrowed at something on the tablet.

Kira did not comment on that one, but her expression shifted to concern and she redirected Alec. "What else do you need done?"

"I... You know that I have been living in the constant danger of being recaptured since leaving Paradigm, right?" Quinn quickly betrayed her, even if unintentionally.

"He means that in order to do things worth doing, sometimes it's dangerous," Kira supplied. She knew Alec's explanation was going to be less than kind. "Mountain climbing is dangerous and yet people still do it."

Alec nodded before handing the pad to Kira. "These are the ones left. I just need everything routed to the primary controls."

"Ah." Quinn had a blank look on him, indicating he was conferring on his net. He glanced off to the side as he read out the inputs that were given to him. She'd grown so used to it, she barely paid attention anymore as he did so.

They broke apart from Alec and she tried to explain further, "Quinn, there is." She hesitated. "There might be things I do you may not understand. Things that put me in situations that make you uncomfortable."

She didn't wish to do so, but she knew she would, especially with unfamiliar territory coming up. Going down on a planet's surface because she would not subject the rest of the crew to things she wasn't willing to do was one.

"I mean, I don't understand why you would make choices that increase your chance of risk." Quinn's expression was unreadable, as if he were trying to sort out how to feel. "I really don't think there is an explanation you can give me that will make that make logical sense, but I am not upset. If that is what you want to do, you will do it. I have no desire to change that part of you because without it, I wouldn't be here with you now. However, just because I will not object to it doesn't mean I will like it."

"I understand."

"Thank you."

Kira stole a kiss after assuring they were out of Alec's range of vision.

"You are terrible at following your own rules," Quinn wasn't arguing, his grin enough to say he didn't care.

"Remember, I don't follow safety regulations."

Kira started crawled in and out of the mining equipment. They resembled classical skid steers, large attachments able to be placed on a slotted section, heavy treads over the thick wheels, allowing it to move. Thrusters came installed on the bottom and sides for movement in space. Magnetic locks allowed it to travel on the outside of a ship.

Manual calibration typically wasn't necessary, but the physical checking of all the components, the walk around, and reaffirming the systems readings was a tried-and-true way to catch any last-minute issues.

Kira wiped her hand across the side of her face, a dark substance akin to grease smeared over her cheek. The engine on Kira's craft needed a replacement filter. She'd launched right into fixing it.

"Do you want to go up to the galley and eat lunch with me?" Quinn's voice called up to her.

"Is it that time?" She popped up out of the hatch.

"Yes, it is that time," Quinn said with a shake of his head. "So, is that a yes?"

"Yeah, of course. Let me finish this. I'll be down in a second." She dropped back down into the machine, promising to be out in a moment. There was a safe way down, but she didn't take the ladder on the back. She instead leaped down onto the treads and then popped off of those by scooting to the edge and coming down. Making a good leap, prepared this time, she reinforced her ankle from her last fall.

Quinn took the moment to practice something he'd seen Morgan do, rolling his eyes.

"Did you roll your eyes at me?" Catching it, Kira wasn't chastising but felt a blossoming warmth for the man with the action.

"Yes."

"And I can't even be mad about it." She sighed playfully, giving him what was supposed to be a mad face, but it only lasted for a few seconds before breaking. "Next time though," she assured him, using her free hand to make an 'I'm watching you' gesture.

"I will bear in mind that I have a finite number of times I can roll my eyes sarcastically at your behavior." Quinn snorted.

"You're already down one."

"And am I correct in assuming that I only get a finite number of times I can roll my eyes, but the number of times you can do things that will make me want to do so is unlimited?"

"You are." That was what broke the dam of laughter which echoed down the hallway towards the mess hall as they stepped out of the lift. Kira couldn't keep from doing so. Everything bright and loud and enthusiastic about her encompassed in how free it was.

Naturally, her laughter prompted his own, and he joined her. She thought it provided a glimpse of the sort of man he would have been without Paradigm's influence. Then again, without it, he would have never been born, so it was impossible to say for sure.

He'd been so good at sharing himself lately that she almost felt bad when she took him out of the galley and they ate alone, having a picnic lunch, but she wanted him to herself for a second. To memorize as much as she could while trying to forget why she was doing so.

QUINN

After finishing calibrating the machines assigned to him, Quinn found and offered to help Kira finish her work. With his help running calculations, the work would take a minimal amount of time. Except he swiftly learned that Kira preferred her help in the form of small talk and not in him doing the work for her. Which he didn't mind in the least. Even if their small talk was more her talking at him, as he occasionally thought of a good question.

Alec's arrival with a question helped to distract him from being a sounding board to being useful to their engineer instead.

Quinn reviewed the testing algorithm on the machine. They had a testing sample of Listium to use. Despite that, it only calibrated to about 76% accuracy. Everything appeared to be in order. It didn't take long for Quinn to figure out the problem, and he handed the solution to Alec with a slight smile.

"Could have used you years ago, lad," Alec said, looking at it with a smile.

Kira popped up about the time that he finished, peering over Alec's shoulder curiously. "I've told you I'd get a computer engineer on board, but nooooo."

"I don't need no bloody computer engineer." Alec's mustache ruffled itself. "Things were fine."

"We're both finished. Are we free to go, boss?" Kira asked.

Alec hadn't even been looking up, nor did he when he scrolled to the bottom of the code. "Yeah, be gone, both of you."

Alec's dismissal was casual, which didn't really surprise Quinn. He readily followed Kira out of the storage bay. The man's affection, trust, and desire for her only seemed to grow by the day. Perhaps such seemingly boundless growth should have worried him, but it was the best he had felt in his entire life. He barely ever even felt considered the trauma of his upbringing anymore. It lingered those rare times he was alone in the wee hours with his thoughts, but those were becoming rarer in the last few days.

Kira wanted to check on the progress of the scans. It might not reveal much, but they'd not been to the bridge since that morning, so they made their way there.

What they found was not an unusual sight for Kira. Morgan had his feet up and propped as he watched information flash upon the HUD.

Kira barely gave him a cursory glance as she asked, "How are things coming along?"

"Nothing so far of note," Morgan replied, feet coming down, but he remained seated, his hands locked behind his head. "Not that we expected anything this close."

"Still have to scan," she noted to Morgan.

Morgan shrugged, getting up out of his seat to stretch. "Picked over already, no doubt."

"Potentially, the route you took is fairly popular for deep space explorations." Quinn had been involved in watching the calculations.

It was not outside of the realm of possibility that someone had jumped to the same star they had since Morgan had picked one of the brighter, and therefore closer ones.

"Most likely," Kira agreed. "But we are doing it sector by sector. You've just sped up the process quite a bit."

What took weeks would now only take days.

"It was no trouble."

It really wasn't. Most of the equipment on the ship had already been designed by him previously and he hadn't had to foot the cost of the materials. So for him, it had just been a matter of building the ship, which he'd enjoyed. There was a slightly better than non-zero chance that he would build his own ship once he had settled in and could get to work.

Morgan half laughed and said, "Looked like it was loads of trouble, but we appreciate it."

Kira echoed the sentiment through a smile and a slight squeeze of his hand. They bid Morgan adieu not soon after and checked in on the other crew members, even catching Jaden, rigging up purple paint.

Kira walked right by like she didn't see what he was doing and Jaden pretended he didn't see her, either. He offered a half wave at Quinn, which he returned.

Walking away, Kira turned her head and answered no one, "I will be down momentarily."

Waiting another beat for the reply, she looked at Quinn. "Watson is retrofitting one of the shuttles. He needs my opinion on something. I can go down alone."

"I can go. Unless you think it's better I don't." He didn't want to preclude her asking to avoid upsetting the A.I..

"If you can both behave."

"*I* can behave." There was very little that Watson could say at this point that would get under Quinn's skin. The insecurities the A.I. had picked at regarding Kira were no longer a sore spot.

"Well, that's one of you."

He couldn't speak for Watson. Well, he could, but he was fairly certain that if he looked up the A.I.'s inner thoughts, Kira would be rather cross with him. Thus far, he hadn't done so out of respect for the A.I.'s core intelligence, and he saw no reason to violate that particular sanctity of thought.

Watson held up the tracking device for their inspection. "I had a feeling," Watson said when they came in separately, keeping things professional. "That there was more than met the eye to their visit."

The sight of the tracker made Quinn frown. If such a thing was on the ship, he should have detected it. His neural net blinked back on and he scanned over the logs. It depended on some kind of trigger. The device hadn't sent its signal until they'd been in the same location for a few hours. Since it sent a subspace transmission, the Praetorians didn't want it to trigger constantly, too high of a chance to get caught, but they couldn't have it trigger randomly since subspace shots took time to line up. So, it had a sensor that could track time between jumps.

It had triggered, and he'd missed it because he'd been with Kira and his neural net had been off.

"They were more concerned than they let on then. They've never hassled us like this before." Kira took the tracker. No larger than a little Bluetooth speaker and squared like one, but the tracking from it was great if you were in a good range.

Watson looked at Quinn when Kira spoke before returning his gaze to hers. "Yes, well, they've never had a reason to before. I've been monitoring chatter for Paradigm. They're working with most governments doing a contract for repossession of property."

"Well, I can reprogram the tracker to send a spoof signal so they don't know we've located the tracker. That way, they won't know where we are and won't know we found it." Quinn made a priority alert for any outgoing signals, not in standard broadcast frequencies. He kept his systems running. He'd die if that happened, but it could go into sleep mode and it had a small emergency battery that could save his life in the event of a strong enough EMP.

"Even with a signal like that, they still might have something on the device itself. Better to just jettison it as well."

Watson gingerly took it back from Kira. "This may not be the only one. Leading them on for a few sectors will give us a chance to find them all and do it properly."

"If there is more than one, they should all be of similar make and production if not identical. I'll have my detection drones do a sweep of the ship." It wouldn't take long for them all, if there were more of them, to be found. He didn't argue with Kira about the spoof signal. He could set it up in such a way that there was zero risk, but he assumed she was aware of that and was being overly cautious.

Kira nodded tightly. "We'll scramble the signal then after they're found and drop them on our next jump."

The drone that Quinn had activated swiftly entered the room before anyone could speak. The floating octopus mechanical wonder grasped the tracker, scanned it, and broke down its composition for him so that it could be programmed for the others.

"Thank you, Quinn," Kira's voice still sounded tight.

"Captain," Watson started, his voice overly gentle with her. "Should we move ahead of schedule? Jump a few sectors to put distance?"

Folding his arms, Quinn offered no comment on this as the scanning drone did its work. A diagram of the tracker and its components appeared as the ultrasonic vibrations mapped the interior components. Once he had a full analysis, he loaded the easiest to track variables into some drones and sent them whirring through the ship.

"I'll call a meeting to discuss it." Kira sounded distant.

"I'll come once the scan of the ship is completed." Quinn's full on work mode had hit, preparing a multitude of counter measures should something like this happen again, he'd leave without so much as a goodbye.

KIRA

Kira had been about to explain the issue when Quinn arrived on the bridge. An accompanying drone set three more of the trackers on the table. Alec got up, taking one. He'd been earlier than the others and he'd gotten a partial rundown.

"They came on board to plant tracking beacons," Kira finished her train of thought with that. "Watson suggested we jump quickly and avoid the next few quadrants. Quinn is going to scramble their signal and we'll drop them on the next jump as well for extra safety. Their vessel isn't equipped to follow us for too terribly long."

None of the crew looked overly concerned. They lived a smuggler's life under the pretense of being legal. They all knew that. It came with certain dangers.

Hela sat next to Rick. Rick looked furious, not with Quinn but with himself, his expression cold. Hela touched his shoulder, and he softened only a little.

Alec held the tracker and said with a sigh, "We have to consider other ways they could track us as well if they're sending a different vessel, lass."

Kira nodded.

Morgan grinned and took it from Alec. "Let them try to catch us." Always confident in his abilities, and he wanted to play with them.

"Statistically, the Praetorians would win through numbers if nothing else," Quinn rationalized. "Sorry, you were just displaying bravado, weren't you?"

Alec clapped Morgan's shoulder and chuckled.

Even Max let out a tight smile at that one. Kira tried to keep hers hidden.

Rick stood up. "More than one jump," he put in his vote. "It would be safer until we get far enough that we are a needle in a haystack."

Quinn spoke up again. "I've already prepared an interception for the subspace signals the tracker broadcast on. The next time they transmit, it will send out a set of coordinates in a random direction, tracing them away from us. The number of jumps is irrelevant."

"It doesn't matter, they might guess we found them," Rick clarified. "Those should still go as soon as possible. We should make a cluster of jumps until we can scan again."

Kira did not disagree with his logic. When they scanned, it left them in one place for quite a while, and she did not want to be vulnerable for any reason. "That's fine," she agreed.

"Does anyone have any other suggestions?" Kira would hear everything, even if it was not helpful. Sometimes the smallest things made a difference.

With the consensus being no, she said, "We'll keep to the schedule and make consecutive jumps in the morning. After the first, we will drop the tracking beacons."

With the matter being settled, everyone dispersed, save for Morgan, Watson, and Quinn.

"I will take the watch tonight, Morgan."

Morgan looked a little crestfallen at that, but nodded.

"I can stay as well, Captain. It will be a long night." Watson's offer came quickly.

"I was going to stay," Quinn replied.

Kira may not have been looking at either of them, but she didn't need to. The peacocking would have to come to a halt quickly.

Watson merely glanced at Quinn and replied shortly, "I do not require sleep and I do not tire. My offer is to keep the Captain awake or to monitor when she cannot."

"My offer is because I enjoy her company. However, I think it is her decision if either of us stays with her this evening." Quinn sounded a bit clipped, slipping into a monotonous drone.

"Both of you stop." Kira snapped. Quinn had said he could mind his manners, but he was losing them at the baiting of Watson.

Watson let out a soft, "Sorry, Captain."

The glance that Kira gave Watson was one of exasperation in the face of uncertainty. "You are right, Watson. I cannot monitor throughout the night without some fatigue. I will stay until midnight and turn it over to you, then."

Watson nodded. "Kira," There was emotion in his voice when he said her name. "This is only one attempt."

"That's all, Watson," she said dismissively.

Quinn was blissfully quiet.

"Yes, Captain." Watson moved past them both. Morgan had somehow gotten away unscathed and stayed that way, slipping out alongside him.

Kira walked to the HUD, putting her hands on the edge, her knuckles pale.

"I'm sorry. The thought of you spending the night alone with him, even knowing that nothing would happen, made me... irrationally jealous. I tried not to snap at him, but I didn't want him or you to think I was unwilling to stay up with you."

"You do not have to apologize." She looked out the view screen still as she spoke, "Watson purposefully egged you into it. He is much more skilled in guiding a conversation than he lets on."

"I'm still sorry." Quinn wrapped his arms around her from behind, kissing the edge of her shoulder. "Since I know I am part of why there is a problem at all."

"You should not apologize for how you feel on a matter." Turning towards him, she embraced him in return, "Watson is handling this poorly and that is not your fault. Nor should he try to upset you purposefully just to prove a point."

"I suppose. I just dislike seeing you so annoyed." Quinn admitted. "I love you, Kira."

She felt... the same, but the words caught on the tip of her tongue and would not emerge. She loved him, and yet he would leave, to protect her, to protect the ship, to protect her crew. There was such devotion in remaining steadfast and committing to the plan he'd devised, but it broke something in her and she could not say the words back.

And I'm supposed to be the adjusted one.

Looking For more?

We have a special bonus chapter in Watson's POV just waiting for you.

Sign up at our mailing list at:

www.mossandwolf.com

Flip the page to see the 'Crew Files'

- CREW FILE -

DESIGNATION:	KIRA STARLING
POSITION:	CAPTAIN
RACE:	PRAETORIAN
SEX:	FEMALE
AGE:	27
EYE COLOR/HAIR COLOR:	AMBER/BLACK (PURPLE)
OUTWARD COLORING:	LIGHT/MEDIUM
HEIGHT/WEIGHT:	5'7/145

- CREW FILE -

DESIGNATION:	QUINN
POSITION:	PASSENGER
RACE:	HUMAN
SEX:	MALE
AGE:	24
EYE COLOR/HAIR COLOR:	LIGHT BLUE/WHITE
OUTWARD COLORING:	FAIR
HEIGHT/WEIGHT:	6'2/170

- CREW FILE -

DESIGNATION:	SEBASTIAN WATSON
POSITION:	SHIP'S AI
RACE:	PREVIOUSLY PRAETORIAN
SEX:	MALE
AGE:	N/A
EYE COLOR/HAIR COLOR:	N/A
OUTWARD COLORING:	N/A
HEIGHT/WEIGHT:	N/A

- CREW FILE -

DESIGNATION:	MAXIMUS CAIRN
POSITION:	VICAR
RACE:	HUMAN
SEX:	MALE
AGE:	63
EYE COLOR/HAIR COLOR:	BLUE-GRAY/GRAY
OUTWARD COLORING:	FAIR
HEIGHT/WEIGHT:	6'2/175

- CREW FILE -

DESIGNATION: ALEC O'MALLEY
POSITION: CHIEF ENGINEER
RACE: HUMAN
SEX: MALE
AGE: 45
EYE COLOR/HAIR COLOR: BROWN/GRAY
OUTWARD COLORING: FAIR
HEIGHT/WEIGHT: 6'0/210

- CREW FILE -

DESIGNATION: MORGAN KITE
POSITION: SHIP'S PILOT
RACE: PRAETORIAN
SEX: MALE
AGE: 26
EYE COLOR/HAIR COLOR: BROWN/BROWN
OUTWARD COLORING: LIGHT/MEDIUM
HEIGHT/WEIGHT: 5'11/180

- CREW FILE -

DESIGNATION: RICK
POSITION: HEAD OF SECURITY
RACE: HUMAN/MODIFIED
SEX: MALE
AGE: 30
EYE COLOR/HAIR COLOR: BLUE/BROWN
OUTWARD COLORING: LIGHT
HEIGHT/WEIGHT: 6'1/235

- CREW FILE -

DESIGNATION: JADEN MORRIT
POSITION: NOT DESIGNATED
RACE: VERDISSIAN
SEX: MALE
AGE: 15
EYE COLOR/HAIR COLOR: BROWN/BROWN
OUTWARD COLORING: MEDIUM
HEIGHT/WEIGHT: 6'1/235

- CREW FILE -

DESIGNATION: .... BREE MORRIT
POSITION: .... SHIP'S DOCTOR
RACE: .... VERDISSIAN
SEX: .... FEMALE
AGE: 25
EYE COLOR/HAIR COLOR: ... BLUE/BROWN
OUTWARD COLORING: .... LIGHT
HEIGHT/WEIGHT: .... 5'3/135

- CREW FILE -

DESIGNATION: .... HELA WILLISON
POSITION: .... QUARTERMASTER
RACE: .... HUMAN
SEX: .... FEMALE
AGE: 29
EYE COLOR/HAIR COLOR: ... BROWN/BLACK
OUTWARD COLORING: .... DARK
HEIGHT/WEIGHT: .... 5'4/235

Social Drop

Thank you for reading!

If you're interested in continuing the series a bit more in-depth as a BETA or ARC reader, join us on Facebook at Written by B. Williams ARC Team.

As always, as an indie authors, the best way to support us is to leave a review on Goodreads, Amazon, or your own social media pages. We'd love to see it if you do and tag us @written.by.b.williams on both Instagram and Tiktok.

Have questions? Email us directly at mossandwolf@gmail.com.

Want more? Check out:
No Bones About It: Moss and Wolf Case Files 1

Acknowledgements

To those who believed in a world full of stars with us, thank you.

Special thanks to the first beta reader, Gretchen, without your encouragement this may have never have gotten finished.

And to Alissa, Alex, Anant, Arindam, and Jessi, you're the best. Please keep writing too.

Art Credits:

The Eikos
The Valstar
The Callistar
Chapter breaks – Werner Ferrufino

Kira and Quinn – Oxonoo(on Fiverr)

ABOUT THE AUTHORS

J.J. is a Canadian writer who lives in Southern Ontario. He enjoys reading, writing, and playing stories about fantastical things and settings. He is an avid fan of Magic: the Gathering, works a job he wishes he didn't have to, and currently lives alone, though he hopes to get an apartment that allows pets someday, as he would like a dog.

B. Williams is an American writer who lives in Missouri. She works in healthcare and writes in her spare time when a tiny terror allows her to. Writing to her is about sharing the imagination of another person.

Made in the USA
Monee, IL
27 February 2025